Adam wrapped his arms around her shoulders and ran his hands down the small curve of her spine. His fingers encountered the thin scar that ran down to the cleft of her buttocks.

"Don't let me hurt you," he said, suddenly easing his embrace, restraining himself with obvious effort.

"Adam," Aldy said, wrapping one leg over both of his and running the sole of her foot seductively along his thigh and calf. "I won't break." She smiled at his concern and leaned to flick at his mouth with the tip of her tongue.

"God, Aldy," he whispered, burying his face in her neck. "I need you...."

Dear Reader,

It is our pleasure to bring you a new experience
in reading that goes beyond category writing.
The settings of **Harlequin American Romances**
give a sense of place and culture that is uniquely
American, and the characters are warm and
believable. The stories are of "today" and have
been chosen to give variety within the vast scope
of romance fiction.

Atop a spindly scaffold, Aldora Cassidy paints the
fairy tales that children dream of, while below her,
Adam Holcomb—the hero and her patron—patiently
waits to tell her of her beauty and her talent.
Rayanne Moore writes about a muralist from the
experience of being one. You will enjoy the beauty
and sensitivity of this love story.

From the early days of Harlequin, our primary
concern has been to bring you novels of the highest
quality. **Harlequin American Romances** are no
exception. Enjoy!

Vivian Stephens

Vivian Stephens
Editorial Director
Harlequin American Romances
919 Third Avenue,
New York, N.Y. 10022

Thin White Line

RAYANNE MOORE

Harlequin Books

TORONTO • NEW YORK • LOS ANGELES • LONDON
AMSTERDAM • PARIS • SYDNEY • HAMBURG
STOCKHOLM • ATHENS • TOKYO • MILAN

Published May 1983

First printing March 1983

ISBN 0-373-16008-9

Chapter One

Aldora's slim fingers shook slightly as she slid her thumb under the flap of the cream-colored envelope. Scanning the letter, her dark eyes began to glow with excitement. She reached for the telephone, uttering a cry of alarm when her hand tipped a bottle of drawing ink. The black liquid puddled out across the drafting table as Aldora grabbed for the paper towels and frantically shuffled her sketches out of the way. Those sketches were to seal the decision of the Edgely Foundation and possibly her own fate as well.

It had been nearly two and a half years since the surgery and Aldora had experienced only a negative cash flow ever since. As an author/illustrator of children's books, she received advances on a new work that barely covered the cost of the art materials, and it took at least two years for the royalties to pay back those advances. That was the way of things when one was working, but Aldora had been unable to work for many months. She desperately needed to augment her income while she waited for her latest picture book to be accepted.

Dumping soggy paper towels into the trash bag by the drafting table, Aldora dialed and listened impatiently to the busy signal. She glanced at the clock. Eleven forty-five. If she couldn't get through now, the offices would probably be closed until two o'clock. That is, if the hospital staff took the kind of lunch breaks that doctors took.

Setting the alarm for two thirty, Aldora started assembling her portfolio. Down on her knees on the hardwood floor, she trimmed tissue and cover-stock papers to fit each of the three color composites. She pasted them to the backs of each mounting board and folded them so that they formed a protective "flap" over the art surface. She was just flapping the last composite when the doorbell rang. Struggling painfully to her feet, she gasped as the now familiar stab shot down her left leg. "Just a minute!" she shouted and made for the stairs.

"Ellen!" she cried as she flung open the sliding glass door. "I tried to call you this morning."

Ellen stared at Aldy's ink-stained fingers, her smudged face. "Were you working? I can come back later if—"

"Don't be silly!" Aldora almost dragged Ellen into the house. "I was just putting my portfolio together." Laying special emphasis on the word *portfolio*, Aldy waited for a reaction.

"Your portfoli-o-o-o, oh, Aldy! You got the job!" Ellen's short blond hair bobbed around her face as she spoke. "Tell me!"

"I've got an appointment. Monday, ten o'clock." Aldora tried to suppress her own excitement as she calmed her friend. "How 'bout coffee?"

"Coffee?" Ellen said in disbelief. "How can you even think of coffee at a time like this?" Ellen threw herself into a wicker chair and beamed. "I just knew it!" Her feet waggled over the arm of the chair as she babbled happily. "They couldn't pick anyone else. The kids'll love your mural as much as they love your books."

"The *kids* aren't on the committee," said Aldora reasonably. A look of apprehension in her eyes, she turned toward the small galleylike kitchen, trying to conceal her fears in the flurry of setting up the coffeepot and laying out the cups.

"How can you be so calm?" Ellen said. "You've thought of nothing else for weeks. Now it's happening!" Ellen's blue eyes twinkled triumphantly.

"Nothing is 'happening' until final sketch approval, Ellie. Besides. . ."

"Besides what?" Ellen looked sharply at her friend and saw that quirk of the right eyebrow that pulled down and slightly inward when Aldy was worried or in pain. "You hurting?" Ellen asked with almost motherly concern.

"No," Aldy said quickly. "I mean, what if it's a really tall wall? I'd need *scaffolding*." On the final word, her voice dropped to a low throatiness.

"You'll manage. It's probably low and rambling anyway," Ellen said. "Kids are too short to appreciate a vaulted ceiling." Ellen laughed at her friend's look of horror. "Oh, I get it—Michelangelo Aldora—you see yourself suspended from the rafters, doing a ceiling mural for all the patients who have to lie flat on their little backsides!"

"Well, the guidelines didn't mention ceilings, but" —Aldora leaned across the counter— "a double-height wall could do it. That might require me to work as high as twelve or thirteen feet off the ground!"

"Aldy, we did discuss getting right back on the horse, didn't we?" Ellen spoke firmly and wagged an index finger at Aldora for emphasis.

"It wasn't a horse I fell off of!"

"Do the scaffold stuff on good days," Ellen said. "When you're not up to climbing, work at floor level."

"Oh, you've got it all figured, huh?" Aldora shook her head. Ellen was a good friend and positively inspired confidence.

"Yup!"

"Well, I don't have the job yet, so—"

"You will, Monday!" Ellen said. "Sugar, no cream."

"What?"

"The coffee, Aldy. It's ready. Sugar, no cream."

"No cream?" Aldora registered surprise.

Ellen puffed out her cheeks and crossed her eyes. "I

gotta cut down. Not lucky like you: all curves, no appetite.''

Aldora rolled her eyes toward heaven. ''Give me strength!''

Two cups of cinnamon coffee later, Ellen picked up her purse and gave Aldy a hug. Aldora walked Ellen to her car, waving as she pulled away from the curb. She wished she had the confidence in herself that Ellen had in her.

Climbing the stairs of the front porch, Aldy heard her alarm ringing. She ran up to the studio, snapped it off, then placed her call to the Edgely Foundation and Hospital to confirm her Monday appointment.

ALDORA worked through the weekend and by Sunday evening she had all her sketches and composites in order and had combed her wardrobe for an appropriate outfit. She sat at her sewing machine and took in the seams on the slacks of her rust pantsuit. Then she deepened and lengthened the darts of the flared jacket. ''All curves,'' Ellen had said. ''Ha! Where?'' Aldy mumbled as she tried on the suit and looked in the cheval glass. She buttoned and unbuttoned the jacket, fluffed impatiently at the soft, ruffled blouse. Rust and cocoa, the combination was great, she thought as she undressed, but... well, not too bad for all those weeks in the hospital *and* the months afterward. She hung the suit on the closet door and a gleam of metal caught her eye. She slammed the closet door angrily. It closed, clamlike, on the hanger hook and bounced back at her, spilling the rust suit on the rug. Tears stung Aldy's eyes as she stooped to pick it up and her hand shot out to grab the wall for support. Slowly she straightened up and laid the suit over a chair. Then she reached into the closet and dragged out the mass of cloth and metal. She held it in front of her and visions flashed through her mind. Six months in this nasty bit of work! She ran her hand through her long, dark hair and remembered the fifty-three days in the hospital. "Hey," she chided, "then you thought this back brace was salvation itself. The way out of that hospital bed at last."

Another image began to crowd in. The accident. The months of imprisonment in this three pounds of steel, straps, and buckles that drove Ken to... well, out of her life, anyway. The hurt welled up again and she shook her head to drive the image away. Her right eyebrow pulled inward and she turned to the door.

Down in the garage, Aldora jerked the lid off the trash barrel and dumped the brace into the can. Then she grabbed an old blanket off a pile of camping gear and stuffed it down over the brace. She chuckled at the symbolism as she replaced the lid. "Brace *yourself*," she punned, climbing the stairs, "the last prop is gone."

Chapter Two

When the alarm sounded Monday morning, Aldora groped gratefully for the shutoff. Her sleep had been troubled by dreams of towering ceilings and endless scaffolding. She rubbed her hand over her eyes. The fairy-tale characters of her stories still danced behind her lids as they had cavorted up that vast dream-wall, daring her to catch them with her brushes and paint them into obedient stillness.

Swinging her feet to the floor, she pulled herself up with the aid of the bedpost. Not too bad, she thought, ignoring her cane and walking to the bathroom. Aldora pulled her nightshirt off over her head and tucked her thick, heavy hair under a showercap. Leaning against the cool tile, she let the hard, hot needles of water beat against the small of her back. She massaged the stiff muscles and tried to avoid feeling the narrow white scar that followed the line of her backbone from several inches above her slim waist to the base of her spine.

ALDORA guided her VW Bug down the winding road to the city and hoped the Los Angeles traffic wouldn't be too heavy. She reviewed the names associated with the Edgely Foundation and some of the material she had looked up in the library. The Edgely Foundation and Hospital was dedicated to the research of crippling childhood disorders. It had been the dream of Mrs. Theodora Bishop Edgely who had lost a child to a crippling disease. Stricken, herself, with painful arthritis in her early forties, she began to set up the trust that made this foundation a reality. Her dream was not for herself, nor others with her affliction, but for the children. The

Edgely Foundation was equipped with the finest that money could buy and children from all over the world were flown in for treatment. Her keen business acumen and her prominence in the social registers of the world allowed her to generate an almost unending flow of generous contributions. Now the hospital was adding a new rehabilitation wing to accommodate the Foundation's success stories: children cured of progressive deterioration, but needing specialized assistance in reentering the mainstream. It was this new wing that was being endowed with the mural Aldora hoped to paint.

Who would be on the committee for the final decision? Adam Holcomb, director of the Edgely Foundation? No, certainly he'd leave the details of the art selection to his staff, Aldy decided. Grant Curtis, the young architect who had been commissioned to design the new wing? Yes, definitely, and doubtless an interior designer or two who would be frantic that the mural might upset his or her color scheme. Aldora had only seen the new wing from the outside, but if it was as much a tribute to fine design and brilliant imagination inside as it was from the street, then just working there would be a pleasure. Aldora glanced at her watch and gave up trying to second-guess her appraisal committee. At nine forty-five she was just taking her ticket from the meter at the underground parking lot. Seeing the soaring lines of the new building reaching skyward, dwarfing the original wing, Aldora thought again of ladders, scaffolds, and high places. She wanted this job. Needed it. But the memory of her own body hurtling down that embankment brought beads of perspiration to her brow. *Stop it!* she thought angrily. *This is not going to beat you, Aldora Cassidy. You need that income. You need the publicity as an artist. You will do it.* If *I get the job,* she added anxiously.

At five of ten Aldora walked into the second-floor office of the Edgely Foundation and Hospital. The office was a picture of modern luxury. Thick chocolate carpeting gave beneath her feet, telling of the plush cushioning underneath. The walls were soft beige with contemporary geometric panels painted on the surface in rust, orange, and sandalwood with accents of bright yellow. With murals on the office walls, Aldy thought, it was little wonder they had commissioned them for the new wing.

"May I help you?" A plump redhead looked up from her typing and smiled at Aldora.

"I have a ten-o'clock appointment with the committee about a mural for—"

"Oh, Miss Cassidy!" The girl's eyes widened. "You look just like the dustcover picture on your books." The red curls fell forward as the girl leaned across her desk and peered up at Aldora's face. "My nieces love your work!"

Aldora, always uneasy with praise, smiled at the girl and shifted her portfolio to her other hand. "Thank you."

"Just have a seat." The girl motioned to a sofa. "I'll buzz Mr. Curtis."

Aldora sat on one of the soft leather love seats. No expense had been spared in the office, she thought. The article she had read in the library had revealed that this place was extravagantly funded. Now Aldora could completely understand what the writer had meant by "extravagantly." The article had also hinted that if the fabulous Edgely wealth couldn't supply what was needed for its small patients, then what was needed didn't yet exist. And that same article had concluded by stating that if the needed tools did not exist, the Edgely staff of researchers and scientists would invent them, build them, or discover them. That article had been seven years old, but the more recent reports Aldy had found only confirmed that original prognosis. The Foundation had made quantum leaps in the area of reconstructive surgery, transplants, joint replacement, and prosthesis research. The necessity of this new wing, specializing in rehabilitation therapy, was further testimony of the dream Mrs. Edgely had initiated, that of relieving the children of pain and suffering and relieving their parents of the heartache she had borne, becoming a reality.

"You may go in now, Miss Cassidy."

Aldora forced her attention from her reflections and picked up her portfolio. She crossed the reception room and stepped through the door to the inner office.

Her senses reeled for an instant, but it wasn't the vaulted ceilings or the breathtaking wall of glass that opened onto the vivid green of the atrium that upset her equilibrium, it was the rugged young man with the friendly blue eyes and sandy hair who was crossing from behind the mammoth oak conference table, his hand outstretched. His build, the way he smiled at her— Aldora's mind raced back to the last time Ken had come to the hospital. He had moved with the same vitality, his eyes had been just as inviting, but the spring in his step, the light in his eyes, had not been for her.

"Miss Cassidy," he said as he took her hand. "This is a pleasure. I'm Grant Curtis."

As Aldora stammered a greeting, she became aware of the sincerity in those eyes, the way that strong, tanned hand continued to hold hers firmly. Her initial apprehension began to ebb.

"This is Miss Julie Shore, our interior designer. She'll be working with us on the wing."

Aldora saw a tawny blonde step forward and smile a welcome that her rigid posture didn't support. "How do you do, Miss Cassidy." The blonde allowed herself to sway slightly against Grant Curtis as she leaned to offer Aldora her hand. "Grant has been extolling your virtues since I arrived."

Aldora noticed the possessive purr as the girl used Grant's first name. "Well, the interiors of this building have been extolling *your* virtues since I arrived," Aldora said pleasantly. No sense in allowing any antagonism to build, she thought. Aldora wished desperately that Mr. Curtis's athletic build didn't bring memories of Ken so strongly to her mind.

"See, Julie." Grant smiled triumphantly. "She's good with the words."

Julie forced a smile at Grant and walked to the door. "How do you take your coffee, Miss Cassidy? Grant is virtually tongue-tied without a mug in his hand."

"Black, please," said Aldy. Apparently the designer/architect relationship was a bit more than a business one, but Aldora had the feeling that she must have walked in on the heels of a minor quarrel.

"Why don't I take that," Grant offered, reaching for her portfolio. He placed it carefully on the polished wood surface of the conference table.

The care he took with her artwork did not escape Aldy's notice as she stepped forward to unzip the case. "I'll lay out the composites first," she said. "If you need more, I have some alternate layouts in these sketches." She folded back the tissue-paper flaps and nervously arranged the work.

Grant moved from one to another. A slight furrow creased his brow and Aldora assumed the worst. *He doesn't like them,* she thought in a panic. Time dragged. Aldy wished he'd say something, anything. Then Julie came back with a tray of cups.

"Here's your transfusion, Grant." Julie seemed to be making an effort to smooth things, but as she handed a cup across to Grant, the container tilted slightly and coffee ran down the side of the cup. Aldora drew in her breath sharply and made a dive for her artwork. Grant, way ahead of her, whisked the composite aside; coffee spilled only on the wide, white border. "Dammit, Julie!" he snapped. "This stuff is good. You could have ruined it!"

Looking contrite and apologizing profusely, Julie gathered towels to repair the damage. Grant grabbed the towels from her hands. "Don't ever wipe! Blot!"

He glanced at Aldora. "Sorry." He blotted carefully at the edge of the illustration board. "Julie, get the white-out from my desk." As he spoke, tension filled the room.

When Julie left, she took the prickly atmosphere with her. "Adam has to see these," said Grant enthusiastically. "He was supposed to be here this morning, but had a family emergency. Sorry."

Aldora fought rising hope and excitement. "That's high praise, Mr. Curtis," said Aldora evenly.

The director of the Foundation wasn't going to leave the selection of the art to his staff after all! Aldora's heart pounded and hope rose in spite of her endeavor.

He grinned. "Call me Grant. I've a feeling we'll be working together on this. Can I keep these until tomorrow?"

Aldora smiled. "I'm very glad you like my work, Grant. I'll leave the whole portfolio. The alternates I mentioned are in here."

Julie returned with the white-out and Grant and Aldora touched up the spill mark on the border. "That's fine, Grant," said Aldy replacing the lid on the white-out. She saw Julie stiffen when she used Grant's first name.

"I don't expect much in the way of changes, Aldora. We can discuss that tomorrow. Same time, okay?" Grant watched her putting the composites back in the portfolio. "Leave that one to dry. I'll put it away later," he said. He looked over at Julie. "Your work is safe with *me*." Tension crackled in the room again and Aldora felt the color rise to her face.

"Ten o'clock will be fine, Grant," she said, shouldering her bag.

"It's been a pleasure, Aldora," said Grant. He held out his hand to her.

Aldora was just about to return the handshake when Julie thrust her hand quickly into Aldora's. "Oh, yes, and please, forgive my clumsiness." Julie looked

pointedly at Grant. "So glad there's no harm done."
Her grip tightened slightly on Aldy's fingers.

"Don't think any more about it, Miss Shore," said
Aldy sincerely. "I nearly drowned them with black ink
myself the other day." Then to Grant. "Tomorrow
morning, right?"

"Right." Grant stepped over to hold the door for
her. "Thanks for being so understanding," he said
quietly.

As Aldora crossed the reception room, she thought
she heard the sound of raised voices from behind the
closing office door. She hoped Julie wasn't getting the
rough edge of Grant's tongue for the coffee mishap. If
she did get this job, it would be difficult enough without
antagonizing Julie.

ALDORA drove slowly but her mind raced. Grant had
said nothing about the dimensions. That could mean
that the long, low wall mentioned in the guidelines was
still the objective. She sighed with relief. No high scaffolds to climb. Now, if only Mr. Holcomb would like
her work. She detoured past Ellen's and gave her friend
a full report.

"So this Grant took your side against the decorator,
hmmm?" Ellen stirred her coffee and reached for another doughnut.

"Don't read a scenario into it, Ellie. You know my
feelings about work and play." Aldora sipped at her
coffee. "Remember when you had me married and rear-
ing five kids because a box boy helped me with my gro-
ceries?" Aldy teased. But she couldn't really be too
hard on Ellen for her flights of fancy. Her friend was an
incurable romantic. Aldy knew that if she had had as
great a home life as Ellen's, she'd probably want everyone else in that same happy boat too.

"Yeah, *all* work, *no* play!" Ellen sighed. "You can't
honestly tell me that you enjoy being a virtual recluse at
twenty-seven!"

"No," said Aldora. "I should have started earlier!"

"That'll look cute in a greeting card," said Ellen, miming the act of throttling Aldora with both hands to show her displeasure at that attitude.

Aldy gave Ellen her stern the-subject-is-closed look but couldn't help smiling. She knew Ellen reverted to sarcasm only with her dearest friends, and Bill, Ellen's husband of two years, often claimed that he must be the dearest friend Ellie had.

Aldy was sure that she no longer had the stamina for running two careers and a relationship. She was equally sure that she'd never again abandon her art. Never let anyone submit Ken's brand of ultimatum along with a bid for her heart. Aldora gathered up her keys. "I know, Ellen, you care." She gave Ellen a quick hug. "Gotta run."

Ellen glared at Aldy with her "fierce" look. "*Run* is accurate in this instance." Then she returned the hug. "Call me tomorrow, first thing, okay?"

"Okay," Aldora promised and turned to leave.

SITTING down to a solitary supper, Aldora tried to balance her monthly statement for the third time. *It's hopeless,* she decided; even without the tomato bisque spatters it didn't work out. Aldora had balanced her checkbook to the penny; what wasn't working out was how she would purchase all the replacement materials to begin illustrations for a new story she'd written. She needed another roll of acetate for color separations, more sheets of color-aid, hot-press illustration boards, and more. It was endless. That was the problem with illustration: Advances never quite covered the material outlay. Aldora sighed and slapped the cover of her checkbook impatiently.

One thing was certain, if she was lucky enough to get the mural commission, she'd take that job even if the wall *was* huge!

If only.... Aldora recognized that her spine wasn't

all that accident had shattered. Her confidence, her fledgling career in fine arts, her optimistic trust in the basic kindness of others; all had fallen victim to the vagaries of a man's heart. Well, Ellen could just grow hoarse with prodding! Aldy wasn't going to let it happen again. She could take care of herself. She'd get that mural. Pay off her bills. And maybe, soon, she'd work again on her oils. She had been *so* close to that one-woman show!

Aldora stood up and turned out the kitchen light. She massaged the stiff muscles of her lower back as she walked to the bedroom. *Don't go into spasm now,* she prayed, *not now. There's so much to do.*

Chapter Three

"Welcome co-worker!" said Grant as he wrapped both his hands around Aldora's and led her into the conference room. He was wearing a pair of faded jeans and a blue work shirt and Aldora was relieved to note that he looked a great deal less like Ken than she had first thought. He perched on the edge of the table and grinned at her.

"Are you saying that—"

"I sure am," Grant cut in. "Adam loved your work." He motioned to two composites laid out on the table. "I just have one or two small changes—some good and bad news."

Aldora felt her right eyebrow pull in just a bit. Her confusion must have been obvious because Grant reached over and patted her arm. "Adam was impressed, that's good news," he defined patiently. "Extra work for you is the bad news." Grant's blue eyes sparkled with mischief at this last remark. "But I doubt you'll mind," he continued. "Adam compensates well for overtime." Picking up one of the composites with notes on the tissue overlay, he held it out to Aldora. "This was our favorite."

Aldora looked at the work. It wasn't her personal favorite, but it came in second. She stared at the notes on the overlay. Lines and arrows seemed to be truncating the horizontal format so that it became vertical. She looked up at Grant.

"Adam wants to use this one in an expanded version on the full-size wall facing the entry door of the recreation room." Grant smiled at Aldy's look of astonishment and reached for a second drawing. "He approved

this one for the long hall in the admissions section.''
This was Aldy's personal favorite of the three compositions she had submitted. ''We both thought it would be selfish,'' he went on, ''not to put one of your murals where the parents could enjoy it too.''

Aldora didn't know how to react. Good and bad news was right. Double honor, double pay, perhaps, but what was this ''full-size'' wall going to be like? Visions of scaffolding crowded in again.

''Hey, I know it'll take some time to alter the proportions on that first piece, but Adam said he didn't need final approval; you're the boss.'' Grant had apparently assumed that her hesitation was due to the fear that an all too familiar pitfall of commissioned work was involved here. ''I mean,'' he continued, ''that the revisions won't drag on and on while we sit on our wallets.'' It was unfortunate but not uncommon that contractors would order countless revisions for free and then turn down the finals in the end.

''Oh, no.'' Aldy felt her face grow hot. ''I wasn't concerned about that, honestly.'' She rushed on to cover her embarrassment. ''I'm delighted that Mr. Holcomb has such faith in my work that he's willing to spread me all over his walls, but—'' She realized her error and blushed redder as Grant threw back his head and laughed. ''Well, so to speak,'' she finished lamely.

Grant looked delightedly at her. ''Your art isn't your best use of color, I see,'' he teased. He slipped an arm around her shoulder in a big-brotherly way. ''Let's show you these walls. You'll probably want to make notes on the sizes and lighting.'' He steered her toward the door.

Aldora felt encompassed by his friendly affection as well as his arm. As Grant held the door for her, Julie came into the reception room.

''Oh, Grant—'' She broke off, staring at Grant's arm around Aldora's shoulder. Her body tensed. ''Miss Cassidy, I thought you'd gone.''

Aldora felt herself blushing again. "Mr. Curtis was just going to show me the new wall," she stammered. "I need notes—" Realizing she was babbling on, Aldy closed her mouth on the words and rummaged in her bag for a notebook.

Ignoring her completely, Julie stepped up to Grant. "Adam wants those remodel plans for the lobby by four this afternoon."

Grant let his arm drop casually to his side as he moved to a flat file. "Right here, third drawer," he said and tapped the handle. "They're all ready to go." He took Aldora's arm. "We'll be in the new wing, Julie. See you later."

ALDORA's heart pounded wildly against her ribs as she looked up at the wall in the recreation room. Her eyes tracked the distance from floor to ceiling and her chest grew tight. "Do you have the measure to the nearest inch?" she asked abstractedly. *Fool,* she thought too late, *he's the architect, of course he has the measurements.*

"Twenty-two six by thirty-two."

Aldora scribbled furiously in her notebook. She hoped her shaking wouldn't make the notes entirely illegible. "That's twenty-two and a half feet high?" Her voice trailed off.

Grant took her expression for one of awe and admiration. He was only half right. "Isn't it magnificent? Kids won't feel closed in." He threw out his arms as if to encompass the expanse of it all. "The Edgelys thought the worst thing about hospitals was that they looked like hospitals!" He was obviously quite proud of flying against such conventions with his soaring ceilings and glass walls opening to lush, green atria. "Same light in here as in the conference room. Great for your work. Trees outside and trees inside, thanks to you."

Aldora realized that he was referring to her wooded scene with the dwarfs and elves and forest creatures.

"Yes, great!" she said with forced enthusiasm. She pulled her gaze from the height of the wall with a sick feeling in her stomach. *I won't dwell on it,* she thought.

"There is a minimal need for artificial light in daytime hours. Those track lights are for evening viewing." Grant pointed to the fixtures in the ceiling.

Aldora had to put her head back at an uncomfortable angle to look up that far. She felt momentarily dizzy. She must have swayed slightly because Grant's hand shot out to steady her. "Gotta watch this floor," he said, misunderstanding her loss of balance. "It's uneven, not finished yet."

Aldy looked at the floor and straightened a wrinkle in the drop cloth with her foot. *Let him believe that,* she thought; *drop cloth, I love you!* "I'll be wearing sneakers when I work," she said quickly. *Oh, Lord, hoof in mouth again,* she thought. *Like he wouldn't have enough sense to assume I wouldn't be painting a mural in Gucci originals with four-inch heels! Get yourself together, girl, it's only a wall!*

"Now through here...." Grant was leading her on to the next work area. She hurried to catch up. For the next half hour, Aldy took down measurements, made notations on light sources, wall surfaces, proposed floor-furniture plans. Then they returned to the office.

As Aldora read over the contract, Grant handed her a check. "An advance. The least Adam could do for the change in plans."

Aldora looked at the check and nearly gasped out loud. There was no way she could afford to turn down this job, scaffolding or no scaffolding! She looked at Grant in disbelief.

"I told you he was generous." He grinned at her. "Incentive."

"It certainly is," said Aldy. She shook her head, picked up the pen, and signed her name to the contract, hoping the trembling wouldn't show in her signature.

"Let me know when you want to start. My men will put up the scaffolding."

Aldora felt her stomach tighten and do a flip. "Oh, yes," she said levelly. "Could I watch?"

Grant looked surprised. "If you want to."

"It might make a difference as to how the verticals are positioned," Aldy lied. She could work around a vertical the size of a redwood, but if she were going to be up in the air, she felt as if she just had to know how the supports had gone together.

Grant seemed to accept her reason. "I hadn't thought of that. Give me a day's notice, okay?"

Knowing she'd hold to her word, Aldora glued her courage to the sticking point. "I think by the end of next week, tentatively." She was glad that she was still sitting down. That confident voice didn't even sound like hers. "The cartoons should be ready to transfer by then." She shifted in her chair. "I'll still call to confirm, though."

"Ah, a professional to her toes." Grant smiled appreciatively. "I'll wait to hear from you."

Aldora got up, amazed that her legs didn't buckle under her. "Thank you, Grant," she said as she folded the check and her copy of the contract into her purse and picked up her portfolio. "I can get a preliminary on the revisions to you before—"

"Adam said 'carte blanche,' Aldora," said Grant quickly. "You're the artist." He held the door for her. "Need some help?"

"Thanks, no," Aldy said. "Artists are used to weird bundles. This stuff is tame."

Out in the hall Aldora leaned against the nearest wall, breathing deeply. Her real reason for not wanting Grant to escort her stemmed from a strong desire to collapse in private. She pictured the scaffolding. *Twenty-two and a half feet,* she thought gloomily. *My God, what have I done?*

TUESDAY evening Aldora dressed and did a quick check on her makeup. She didn't really feel up to going to Ellen's for the "celebration dinner," but Ellen had been so excited that she couldn't refuse. Even Bill had whooped his congratulations over the extension phone. Aldora braided her long hair into a queue, fluffed the shorter hair into waves around her face, brushed a hint of blusher across her high cheekbones. *Can't go over looking like death,* she thought to rationalize her unaccustomed use of the blusher. She gathered up her preliminary sketches of the revisions and the approved color composites to show Bill. Ellen had seen most of the work during the course of the creative process, but neither she nor Bill had seen the revisions for the large wall.

"FANTASTIC," said Bill as he leaned over the cleared dining table and lit an after-dinner cigar. "Kids will be crazy to get into that hospital just to see your work."

Aldy laughed.

"I can't wait to see this on that wall," Ellen said. "Imagine those trees and that waterfall reaching up that expanse!"

"Yeah," said Aldy dismally. "I can wait."

Bill looked at her sternly. "You'll be fine," he said, adopting Ellen's confident air. "Just do the tall stuff when you're up to it."

"That's what I told her," Ellen put in.

"How would you like a helper's job, Ellie?"

"Me? I can't draw a breath, let alone paint!"

"Not painting," Aldora said. "First-aid assistant for when I fall on my head."

Bill shook a finger at her. "Once you get up there it's like standing on the ground." Bill knew his stuff. He was in construction; they used to joke about him spending a lot of time in high places.

"I know." Aldora forced a smile. "It's just the thought of getting started."

"Get a helper or two," Ellen suggested. "All the old masters did it. You do the creative stuff and they fill in."

"Oh, I'll have that much help. Two of my students, Eddy and Kate."

"Just don't get so absorbed you forget to take breaks," Ellen said in her maternal tone.

Bill laughed. "That's asking a lot! The building could go in a quake and Aldy would be painting when they came to dig out the survivors."

Aldora laughed, but shuddered inwardly at the idea of weathering a California quake on a scaffold.

Ellen brought coffee and they retired to the living room.

"A toast!" said Bill.

"With coffee?" Ellen asked.

"The artist doesn't drink, remember?" He raised his cup. "To our muralist and her talent!"

Ellen said "Here, here!" and Aldy felt her eyes go moist with affection for these two. She only hoped their faith in her would be justified.

Chapter Four

During the next week Aldora worked furiously on the cartoons. All the elements of her composition had to be enlarged to the final size and sketched out on long rolls of sturdy paper. At the time of positioning, these cartoons would be backed by transfer paper and pinned in place against the wall. Then Aldora would have to trace each section onto the surface, adjusting and adding details as she worked.

Even her huge drafting table was not large enough to accommodate such giant sketches. To get the proper perspective Aldora had to use her living room floor. Down on her knees, she roughed out the figures, then ran up to the studio loft and looked down at them from the interior balcony. Even with this method, Aldora could see only sections at a time. All the sections had to be grid-patterned and coded with letters to identify their position in the small color composite.

It was brutal work. By the time Aldora had gone up and down the stairs a half-dozen times and spent hours on her knees hunched over rolls of paper, she was in agony. The awkward positions forced her to take frequent breaks. The frequent breaks forced her to work late into the night to keep to her schedule. If she backed off now—procrastinated—she feared she would never be able to force herself to actually get to climbing around on that scaffolding.

By Thursday afternoon she loathed each and every inch. Hated all the characters.

"He'll detest it!" Aldora muttered as she hung over the balcony and stared down at the next-to-last section. "Grant will rip up my contract."

She gripped the railing and tried to straighten her back. The stabbing pain down her leg brought tears to her eyes. *Time to quit,* she thought. *I'll go to the spa and work out these kinks. It'll all look better to me tomorrow.*

Aldora changed her clothes and drove to the health club. It seemed like a bit of a luxury, but it was a necessity. Only the hot tub and laps in the pool could force her back muscles to loosen, enable her to function, to move without her cane again.

She pulled into the lot and grabbed her tote bag with her free hand. Leaning heavily on her carved cedar cane, Aldora limped to the rear entrance.

"Hi, Aldy," said Karen, bursting through the door and nearly knocking into her. "I haven't seen you in a while."

"Good!" said Aldora. She smiled at the manager as she maneuvered inside. "Less is definitely more."

Karen laughed. "The *less* we see of you, the *more* you like it, right?"

Aldora nodded.

She changed into her suit and limped to the pool. As she did her laps she could feel the water do its work. *Thank heaven,* she thought. *Grant would cancel me in a minute if he thought an invalid would be scrambling around on that scaffolding! Better put in a short day tomorrow again, then work through the weekend.*

By the time Aldy climbed into the hot tub, she had the swirling waters to herself. The Jacuzzi pummeled her gently and the aching began to float away on the myriad bubbles that tingled against her skin.

Too exhausted to discipline her thoughts, Aldora drifted. Looking at the cedar cane lying by the side of the tub brought back visions of the day she had first used it. Ken had come to the hospital after work. She had stood in her new back brace, clutched this gift from Ellen, and tottered proudly toward him. She had only been up twice before.

"It won't always be like this!" she had cried when she saw the look of horror, the revulsion that crept into Ken's eyes. "Only six months in this...I'll be fine!" Aldy said desperately.

"Sure, hon," Ken said, trying then to conceal his shock. "So, what's this surprise?"

"If I work hard, I can go home in a week," said Aldy triumphantly. "Will you do the honors? Escort me?" She smiled happily up at him.

Ken didn't respond immediately. He pulled a small pocket calendar from his jacket and examined it for a long moment. "Gee, hon," he said slowly, "I'm afraid I'll have to be in San Diego all that week." He tried to look genuinely hurt, but Aldy could see a look of vague relief creep in behind that act.

"Could you postpone it?" Aldy pitched.

"'Fraid not, hon. A really big opportunity for me...for us," he amended quickly.

"Oh...all right," said Aldy levelly. "I guess I can make arrangements with Ellen and Bill."

By the time Aldora got out of the hospital, Ken had walked out, out of her life forever. She tried to tell herself that it was just guilt. That Ken would stop blaming himself for the accident, come back to her. Then she heard that he'd married and that he and his bride were buying a house in San Diego! Aldora vowed that she would never again allow herself to be in a position of seeing such revulsion on any man's face. Only Ellen and Bill kept her from losing her sanity, breaking down completely. Brick by bitter brick, she walled society out.

Aldora felt hot tears run down her cheeks and mix with the swirling waters of the spa as she recalled Ellie's selfless devotion. Grabbing her towel and cane, Aldy climbed from the Jacuzzi. She walked with less effort now. She tucked the cane under her arm and went to the locker room to dress.

ALDORA'S rigid timetable had her finished with the cartoons for the large wall by Tuesday. She wanted to call Grant and arrange for the scaffolding for Thursday, but she had said the *end* of the week. A solid knot of anxiety lodged in the pit of her stomach as she reached for the phone. *One more day,* she thought. *I deserve one day off. He's not expecting me to call this soon. Procrastinator. Coward.* The words ran in her head. *Last chance to work on the next book,* she rationalized. *I should get it started, get the rough sketches and story line to an exciting turn so I can look forward to digging in as soon as the murals are finished. I owe me that.* At last, Aldy managed to alibi her hand away from the receiver.

On the following day Aldora allowed herself no more excuses. She dialed the hospital number and tapped nervously with a pencil while she waited for the call to be put through to Grant's office.

"It's Aldora, Grant," she said when he came to the phone. "I guess I'll need that scaffold on Friday, if you can manage." Her voice sounded strange, quavered a bit as she mentioned the day. So soon!

"Wonderful," said Grant. "You got it. What time?"

"I'm open."

"Great. Be here first thing, about eight thirty. You can supervise in the morning and I'll take you to lunch."

Aldora felt a rush of apprehension. "Lunch?"

"Have to celebrate opening day," he said. "Julie and I will take you to our favorite dive."

At the mention of Julie's name, Aldora breathed easier. "Well..." She hated to mix business and pleasure, but with Julie along it would be a way to get to know her better, smooth things, make sure that the girl harbored no odd notions about Aldora where Grant was concerned. "I'd love to," she said, meaning it.

"Fine. See you at eight thirty."

Aldora's hand shook as she hung up the phone. It was done. Friday the men would bring the boards and pipes and then there would be no more excuses, no way to get out of climbing up ladders and walking out on the planks, finding out what she was really made of. *Concentrate on the lunch, Aldy,* she scolded. *It'll be fun. This is your chance to put Julie at ease, make a friend of her.* Aldora thought of how anxious Julie had been that first day. How shocked the girl had looked to see Grant with his arm around Aldy's shoulder the second time they met. She knew too well how awful it was to feel so much for someone and then find it wasn't mutual. Aldy was sure that Grant and Julie had a talk about that "embrace" later on that day. Julie's expression hadn't hidden her hurt or confusion. It was plain that Julie cared a great deal where Grant was concerned. Aldy hoped that Julie's being included in the lunch date revealed that Grant returned that affection. Aldora laughed at herself. *And you talk about Ellen being a matchmaker, Aldy Cassidy, just look at you. You don't even know these people!* But a small inner voice added: *At least not yet.*

ALDORA pulled a magenta sweater on over her tailored mauve shirt and tugged the bottom edge lower on her slim hips. She braided her dark hair into its workday queue and applied a touch of light pink lipstick to her full mouth. She looked critically at her reflection. Just right, she thought, neat, but no fashion plate, no threat. She brushed at a bit of lint on her jeans and gathered the rolls of cartoons and transfer paper into her arms. This afternoon would be the killer; then she'd have done it, dared the scaffolding; she'd be home free!

As Aldora walked into the new wing of the hospital, she noticed that workmen were already assembling the pipes and planks for her scaffolding. She leaned against a wall and tried to steady her quivering knees. *Concentrate,* she scolded. *Get absorbed in the work. Don't think about this afternoon.* Aldora walked over to one of the workmen. She introduced herself and was quickly involved in the setting-up procedure. She checked her composite and made minimal requests concerning vertical supports as she anxiously watched the scaffolding rise toward the vaulted ceiling.

By the time Aldora had watched the first two tiers go up, she was satisfied that the structure was well put together, safe, sturdy as the floor it stood upon. She assured herself of this and tried to forget that the top tier would be about eighteen feet off the ground! Aldy stepped back to get an overview. A hand touched her shoulder and she started.

"Sorry, Aldora," said Grant smiling down at her. "I didn't mean to frighten you."

"It's not your fault," she said. "I was lost in concentration. I do it all the time," she laughed. "It drives most of my friends crazy." She thought about poor Ellie who swore that Aldy would give her perma-guilt for the next hundred years for scaring her friend into heart failure. "There's no way to avoid it, it's an occupational hazard."

"Hazard is right," Grant agreed. He looked up at the scaffolding. "I can't have you jump like that if you're up there!"

Aldora shivered at the thought.

"How 'bout I whistle as I approach?" Grant said only half teasing.

"We could try it; it might work."

Grant let out a long wolf whistle and grinned at her. "That sound will be me trying to get your attention."

Aldora blushed a deep red as two of the workmen turned around and looked. One of them echoed his boss's whistle and Aldora covered her face with her hands. "It'll never work," she groaned. "If I don't fall to my death, I'll blush myself out of existence!"

Grant laughed and lazed against the wall. "Okay, from now on it's 'Yankee Doodle' or nothing." He looked serious for a moment. "I do love a lady who can blush like that." He winked at her. "Those blushes are already legend. Adam agrees, it's a fine, feminine trait."

Aldora was speechless!

"I'll send the guys back to plastering for a while and we'll go to lunch." Grant moved toward the workmen.

What was going on? thought Aldora as she watched Grant's lithe, retreating form. She felt her composure slipping away. The subject of her personal blood flow to her face was hardly one that could have come up in the discussion of her artwork. Apparently Grant and Mr. Holcomb had a friendship paralleling their business association. Grant returned whistling "Yankee Doodle" under his breath.

"Let's go," he said. "Julie's waiting in the car." Grant took her arm and steered her toward the elevators.

"There she is," said Grant as they stepped out at parking level B.

Aldora followed Grant's gaze and saw Julie wave from a yellow Mustang convertible.

Grant helped Aldy into the backseat.

"Hi," said Julie as she slid over and let Grant take the wheel. "We're in my car; his is selfish!" She gave Grant a quick hug.

"A two-seater, she means," Grant explained as he pulled the Mustang up the ramp to the street.

"A maroon MG." Julie turned around to Aldora. "The *real* love of his life."

"No comment," Grant teased, looking in the rearview mirror at Aldora. But he put his arm around Julie's shoulders and gave her a warm hug.

Aldora laughed. She was glad to see that Julie and Grant were close again, that Grant was giving Julie the kind of reassurance she'd never felt from Ken.

As they drove along, Julie sat facing the backseat and talked to Aldy. They were on a first-name basis in no time and Julie was filling Aldy in on her own job by the time they pulled into the parking lot of a cozy-looking little delicatessen off Santa Monica Boulevard.

Aldora learned that Grant's family had known Julie's since moving to Los Angeles in the forties. Grant had met Adam Holcomb while Grant was earning his degree at the USC School of Architecture.

"Yeah," Grant put in, "Adam was an alumnus of USC himself. I met him at a fraternity bash." Grant smiled as he recalled the incident.

Julie looked at him. "Grant can be pretty unforgettable when he chooses," she teased.

"She means the scale model we built for Adam that first semester." Grant continued the story for Aldy's benefit. "Adam had donated a new poolroom and lounge area to the fraternity house and we threw a 'thank-you bash' one Saturday night."

"He does mean 'bash,' " Julie said, smiling at Aldy.

"Adam wasn't at all the old stuffed shirt we'd anticipated," said Grant, easing the car to a halt at a light. "When we all recovered from our hangovers on Sunday, a bunch of the architecture students got together and built a scale model of a real den of iniquity, complete with pool table and smoke-filled bar. We sent it to him in a rented beer delivery truck."

"Adam still has that model in his living room," Julie put in.

"So how come he happened to single Grant out?" Aldy asked.

Julie chuckled and pointed a finger at Grant. "He was driving the beer truck."

Aldy laughed. "How'd you get hold of a beer truck, Grant?"

"I drove it three days a week to help with school expenses," Grant said, maneuvering the Mustang into a parking space and setting the hand brake.

"They hid the model in one of those big metal beer

kegs," Julie added. "They cut it in half and then soldered hasps on the outside."

"Sort of a takeoff on the old ship-in-the-bottle routine?" Aldy said.

Grant nodded. "I've never seen Adam laugh so hard before or since." He got out and held the door for Julie, then pulled the seat forward for Aldora.

"Well, with all this important stuff going on, how did you ever get around to architecture?" Aldy asked.

"That came years later," Grant joked.

"Yeah," Julie cut in, "after the hangovers really wore off."

Grant poked her lovingly in the ribs. "I submitted the best bid for the new hospital wing designs, although I'm sure Julie, here, would have you believing it was all nepotism."

Aldy laughed and widened her brown eyes to mock innocence. "Why, Grant, Julie wouldn't do anything like that!" Then to Julie: "Would you?"

Julie laughed and carried on with the story as they went into the delicatessen and waited for the hostess. She explained that she had studied at UCLA and that she and Grant had fought battles each football season. The rivalry led to camaraderie, and that led to... well, Julie declined to say just what that had led to, exactly.

The hostess greeted Grant and Julie as if she'd known them a long time. Taking menus, she led them to the back of the restaurant.

"Get us closer to the bar, eh, Cora?" Grant teased the hostess.

Aldora, hoping she wouldn't have to go through a song and dance about not drinking, was following Julie when she saw a very tall, handsome man stand up and look directly at her. Even from across the room, Aldy could see the distinguished touch of gray at his temples and the welcoming sparkle in his green eyes. She looked over her shoulder to see if there was some fantastic-looking woman who was drawing his attention. But then she saw Grant raise his hand in greeting and the man smiled. *Oh, goodness,* she thought, *we're having lunch with him!*

The man's smile widened as they drew near and he riveted his gaze on Aldora. He looked down at her from his lean and lofty height but spoke to Grant. "You're absolutely right, Grant, she's lovely."

Aldora felt the detested rush of blood to her cheeks. *Oh, no,* she prayed. That comment was designed to cause her to display one of the blushes Grant had teased her about earlier. She'd been set up! She glared at Grant. Being the object of a good joke didn't bother Aldy one bit, but this smacked of chauvinistic cruelty at her expense. She was about to vent her temper when Grant cut in quickly: "Aldora Cassidy, I'd like you to meet Adam Holcomb."

Aldora nearly fainted into her chair. Thank heavens Grant hadn't let her make a complete fool of herself with an outburst of anger before she realized that this man was the head of the whole Edgely Foundation! All her temper drained away as she looked up at him. "Mr. Holcomb?" she murmured in disbelief. "I—I've heard such nice things about you from Julie and Grant, but...I never expected...that is, Grant didn't mention—" She quit stammering and lifted her hand in helpless protest.

Adam tipped back his head and laughed. The deep, sonorous sound caused Aldy to catch at her next breath. He had such an infectious laugh. It soothed away all her residual anger at Grant's prank. She joined in and Grant and Julie laughed too.

"Knew she was a good sport," said Grant, patting her shoulder.

"Artists have to be or we don't survive," Julie said joking back at Grant. "Especially women. It takes a strong sense of humor to work with you."

"Even more vital to a writer?" said Adam, looking at Aldora again.

"Please," she said, "three wordless picture books and a short fairy tale hardly qualify me for a Pulitzer!" Aldora noticed that Adam's chair was against the wall and he was so tall that he had to fold himself into the space rather than just sit.

"Well, maybe a Newbery?" He leaned slightly toward her as he spoke, making his words seem almost intimate. "I love the work you're doing, Miss Cassidy. Grant showed me the composites. Those murals will be just what the children need to give them hope and a friendly, family feeling."

"Thank you, Mr. Holcomb," said Aldy. She dropped her gaze to the napkin on her lap. There was no way she could look into those green eyes right now. What was wrong with her? A few compliments from a man she'd just met and her stomach felt tight, fluttery, every time he spoke to her! It was just the shock of meeting the head of the Foundation in this unusual manner, she thought. She drew a breath as quietly as she could and looked up. Certainly she could meet Mr. Holcomb's gaze, handle herself with some degree of control now that she was used to the idea of lunching with *both* her immediate supervisors.

Grant and Julie were filling Adam in on some remodelling plans. Aldora looked at Adam Holcomb. What a fantastic face, she thought excitedly. Without thinking, she pulled a pen from her purse and doodled on the corner of her napkin. *I'd love to do a painting of him,* she decided. *Maybe a more casual look, though; that brown tweed is too formal for the sort of work I like to do.* She sketched rapidly as she mused. As she added the final touches to her drawing of Adam's rugged features, she was aware that all conversation had stopped. She looked up from her napkin. All three of her luncheon companions were watching her intently.

Aldora slid the napkin back into her lap and fumbled for her purse. "Don't mind me," she said, "just go right on with your conversation, I. . ."

Julie smiled and Grant grinned at Aldy. "And *that* is why I'm going to be whistling a lot of 'Yankee Doodle' every time I'm within twenty feet of your scaffold."

Adam and Julie looked bewildered. "'Yankee Doodle'?" said Adam looking at Julie. "Have you been driving with the top down on that Mustang, again?"

Julie shrugged, as confused as Adam.

"Aldy gets rather absorbed in her work," Grant explained. "She jumps a mile when you speak to her."

Julie laughed delightedly. "I love it."

Adam nodded. "Concentration like that is a valuable commodity," he soothed. "Only way to get anything done."

He understood! Aldora felt flooded with relief. He had taken the sting out of her perpetually embarrassing trait. He made her feel it was a gift.

"Do the same thing," he added. "Maybe you should 'Yankee Doodle' your way into my office, Grant." He smiled at Aldora, showing an even row of white teeth that made his face look even more deeply tanned.

The waitress came and took their orders. The men had wine but Julie declined, asking for coffee along with Aldy. Lunch conversation drifted around to a comparison of the best deli sandwiches in Los Angeles.

Grant held out for the restaurant they were in, but Adam argued that he knew of one place that was better. Julie looked mysterious and said nothing.

"We'll settle in the usual way," Adam said. "You and Julie have brought Aldora here, I hope that she'll let me take her to my favorite place very soon." He looked at Aldora. "She can be the judge."

Aldora's heart began a small dance in her chest. She nearly missed the rim of her coffee cup with her mouth. Why did she feel so uncomfortable each time Adam Holcomb looked at her?

"My daughter swears by this place and I need someone on my side."

Daughter? He was married: safe ground! So why did

Aldy suddenly feel that the ballet her heart was doing was from the dying swan?

"...so, Saturday evening, then?" Adam was speaking to her.

Aldora looked up from her plate. *A family dinner,* she thought, *might be nice.* "I'd love to, Adam, but I'm afraid I have a business appointment with my publisher on Saturday." Why had she said that? Why did she feel that she should make it clear that her engagements were of a business nature only? She glanced at Julie and Grant. They looked disappointed.

"Monday, then?" Adam offered. "You, Grant? Celebrate the first day's work on the mural?"

"Fine with us," Grant said and put an arm around Julie.

Aldora's mind raced. Another couple, a family dinner. Should be perfectly safe. "Count me in," she said and smiled.

"Great, Jessie will be so excited. Hasn't given me a moment's peace since she learned you were doing the mural." Adam sipped at his wine. "She has all your books."

"How flattering." Aldora flashed Adam a smile that lit her dark eyes with gratitude. Ellen was always saying she was too much of a recluse. This outing should quiet her for a while.

Adam picked up the check and they all walked to the front of the restaurant. "I have your address, Aldora," said Adam as he waited for his change. "About seven o'clock?"

"Seven's fine," said Aldy, smiling.

"All right. I'll be looking forward to it."

As Grant drove her and Julie back to the Foundation, Aldora wondered about Adam's choice of pronouns: "*I'll* be looking forward..." he had said. *You're too suspicious, Aldy,* she scolded. *A nice* family *outing. You'll enjoy it.*

All the scaffolding was in place when Aldora returned

to her work area. She examined the layout of the top tier of verticals and planks and then set to work pinning up the floor-level row of cartoons and transfer paper.

At three thirty Aldora pinned the last of the bottom row in place and straightened her back. She took a deep breath and looked up at the waiting platform. Sighing, she pulled a ladder over to the end of the scaffold and started to climb. With clammy hands she gripped the ladder rails and placed one foot on the first rung. Then she stepped off and retrieved her tote bag from the corner. She loaded transfer paper and sketches and the color composite into the bag and looped the handles over her arm. No way was she going to get all settled up there and then have to come down for supplies. She began again. One step up. Two steps. The platform edge loomed just above her head. *Come on, girl,* she encouraged herself. *Only a bit more.* The tote bag bumped against the ladder rungs and slapped against her hip on the return swing. *Tomorrow, I bring a basket and handline,* she vowed silently. *It's all I can do just to get* me *up the ladder.*

Reaching the first plank, Aldy transferred the tote bag to the board and took another deep breath. Letting it out very slowly, she forced herself to relax, then stepped cautiously from ladder rung to platform. There! Not too bad. But she had to repress an inner voice that tried to remind her that this was the lowest level, only six feet from the floor. Two more remained; the highest was about eighteen feet straight up.

Aldy forced her mind to concentrate on work. She had just put four more pushpins in her mouth when she heard the strains of "Yankee Doodle" wafting up to her. She looked down and saw Grant at the base of the ladder, grinning.

"Don't you ever quit?" he asked. "I'll have to alert the night shift."

Aldy stared at her watch, unable to believe that it was almost six thirty! "Sorry," she said as she made her way slowly along the plank to the ladder. "I guess I lost track of—"

"I know," Grant cut in, holding up a protesting hand. "Why do you think I was whistling that dumb song? You were very far away." He helped her down from the ladder. "This will wait," he kidded. "It'll all be here Monday morning." Looking up at the confusion of pins and paper, he added, "No one else could possibly figure it out. Unless you believe in those elves you draw."

Aldora laughed. "I wish."

"How do you know what's what?"

"The same way you know your buildings are going well with just a mess of framing and girders," she countered.

"Touché." Grant picked up her notes and sketches. "I'll walk you out," he said. "The lighting isn't on in the hall yet."

Grant helped Aldy into her car and closed the door. "Monday," he called as she drove away.

Aldora was too happy to go home to an empty house. She went past Ellen's to tell her the good news.

"I did it!" she crowed as Ellie opened the door. "My first day on the planks and I'm still in one piece!"

Bill came into the hall with a dish towel in his hands. He gave her a soapy hug. "Sure seem to be all in one piece," he teased.

Ellen swatted at him playfully. "Let her get in the door before you make a pass."

They had coffee while Aldy recounted the details. Ellen got a gleam in her eye as Aldy built up a bit of a tale around the meeting of Adam Holcomb. Leading Ellie on, she described how completely gorgeous the man was and how gallantly he'd defended her annoying trait of absorption in her work. Then she casually added that she had a date with him Monday night.

Ellen was all set to go into her shoes-and-rice number. "At last," she said. "He's gorgeous and you admit you like him!" Ellie looked triumphantly at Bill.

Then Aldy lowered the boom. "His daughter has all my books." She was instantly remorseful when she saw Ellie's shocked, hurt expression.

"You tricked me!" She picked up a sofa pillow and flung it at Aldy in mock anger. Then she crossed her eyes and stuck out her tongue.

"Serves you right," said Bill, laughing and rolling on the couch. "World's biggest matchmaker!"

"I'm only five-three in my socks!" Ellen shot back. "And I lost four pounds this week." But a smile threatened to undo her fierce look.

"Okay," Bill leaned over and put his arms around her. "The world's prettiest matchmaker?"

All Ellie's sham temper dissolved in a fit of giggles as Bill tickled her ribs.

Aldora felt a pang of longing accompany the pleasure she always felt at seeing Ellie and Bill so happy. She hadn't felt that way since the breakup with Ken. For a long while it had hurt to see couples being affectionate, but that feeling had passed; she'd healed over the inside sore spot. Why was the pang back now? "I've got to go," she said.

Ellie and Bill walked her to her car. As she pulled away, she could see them in her rearview mirror. They were going into their house with their arms around each other. Again Aldora felt that longing as she drove up the winding road toward home.

Chapter Five

Aldora spent a quiet weekend. A bit sore from·all the climbing on Friday, she worked out at the spa again, luxuriated in the hot tub. Then the dinner with her publisher revealed that her newest book's artwork had been approved, but that they needed a few revisions in the text. These she did on Sunday and mailed the pages off to the publishing house. She pressed some shirts for work and climbed gratefully into bed.

She was just dozing off as the phone rang. She groped for the receiver.

"Hello, Aldora? Adam Holcomb. Hope I didn't wake you."

His voice sounded rich and full even over the phone and Aldora was instantly and totally awake at his first words.

"I wanted to confirm our date for tomorrow and ask you if my daughter, Jessie, could bring some books for you to autograph." He paused and then rushed on, almost nervously. "She's been driving me crazy. In the interest of being able to get some sleep myself, I thought I'd call and disturb yours."

Aldora laughed. "No bother, Adam. I'd be happy to autograph them for her."

"Great," Adam said. "She'll be so thrilled. See you at seven."

"Okay." Aldy was reluctant to have that lovely voice stop reaching through the darkness to her in that manner that made her heart flutter just a little. "I'm looking forward to it."

"Good night, Aldora."

Aldy responded and then heard the receiver being

cradled. She lay there in the dark with the phone still in her hand. The harsh buzz of the dial tone brought her to her senses and she hung up the receiver. "Sure, he has a great voice, Aldy, but that's no reason to go strange over a married man and sit up until all hours with a dead phone," she said, angry with herself. In the darkness of her room she noticed that her own voice didn't sound nearly as comforting as Adam's did.

She punched up her pillow and tossed over on her other side. She couldn't seem to get comfortable. What was the matter with her? She was almost asleep when Adam had called, now she was wide awake. She flipped on the light and picked up a book. Her concentration drifted and an hour later she had turned the page only once. Exasperated, she switched off the lamp and pounded her pillow for the last time. But hours later she was still awake.

ALDORA lugged her basket and handline to the bottom of the scaffold and looked up at the highest platform. The apprehension she had felt driving to work caused her to push herself to get the worst over with before she chickened out altogether. She'd need an extension ladder to get up there safely, so she asked a workman to bring one and then began loading her supplies into her basket. She was checking her mental equipment list when he returned.

"Right here, please," she said. "Thanks."

Looping the handline, she tossed it expertly, lofting it over the topmost beam. She fastened the other end to the handle of the basket and turned to the ladder. Rubbing her palms on her slacks, she gripped the side rails and started to climb. Halfway up she noticed that her fingers ached and her knuckles were white from gripping the cold metal ladder. Nervously, she took each hand from the ladder in turn, shook it out, and continued up to the top platform. As she stepped out onto the plank, she heard the sound of two hands clapping below.

Oh, no, she thought. *I can't look down!* She gripped the side of the ladder with one hand and shifted all her weight to her opposite foot. She raised one hand over her head and tried desperately to give the best possible body-language interpretation of supreme exasperation. "What now?" she called out lightly, hoping she could put off looking down indefinitely.

"Masterful," said Grant. "Especially the handline toss."

Aldora shrugged one shoulder. "Thanks, but coming from the world's only Revolutionary War song buff, is it a compliment?" Aldy knew she'd have to look down soon, but she mimed waiting for the response with a hand cupped to her ear. Perspiration beaded on her forehead and trickled down her neck.

"Most definitely," came the answer.

Aldora gripped the ladder until her fingers hurt and turned her head ever so slightly. She glanced down at Grant over her shoulder. "I accept," she said. "But I'm not coming all the way down for a curtain call." She chuckled, wishing the laugh didn't sound so nervous and thin as it drifted out into the void below her. Grant looked so small! She swallowed hard. This top plank was only about four and a half feet from the ceiling so she lowered herself to a sitting position and let her feet dangle from the board. Then she looked down at Grant again. That seemed to help. Sitting felt much more secure.

Grant shook his head. "Sitting down on the job already?" he said.

Aldy risked leaning over to make a face at him. "You'd rather I concussed myself on your roof-beams?"

"The men could lower that top plank for you," he offered.

"No, thanks," said Aldy quickly. "I can reach it all from this position."

"Okay." Grant waved and walked off across the room.

Aldora took the first breath she'd been aware of since she'd stepped out on the platform. *Thank heavens, I'd really rather topple off here in private.* She smiled to herself. *Guess I'm a closet accident case.* She started pinning up drawings. Working feverishly, Aldy tried to crowd out the memory of how completely untrue that had been when she'd taken that big fall in front of a group of sixty over two years ago. Only one of those people had been someone who had mattered, and he hadn't stayed around long after that. Aldy pushed thoughts of Ken from her mind and stabbed pins into the cartoons with vicious intent.

FOUR hours later Aldora had placed half of the uppermost drawings and transfer sheets and was lowering her basket down with the handline. After lunch she'd refill her basket and have a workman move the ladder for her. By the end of the day, the worst would be over. Suddenly Aldy was aware that someone was watching her. Looking around, she saw Adam Holcomb with a curious expression on his face, leaning against the far wall. Aldora waved and started down the ladder. As she reached the bottom rung, strong hands encircled her waist and lifted her to the floor.

"You are remarkable." Adam's voice held astonished admiration. "I never thought our hospital wall could look so good."

"Thank you," said Aldy, looking at the floor. "I don't see how you can tell from all those papers and pins." She began coiling the handline as she spoke.

"But I can," Adam said. "The *mural* looks great too."

Aldy looked up at him. He smiled, seeming to enjoy her startled look. She laughed nervously, picked up her basket, and began rummaging aimlessly to cover her lack of response. Would she never be able to converse with this man without feeling constantly off balance?

Adam took her gracefully off the hook. "Am I too late to take our resident cat burglar to lunch?"

"I really can't," said Aldy, waving a brown bag. "I brought mine and my helpers will be arriving any—" She stopped midsentence at the look of urgency in Adam's eyes.

"I must speak with you, Aldora. How about some coffee with that whatever-it-is?" He pointed to the sack.

"All right."

"So, you see why I had to clue you in?" Adam finished.

Aldora sat numbly and watched her coffee steam into a lukewarm, unpalatable tastelessness. Surely this man had enough power, money, to get his daughter the best. Why didn't he bring her to the Foundation? Aldora forced herself to focus on the rest of Adam's sentence.

"...the child's very sensitive. I realized after I'd rung off last night that I hadn't told you she was semi-invalid. She's more than a little self-conscious about her chair."

Aldora flashed back on her own discomfort when she'd had to use her cane and brace all the time. "I understand," she said quietly. "I wouldn't have thought of reacting—"

"I knew that," Adam said before she could finish. "I just thought it'd be easier on *you* to know in advance." An expression of pain altered his rugged features as he spoke.

"Would she misinterpret if I brought her something special?" Aldora asked.

Adam looked puzzled.

"I thought I would bring her an original sketch from my newest book," Aldy explained. "It's just been accepted as of Saturday so I can spare the composites now, but I wouldn't want her to think it was due to her disability.''

''She'd be delighted.'' Adam backed gratitude with concern. ''Don't go out of your way, though,'' he added.

''No trouble,'' said Aldy lightly. She could see eager affection for his daughter shining in his smile, his green eyes, and she was happy to be able to help. ''I better get back now.''

Adam stood as she left the table. ''Tonight, then.''

Aldora waved and walked back through the building to the new wing.

By four thirty Aldora's helpers had pushed her far ahead of her estimated schedule. ''Let's knock off early,'' she called to Kate and Eddy. She gathered her equipment as Kate swung down from the first platform. ''Thanks, you two,'' Aldy said. ''It's going very well.''

Eddy did a Tarzan yell and landed at Aldy's feet in a bound. ''Jane and I will see you tomorrow,'' he said with a serious attempt at a straight face.

Kate punched him in the shoulder. ''Heights do that to him,'' she said. ''What time?''

''About ten. I've got a''— she nearly said ''date'' and stopped herself—''meeting tonight. Let's not make it too early.''

Eddy and Kate joined hands and went off down the corridor with Eddy singing ''Follow the Yellow Brick Road.'' Kate, making a face, tried to silence him with a hand over his mouth.

Aldora watched them leave. There was that funny pang again. She picked up her workbasket and headed for the car.

''NOTHING fancy,'' Aldora muttered as she glared into her closet. ''Mighty good thing, that,'' she said as she went through her wardrobe a second time.

She pulled out a pair of brown twill flare-leg slacks and held them up to the light. Draping them over a chair she hunted through her dresser for her honey-beige cashmere pullover. After she'd dressed, she added a paisley neck scarf of rust and chocolate, then a small brooch. She turned to examine the effect in the mirror. Not bad, really. The pants looked a bit too flared for current fashion, but she decided that it was the slimness of her legs that gave that illusion of breadth to the cuffs. She pulled on soft leather boots and added a touch of coral lip gloss to her mouth. Smiling widely into the glass, she checked for lip color on her teeth. They gleamed back at her, whitely. All set.

Aldora was just matting the illustration for Jessie when she heard the doorbell. "Be right there," she called down from the studio.

As she descended the stairs she could see Adam through the glass door. He was wearing tan slacks that accented his trim waist and long legs. A gray-green sport shirt, open at the throat, displayed a soft mat of dark hair curling from his chest and emphasized the jade of his eyes. A dark brown sport coat hung over his left arm. *What a great way with clothes,* Aldy thought. *Probably look good in any costume I'd want to paint him in.* She glanced at the easel in the corner of the loft. Maybe she'd get back to serious painting sooner than she'd expected.

She smiled through the glass at her escort. "Welcome," she said as she slid open the door.

"You have the perfect house for an artist," Adam said as he stepped down into the living room of the A-frame. "Studio upstairs?"

"Sure thing. Feel free to look while I get my jacket." Aldora went to the bedroom closet. She could hear Adam take the stairs two at a time. That was one good thing about long legs, she thought, made short work of stairs. When she returned with her wrap, Adam was standing by the front door.

"It looks fascinating, Aldora. How about a guided tour sometime?" He reached to help her with her jacket.

"I'll just carry it for now," she said, slipping Jessie's illustration under the folds. "You can have a tour any time; Jessie's welcome too." Aldy hesitated, knowing Adam would have to carry her up the stairs, but perhaps a tour through a real artist's studio would compensate Jess for any embarrassment she might feel.

"I'm sure she'd love it," said Adam as he latched Aldy's door and took her arm on the porch steps.

"Maybe you and Mrs. Holcomb would like to bring Jess up tonight if dinner doesn't run too late?" Aldy offered.

"Jessie and I would like that," he said.

Aldy's heart jumped in her chest. What had she said? "You and Mrs. Holcomb..." and he had *corrected* to "Jessie and I...." Certainly the man wouldn't take his daughter out to squire his muralist to dinner and leave his wife at home! Aldora looked anxiously at the metallic brown Lincoln in her drive.

A small blond head peered out at the back window. The front seat was empty! Aldy's heart began to pound. What was going on here, anyway? she thought angrily.

A small, shrill voice drew her attention. "Is this her, Daddy?"

"Sure enough, pumpkin," Adam said as he leaned into the car and pulled the seat forward so that Jessie could see out more easily.

"How do you do, Miss Cassidy," Jessie said. "I have all your books." She pointed to the four picture books stacked on the seat next to her. "Daddy said you'd autograph them for me!"

Aldora was immediately captivated by this candid ten-year-old, but her heart ached a bit as she thought of the wheelchair that she knew must be in the trunk.

She could see Adam out of the corner of her eye. He looked so loving when he gazed at his daughter. Almost tender.

"Don't pester Aldora yet, pumpkin." Adam chuckled at his daughter's eagerness. "Let her get in the car first." Adam replaced the seat and handed Aldora into the front. As he walked around to the driver's side, Aldora slid her back against the passenger's door and turned to face Jessie. "I've brought you something," she said, pulling the illustration from under the folds of her jacket. "It's for my most loyal fan." She handed Jessie the drawing and watched the girl's eyes widen in surprise.

"For me?" Jess looked at her father for confirmation and he nodded. Green eyes looked into green as father and daughter communicated wordlessly.

"Oh, thank you, Miss Cassidy. I've never seen this one before. It's not in any of my books."

"That's because it's from my newest book that isn't even printed yet," Aldy explained.

"You mean I'm the first to see it?" Jessie breathed almost reverently.

"You sure are, Jess," Adam said and looked at Aldora. "You've made her day, Aldy, thank you."

Aldora noticed the use of her shortened first name and looked up quickly. "I'm glad," she said. He didn't seem to realize that he'd altered her name as he spoke, but the way he said "Aldy" made her heart clench and her blood race.

"Mama would love this one," Jessie said quietly.

Aldora saw a flicker of emotion cross Adam's face, saw his shoulders tense. "Maybe she'll see it someday, pumpkin," he said stiffly and pulled the Lincoln smoothly out of the drive.

Well, Aldy thought uneasily, Adam must be separated from his wife. Maybe, divorced! That explained her absence tonight, but gave Aldy a whole new set of worries. If Adam was divorced, then she was out on a date in spite of her resolve. She'd never have agreed to come out with a man like Adam Holcomb if she'd realized he was single. Especially since she was aware that his looks, his easy charm, all had a definite effect on her pulse rate and his flattery tended to rather turn her head a little.

Feeling suddenly awkward, Aldy looked back at Jess who was staring fondly at the illustration. *Don't be silly,* she thought, *who'd take his daughter on a first date?* She breathed easier with that rationalization and settled back in her seat.

GRANT and Julie were already at the restaurant when Adam wheeled Jessie up to the table.

"Hi, Jessie," said Grant playfully. "How's my best gal?"

Jess reached her arms toward him. "Just fine, Uncle Grant." He leaned over to hug her.

"Look what Miss Cassidy gave me," she said, lifting the illustration from its place by the arm of her chair.

"That's terrific, Jess. Is it from one of your books?" Grant asked, looking from the drawing to Aldora.

"It's from a new book that isn't even printed yet!" Jess said excitedly. Her eyes sparkled with importance. "I'm the first to see it."

Grant smiled at Aldy. "That's really nice, isn't it, Julie?" he said, but his eyes were fastened on Aldora.

"May I see it?" Julie was across the table and straining for a look.

Grant held the picture for Julie's inspection.

"It's wonderful," she said. "This must be your lucky day, Jess." She smiled at Aldora.

Jessie held out her hand and Grant passed her the picture. "Would you put it in the car, Daddy? Please! I don't want it to get crushed."

Adam took the picture from Jessie's hand. "Back in a flash," he said. He strode out of the restaurant and

Aldora couldn't help but admire his graceful carriage as she watched him go.

The evening was a huge success. Grant was a shining example of a doting "uncle" as he bantered with Jessie. Adam, who carried the responsibility for entertaining the other two ladies easily on his broad shoulders, was a sterling conversationalist. He kept Julie and Aldy laughing when Grant was too engrossed with Jess to speak to the ladies. The only rough moment came when Aldora was reminded that this was a contest and she was supposed to be judging the quality of this deli plate versus the one Grant favored.

Aldora looked at Grant. He and Adam wore identical expressions, both hopeful, expectant. It was a hard choice. She took a deep breath. "I suppose I can't get off with a draw decision?"

"No way," said Julie. "I had to go through this too."

Jess looked as if she were about to burst with excitement.

Aldora squeezed her eyes shut as if anticipating a blow. "In that case, sorry, Adam. Grant's place wins by a cole slaw." She mimed a flinch and held a hand in front of her.

Jessie clapped wildly and Adam laughed that laugh Aldy was beginning to love. "Now Daddy won't have any excuse not to go there," Jess said happily.

Adam ruffled Jessie's hair with a large hand. "I'm a broken man," he teased gently. He reached across and took the check from Grant. "You win," he said.

"Do they bet on everything?" Aldy asked Julie.

Julie rolled her eyes at the ceiling. "You get used to it."

On the drive home Jess babbled on about the fine things Grant had told her during dinner. She was sure that Aldy and Adam had missed all the good conversation and nothing would serve but that she had to fill them in.

When Adam pulled into Aldy's driveway, he turned to face his daughter. "How do you feel, honey?"

"Fine, Daddy. Honest."

"Then how would you like to see Aldora's studio?"

Jessie's mouth dropped open. She looked at Aldy. "Can I?"

"You have a special invitation."

Aldora went ahead and opened doors and turned on lights. She watched Adam as he gently swept Jess into his arms and carried her lightly up the stairs. He placed her in a chair. "Be right back."

Aldy chatted with Jess over the bar as she set up the coffeepot. She didn't want Jessie to fix on her father's errand.

Adam came back with the folded wheelchair and took it right up to the studio.

"Tour time," he said and lifted Jess to carry her up to the loft room.

"Right," said Aldora, following Adam to the studio. She admired the set of his shoulders and the easy way he mounted the stairs even with Jessie's weight. How fortunate that Jessie had a daddy who made it look so easy, so matter-of-fact, as he carried her around. Aldy realized that this was a far cry from her own experience and she was glad that Jess didn't have to suffer the embarrassment so often evident in the faces of those a disabled person had to live with. She felt a wave of affection for this gentle, caring man and his daughter.

Adam set Jess in her chair and let her roll herself around the studio. Aldora followed and explained the equipment and answered Jessie's endless questions. She concluded the tour with a showing of the designs for the murals.

Jess begged to see the mural. Her father laughed. "Soon, Jess, I promise." Then to Aldy: "So, that's what's under all that stuff you have pinned to that wall."

Aldora laughed. "I thought you said you could tell," she teased.

"I lied," he said and winked at Jess. "It'd ruin my image to ask what it all was in my own territory."

They all went back down to the kitchen; Aldy and Adam had coffee and Jess had milk and some of Aldora's homemade apple crumble.

"I love this apple stuff," said Jess.

"So do I, pumpkin." Adam spoke to Jess, but his eyes were on Aldora. "Thank you for a very special evening, Aldy," he said quietly.

There it was again. He used that diminutive of her name, and again, he didn't seem aware of it. Aldora looked at Jessie. She was draining her milk glass and didn't seem to register any reaction to the name or the tone her father had used with Aldora.

"It was my pleasure, Adam." Aldy really meant that. She had enjoyed this evening with this sensitive man and his gallant daughter more than she could say.

Adam helped Jessie into her coat and carried her to the car. "Bye, Miss Cassidy. Thank you," Jess called over her father's shoulder.

Aldy waved until Jess disappeared down the porch steps. She stared at the empty wheelchair and a lump formed in her throat. Not for the first time she wondered about Adam's comment in the lunchroom. "She won't have surgery," he'd said. Aldy wondered if the bitterness in his words as he'd spoken was on his own behalf or a barrier of fear that belonged to the daughter.

Adam bounded up the porch stairs and rapidly folded the chair. Setting it by the open door, he came toward Aldy.

"You made our evening, Aldy," he said. His eyes looked candidly at her and Aldora had the disturbing feeling that he was going to come a lot closer. She was about to move past him to the door, but he reached out and slipped his arm around her shoulders. "Aldy," he murmured. His voice was low, almost a whisper, and filled with need. He brushed her cheek lightly with his lips and the effect was like an electric current through Aldora's body. A current that awakened feelings long buried under layers of pain and anger. As Adam's lips caressed her cheek, her senses reached longingly toward this wellspring of new life, but her mind reeled and drew back from this potential source of new pain, fresh anguish.

Adam moved to draw her body closer to his own. "You really did make *my* evening, Aldy," he murmured, his lips soft against her ear.

There was that change of pronoun again, Aldy thought illogically, as she pulled back a bit and smiled up at Adam. "I enjoyed it immensely," she said. She groped for a way to lighten the mood. "Jessie is adorable company." Afraid of the feelings this man was inspiring, of the look in his eyes, Aldy mentioned Jess to draw the focus away from the two of them, away from these more romantic paths. But the hard look that came over Adam's face made her wish she could slip right through the floor to the furnace room.

Adam stiffened and put her abruptly from him. "I'm glad," he said shortly. "She likes you very much."

Aldora felt a chasm widening between them but couldn't seem to find the words to repair the rift. "Please," she said desperately, "come back any time."

"Right," said Adam, regaining his control and composure. "Good night, Aldora."

The use of her full name after the endearing way he'd shortened it earlier was like an icy shower. Aldy watched him move to the door with purposeful strides. He grabbed up the wheelchair in one powerful hand and went down the stairs without looking back.

Why hadn't she responded to the electricity that had surged through her at his embrace? Why had she made that remark that must have made him feel that it was only Jess that held her interest? Part of Aldora knew why. The rest of her wanted to race down the stairs and call him back. Wanted an instant replay with a change in the script. Tears of confusion filled her eyes as she stood rooted to the floor. She felt as if irreparable damage had been done deep inside her. She swiped at the tears on her cheeks. "Sour grapes time," she whispered to herself. "It's better this way. You can't run a relationship anymore...what could you possibly do for either of them?

"This is what you wanted," she reminded herself bleakly as the silence of the empty house closed around her.

Sitting on the edge of her bed, Aldora brushed at her long hair with firm, angry strokes. Relationships, she thought dismally, they equaled caring; that equaled love; that brought pain *unequaled*!

A picture of Jess clinging to her father and waving to Aldy as she was carried down the stairs swam before Aldy's eyes. Her own father had been a warm, nurturing man like Adam. He traveled a lot, but when he was home, he took Aldy to the zoo and encouraged her to sketch the animals. He'd proudly show her efforts to every passerby, and the guard by the giraffes knew Jim and his daughter by name.

Aldora loved drawing the long-necked, gawky creatures with their huge brown eyes and their splotchy hides. "They are the only animals that can make no sound," her father said. From that time on, Aldora felt a special closeness to these mute beasts who could not cry out even if frightened or in pain.

Aldora's mother, a slim, nervous woman who leaned too much on those around her, was forever demanding silence...and forever getting it. Nothing urged her to anger as quickly as Aldora crying into the house with a bruised elbow or a skinned knee. "I'll give you something to cry about, if you don't stop" was her immediate response to the first hint of a whimper from her small daughter.

So Aldora learned to keep her pain inside. To save it for the dead of night when she could hold her pillow tightly over her face and smother the sounds that made her mother angry with her.

When Aldora was thirteen, her father flew to Chicago on business and never came home. His cab had been hit by a delivery truck, head-on in the rain. He died instantly.

At his funeral Veronica Cassidy had wept copiously for her departed husband and several strong arms were made available to support the young window who looked so lovely in black, so helpless, distraught at the cruelty of life.

No one paid much attention to the stolid little girl who watched dry-eyed as they lowered her father's casket into the yawning ground.

That frail, helpless look that Veronica turned on her friends led to an endless stream of "uncles" who sued for Veronica's attentions and used Aldy as a pawn. After a while Aldora stopped looking for her father's warmth in these men who hugged her overmuch and drifted away when Veronica ceased to be amused by them.

As Aldora blossomed into a beautiful young woman, her mother's nerves worsened and she sent Aldy off to boarding school. Aldora, not a stupid child, knew that this move had less to do with her mother's "nerves" than with the way some of Veronica's suitors had begun to look at Aldora.

Aldy retreated further into her art. It became a living link with her father. In the middle of Aldy's second year at Otis Art Institute, her mother flitted off to Europe with an especially wealthy, attentive man and cabled the news of her marriage from Naples.

Postcards would come occasionally. On birthdays. On the occasion of Aldora's graduation from college.

But Veronica made it clear that she didn't want a daughter Aldora's age at her side, making people wonder about Veronica's own fleeting youth. The postcards came less and less often and the last time Aldora had tried to contact her mother had been when she'd completed her first assignment to do the illustrations for a children's book for a prominent New York publisher. Aldora sent an advance copy to her mother's last known address. Three months later a cable arrived: "Loved the cute pictures, Aldora. Congratulations, Mother."

"Cute!" The four-letter word of the children's book business! Aldora never wrote back. She gave up caring so desperately and immersed herself in work. It didn't take away the hurt, the feeling of abandonment, but it did wonders for her career. Aldora went to New York and stayed for two years. She hated the city, but that was where the work was. Within those two years she became skilled enough and popular enough to move back to the West Coast and deal with the publishers by mail. Some of the houses were setting up branches in the west by then and Aldora began to get job offers from a house in San Francisco. It was on one of the commuter flights to that city that she met Ken Morely. He was a business representative for a large computer firm in Los Angeles and he flew to San Francisco often. The second time he'd had a flight scheduled with Aldora, he'd asked to take her out.

"Hey, pretty lady, we D.P.'s are supposed to stick together," Ken had said when she'd refused him.

"D.P.'s?" Aldora asked shyly.

"Displaced persons. All commuters are displaced."

"I don't feel that way about San Francisco," said Aldy firmly.

"Well, how about a tour of my town when we get back to Los Angeles?" Ken smiled at her and raised his glass. "A welcome home party just for us?"

Aldy felt herself relent just a bit, but parties were

not her thing. "No, thanks anyway." She tried to resume reading her revision notes.

"You're a writer, eh?" Ken smoothly drew her out.

"How did you know?" Aldy looked up from her papers.

"That envelope carries a rather prestigious publishing house's name on its letterhead," said Ken easily. "We do some of their in-house computer setups."

Aldora began to feel more comfortable with this line of talk. She explained that she was mostly an artist now, but hoped to do more of the writing soon. She and Ken chatted until the plane touched down, then parted company and went their separate ways. She was sure that was the end of it.

Two weeks later, in Aldy's Los Angeles studio, the phone rang and it was Ken!

"How did you find me?" Aldy asked after the traditional "openers" had been said.

"You sure don't give a guy much help in that department," Ken said, chuckling.

Aldora wheedled.

He deferred.

By the time Aldy learned he'd used somewhat spurious methods to locate her, she was more inclined to give him points for ingenuity and persistence rather than a jail sentence. After all, he *did* have a legitimate right to peer into the computer at her publishing house.

"All's fair in love and war, pretty lady," he said to soothe her first indignant response to the information. "And I do hope this won't be the latter." He grinned at her and his eyes begged forgiveness.

Aldy laughed and gestured defeat with her hands.

Ken was a partygoer and loved showing Aldora off at social functions. In his line of work the opportunities were endless, so Aldy had to grow to accept the social whirl or abandon her growing love for Ken. She went to the parties, but never learned to like them. The affected chatter, the silly party-antics of gray-flannels liberated by alcohol.

More and more Aldy found herself begging off. Excusing herself to her work. A deadline had to be met. A painting had to be finished for a show or a client. Ken, impressed with Aldy's budding success in both her chosen career fields, accepted this for a time. The relationship deepened and Aldora was blissfully happy when Ken proposed one evening in a romantic restaurant on the Sunset Strip.

Ken couldn't wait to take her to parties after that. Eager to show off the ring he'd given her, the prize he'd won, he became increasingly insistent. Aldora pleaded work just once too often.

"Dammit, Aldora!" Ken raged. "I'm marrying a workaholic!" He fumed at her. She'd never seen him so angry. "It's the books and the illustration or the fine arts, the painting. Make a decision." He flung the ultimatum at her.

"What?" Aldora, close to tears, stared at him in disbelief. "You know I'm almost ready for that one-woman show in San Francisco!" Panic surged through her.

"There isn't room in your life for two careers *and* me!" he shouted. "You decide." He slammed out of her studio, as Aldora stood gaping, her mouth opening and closing like a goldfish out of water.

"I can't," she said bitterly to the back side of the slammed door. "You can't mean it!"

Aldora lasted five days. Five days without a word. Then, shocked, but knowing herself to be deeply in love, Aldora Cassidy, successful illustrator and fledgling comer on the fine art vista, followed the longings of her twenty-four-year-old heart and pulled a drop cloth over her easel. The shine of the ring on her third finger blinded her to all but her love for Ken.

With her schedule eased, Aldora reentered Ken's social world and eventually went to that nearly fatal party at his boss's home. An extravagant affair at their lavish house overlooking the whole sparkling San Fernando Valley from a prestige address high in the Santa Monica Mountains. The food, the guests, and the liquor were ostentatious to say the least. Aldora was so ill at ease; she was more uncomfortable than she had ever been in her life. Hindsight might have tried to show her discomfort to be a premonition, a forerunner of disaster.

Tossing the brush on the dressing table, Aldora shook her head and pushed back the memories of that awful night. She knew what loving could bring and she wasn't accepting delivery. She crawled wearily into bed and turned out the light.

Chapter Six

For the remainder of the week Aldora threw herself into her work with all the passion that she denied herself in her social life. She drove herself until she could fall into bed at night and sleep the dreamless sleep of physical exhaustion.

Kate and Eddy arrived promptly at eight thirty each morning and helped with the mammoth job of tracing the composition onto the primed surface of the wall. As each section was completed, it was Aldora's job to remove the sketches and transfer sheets as carefully as possible and touch up any lines that were faint or that had failed to transfer. Then she had to climb down from the scaffold, walk to the far side of the room and make notes on any adjustments or corrections.

"Good one," Aldy called to Eddy from across the room. "Only have to smooth the joint where sections F and G come together, but you better put the pins back on section E."

Eddy nodded and Aldora climbed back up to the third platform and began touch-ups.

Stepping back to get the scope of each piece relative to the whole was essential, but grueling. By lunchtime on Wednesday Aldora's back and legs were cramping with the strain of all the trips up and down the ladders. Her arches ached from spending so much time draped over the rungs.

Following Eddy and Kate out to one of the atria with her sack lunch, Aldy lowered herself carefully onto a bench and rubbed her feet.

"Sore?" Kate asked.

"Birdfeet," Aldora said, laughing. "Too many ladder rungs."

"I hear that!" said Eddy.

"How could you tell in those?" Kate smiled and pointed to his heavy Western boots.

"I can tell," he mumbled through his tuna sandwich and stuffed a potato chip into his already full mouth.

Kate looked at Aldy and shrugged. "Born in a barn, but I love him." She laughed and nibbled at a carrot stick.

Aldora smiled. She had watched this romance from the beginning. Kate had met Eddy at one of Aldy's painting classes and Aldora had predicted the blossoming of the relationship from the moment she had introduced Kate and Eddy had offered his hand. It was covered with Thalo blue paint at the time. Kate, unaware, had taken Eddy's hand warmly in her own. Too late, she realized her error! Thalo blue was a powerful, electric color and during the time it took to finally get all of the paint to stop oozing, seemingly from Kate's pores, Eddy had wangled a date.

When Aldora had given Ken her prediction, he had hugged her warmly, told her she was a hopeless romantic, a matchmaker. Back then, with Ken holding her close, she had felt as Ellen felt now: get everyone into that happy boat, drifting on a sea of comforting, secure emotions; love. But now, as she listened to Kate's simple declaration, she felt her stomach tighten; its clenching left room for a distinctly hollow place in the center of her body. Though she smiled at Kate, that place was still an aching void. Aldy was annoyed to find thoughts of Adam Holcomb trying to rush in to fill that void. *Stop it,* she thought as she bit angrily into her avocado and sprout sandwich. *You don't need that.* Then her inner voice amended: *He doesn't need you!* The harsh reality of that made her bite of sandwich stick painfully as she tried to swallow. Her eyes watered as the mouthful worked its way down her constricting throat. *It's true,* she thought, *he has one invalid too many already, he* doesn't *need another!*

Aldy looked at her half-eaten sandwich. The thought of even one more bite nauseated her. She wrapped the foil around it and stuffed it back in the bag. "I need some coffee," she said as she stood up. "Can I bring you anything?"

Kate, mouth full of potato salad, shook her head and hurried to swallow. Eddy waved his no, making lettuce shreds fall from his sandwich like confetti at a founder's day parade. Kate glared at the mess and rolled her eyes at Aldy. "What'd I tell you?" she said, brushing bits of lettuce into a sandwich wrapper.

Aldora laughed and walked back into the building. She was just entering the cafeteria when she heard a familiar shout.

"Aldy!"

She turned to see Julie waving her way toward her.

"Hi, Julie. Join me?"

"You bet. I've been looking all over the new wing for you."

"We were out in the west atrium. What's up?"

"I need to show you the sample swatches for the large sofas," Julie said as she fell into the food line behind Aldora. "You were going to tell me if they'll blend with the finished mural."

"Oh, right." Aldy ran coffee into her cup.

"Tonight after work, okay?"

"Fine. Second-floor conference room?" Aldy handed the cashier a dollar. "Take both out of this," she said and motioned to Julie's tea.

"Thanks, Aldy. For the tea too. You're a lifesaver. Swatches and orders have to go in in the morning."

Aldora raised her coffee container in a combined gesture of thanks-and-don't-mention-it and started back to the new wing.

Kate and Eddy were already climbing up the scaffolding when she reached the work area. Aldy looked up at the seam between F and G and spied a place she'd missed. Setting her coffee under a ladder, she grabbed her chalk and started to climb.

At four thirty Julie came by to remind her of their meeting. "Like your coffee cold?" she asked as she watched Aldy step from the ladder.

"Ugh!" Aldy followed Julie's gaze to the cup still standing on the floor, its lid secure. "I guess I—"

"That's why I'm here," Julie cut in. "Your disregard for a clock is legendary!" She laughed and gave Aldy a quick hug. "See you upstairs."

Aldora nodded. "Twenty minutes." And seeing Julie's look of disbelief, she added: "I swear!"

Aldora called to her helpers. They scrambled down and folded things up for the night. As they rolled the cartoons and transfer sheets from the finished sections, Aldy said, "We should be done by Friday morning." She checked the floor for pushpins. "Maybe we can start mixing the paint batches in the afternoon."

"Hooray! Monday we paint!" Eddy grabbed Kate and swung her in a small joyous circle.

"He can't wait to wet a brush," Kate explained as she pulled free. "He told all his friends he's the next Michelangelo."

Aldora laughed, recalling her own former alarm when Ellen had used the same reference to tease her about her scaffold fright. She looked up at the pipes and planks. The top platform didn't look so threatening anymore. She was getting used to it. Five feet...eighteen feet, it felt the same once you got to working, concentrating. She smiled to herself. *It's* not *gonna beat me!*

Leaving Kate and Eddy to finish up, Aldy went to meet Julie.

"You're here!" Julie said, obviously amazed to see Aldy come in.

"Ye of little faith." Aldy smiled smugly and bowed. "Let's see those swatches."

Julie shoved the two thick books of material samples

toward Aldora. "Have a seat. I've marked the possibles." She pointed to the slips of paper between the pages.

Aldy and Julie spread out the selections and finally narrowed to a choice of two. Aldora shifted in her chair. She was starting to stiffen. She'd have to go home by way of the spa or risk a bad spasm in her lower back. "That's it. Either of those," she said, rubbing her back with her hands.

Julie grinned. "This one, then," she said, placing her finger on a muted green swatch with abstract patterns of lighter shades of green overlapping the olive background.

Aldora nodded her agreement. "Good," she said, flexing her tight shoulders. "And for coordinates?"

"I'll pick up that lime green in the piping of the sofa and some occasional pillows." She paused. "Then I'll put accent yellow on the wall benches." Julie looked at Aldy.

"You have definite possibilities," said Aldy seriously. Then, never able to pull off a deadpan when she needed one, she grinned back at Julie and laughed.

"Glad you admit it," said Julie, faking a haughty tone of voice.

Aldora chuckled. She loved Julie's easy way with mock rivalry. It could have been really awkward if the initial mood of jealousy hadn't been so completely dispelled by the close of that first luncheon. The luncheon where Aldy had met Adam Holcomb. Her artist's eye began to flash scenes from that day on the screen of her mind and she felt a smile tug at the corners of her mouth as she remembered Adam's deep laugh and appreciative smile.

"I can't wait to show Jessie the choices," Julie said as if picking up on Aldora's train of thought. "Adam had her bedroom done in lime greens and yellow. They're her favorites."

Aldy smiled thinking of Jess's excitement as she

toured the studio Monday night. "How is Jess?" she asked.

Julie's smile faded a bit. "Fever's back. She's over in the old building, second floor."

Aldora grabbed at Julie's arm. "Jess? Here, in the hospital?"

"I thought you knew," Julie said. "That's why Adam hasn't been by to see the mural. He brought Jess in Tuesday night."

Aldora's brain flooded with questions but her lips couldn't seem to form the words she needed. She stared helplessly at Julie. "Fever?"

"I'm sorry, Aldy. I really thought you knew. It's a staph infection. The asphalt fragments that they didn't get out after the crash. It flares up now and again and she has to come in for antibiotic therapy."

Confused, Aldora sat silent, her fingers still clutching Julie's wrist.

Julie leaned closer and patted Aldy's hand. "Adam didn't tell you, I see."

Aldora shook her head numbly.

"Jess was in an auto accident almost five years ago. Her mother was at the wheel," Julie explained. "Jess had dropped her doll out of the car window and started to scream. Louise took her eyes off the road for just an instant—"

Aldora released Julie's wrist and put her hands over her face, pressed her fingers against her eyelids, and swallowed the hard lump in her throat.

"Jessie was thrown from the car. Louise had some cuts from the windshield. Jess was crippled."

"Dear Lord!" Aldy whispered tightly. She lowered her hands and looked at Julie. "These infections?"

"She hit pretty hard. Lots of fragments, foreign matter in the wounds."

Memories of her own surgery flooded over her as Aldy recalled Adam's words: "She won't have surgery...."

"Want to come along? I'm stopping in on my way home."

Aldora nodded, rose from her chair, oblivious of the catch in her own back as she straightened and handed the sample fabric to Julie.

"Great," Julie said, smiling. "Jess really likes you. This'll give her a boost."

As Aldora followed Julie through the hospital to the main building, the smells and sounds of a working hospital rushed in at her nose and ears and triggered things best forgotten. Aldora fought the memories of her own time in corridors similar to these. Times spent endlessly hobbling up and back as she tried to learn to walk again. Memories of Ken springing lightly down such a hall to greet her.

"You're doing fine, hon, just fine," Ken said, slipping an arm around Aldy's waist. His hand contacted the metal brace and he withdrew as if burned. "Just wanted to come by before I left for San Diego," he said.

"Thanks." Aldy smiled at him but she knew he was glad to be going. "The next time I see you, I'll be at home," Aldy said, trying to lighten the mood. She strove for a hopeful note in her voice.

"This trip will set it up for life," Ken enthused. "A real honey of a deal." He slipped his arms around her then and kissed her gently, as if he was sure she'd break in half at the the first sign of passion.

"See you when you get back," Aldy said and tried to shut out the sensation that that kiss had been almost... sad.

"Sure, baby." Ken got up from the edge of her bed. "Don't bother to walk me to the elevators," he said and waved as he walked from the room.

Ken never completely came back from that trip. His words had made the return trip, just his voice reaching across the miles to apologize. "I didn't mean for it to happen, Aldora. It's just that I missed you so. I mean fifty-three days and hospitals make me so edgy.

Aldora?'' He paused waiting for her to respond. She couldn't speak. "Look, baby, I have to have *some* human companionship! I'm not a monk, for God's sake!''

Aldora had been too shocked to even cry. "I understand,'' she said, her voice barely a whisper. And inside she thought: *It's guilt. He'll be back. This is a panic fling.* But Aldora never saw Ken again.

"Hurry, Aldy! They're holding the doors.''

Julie's voice cut through and Aldy ran to the waiting elevator and squeezed herself in beside a gurney.

An orderly grinned at them, nudged the elderly man he was bringing up from X ray: "Bonus, Mr. Follett, a nice view from the front of the bus.''

The man raised a hand and smiled at Julie and Aldora.

Julie grinned at him. "Good tour guide you have there, Mr. Follett.''

The orderly chuckled and held the Door Open button while the girls got out at the second floor.

"This way,'' Julie said and turned left out of the elevator. "Room Two-oh-six.''

Jessie was dozing when Aldy followed Julie to the side of her bed. An IV needle was taped to one thin arm and the glucose-antibiotic drip trickled slowly down the clear plastic tubing from the bottle at the headboard.

"Jessie. Jess, honey,'' Julie whispered gently. "Brought you a surprise.''

Jessie stirred and opened her eyes. "Julie,'' she said and smiled.

Julie stood to one side. "Look who's here.''

"Miss Cassidy!'' Jessie's eyes widened with delight.

"Hello, Jessie,'' said Aldy, leaning forward to take Jessie's free hand. "Heard you were under the weather.''

"How's the mural?'' Jess asked.

"Be done with the tracing Friday.''

Jess looked at Julie. "Have you seen it?''

Julie nodded. "It looks grand."

"Wish I could see it," said Jess, her smile fading.

Aldy squeezed her hand gently. "There's nothing to see, yet, Jess. Wait till we get some paint on it."

Jess didn't look convinced.

"It's just a mass of fuzzy blue lines now." Aldy chuckled and winked at Jessie. "*I* can't even tell what it's like!" She gave Jessie's hand a squeeze. "But don't you tell on me."

Jess giggled her pleasure at being in on the conspiracy. "I won't," she said, returning the pressure, tightening her own fingers around Aldy's to seal the bargain.

"By the time you're ready to go home," Julie said, "there should be something worth looking at."

Jess looked hopeful.

"I'll have your dad take you out past the mural, I promise." Julie held up her right hand in solemn oath.

"You won't forget?"

"I will *not* forget. Now, you get some rest." Julie patted Jessie's shoulder gently. "The sooner you get well, the sooner you get to see the mural."

"Okay. Tell Daddy." Jess looked over at Aldy. "Bye, Miss Cassidy. Thank you for coming over."

"My pleasure, Jessie." Aldora waved and stepped out into the hall pulling the door closed after her.

"She looks good," said Aldy as she walked with Julie toward the elevators. "But I could tell from her grip that she's still pretty weak."

"The antibiotics work fast; it's the fevers that wring her out."

"Can't anything be done?" Aldy asked, thinking of the international reputation of the Edgely Foundation for "miracle cures."

"Sure. She could agree to have the follow-up surgery the doctors recommended when she was first injured." Julie poked impatiently at the Down button. "But she won't." Julie's mouth was set in a thin, bitter line. "Dear Louise saw to that."

Aldora was sure that Julie was going to explain that last statement but the elevator doors slid open and Julie's face underwent a total transformation.

"Adam," Julie cried, "what fantastic timing!" She slipped her arm through his. "Aldy and I just promised Jess we'd talk to you."

"Hello, Aldy," said Adam, aware now of his double good fortune in timing his visit to Jess.

The way he said her name, the candid way his eyes flowed over every line of her body, made Aldora's heart hammer against her ribs. "Hello, Adam," she said softly. Then she adopted Julie's train of thought to cover her nervousness. "Just the man we wanted to see."

Adam grinned and slipped his free arm through Aldora's. "You girls sure make a man feel welcome," he said. He looked at Julie now, but deliberately let his hand drift along Aldy's forearm as he spoke. Letting himself be escorted from the elevator, Adam continued to run his fingers along Aldy's wrist, up toward the soft skin near the inside of the elbow and back toward the hand again. Just his touch was affecting Aldora like a warm spring day; it was all she could do not to wrench free and rub away the dangerous sensations that Adam was evoking with his touch.

"What's the occasion of my popularity?" Adam asked, grinning at Aldora.

"We just told Jessie we'd give you her escape route," Aldy said, striving for lightness.

Adam paused midstride and looked from one to the other. "Escape route?"

Julie laughed. "Aldy and I promised Jess we'd get you to take her out past the new mural when she was well enough to go home."

"Good! Jess needs all the incentive she can get," said Adam. He spoke to both of them but his eyes, filled with gratitude, were riveted on Aldora. "Terrific idea."

Aldora felt herself blush with this unearned praise. "It was Julie's idea really."

"Well, come on. Let's show Jess how you keep your promises." Adam snugged Aldy's arm tightly against his body and headed for Room 206 before either Julie or Aldora could protest.

The three of them visited with Jessie for a short while and Aldora was moved by the tenderness Adam showed his daughter. Those huge hands were so infinitely gentle as he fluffed her pillow and tucked the sheet around her shoulders without disturbing the arm that held the IV needle. Her heart went out to him as she watched him drop a kiss on Jessie's forehead before they left the room. "I'll look in later," he promised as they went out into the hall.

"How 'bout some supper, ladies?" Adam said as they walked down the hall. "I haven't had a dinner companion since Monday."

"I have to meet Grant," said Julie quickly. "*You* go on, Aldy." She gave Aldora a strange, insistent look and stepped briskly past the elevator to the stairs. "Have fun, you two." She vanished through the exit and the door swung slowly shut.

Aldora stood watching that door and cursing Julie for her hasty retreat and parting comment. She looked over at Adam. He was watching her, holding out his arm, expecting her to take it. "That suits me," he said, smiling.

Aldy couldn't very well leave him standing there in the corridor with his arm outthrust and she had a feeling Julie had guessed at that response. Flinging a final mental curse down the stairs after Julie, Aldy linked her arm through Adam's. "Thank you," she said and allowed herself to be guided into the elevator.

Chapter Seven

Adam pressed the button for the parking level and tightened his grip on Aldora's arm. "I meant to call you sooner," he said, "but Jessie—" He broke off and Aldora thought she'd detected a slight quaver in his voice.

"No problem," Aldy said lightly. "I understand." His look of relief caused her to rush on. "I'm glad we ran into you." Aldora was alarmed at how sincerely she meant that.

"It was nice of you to visit Jess. She's very taken with you, you know." Adam was looking at Aldora with almost the same tenderness he reserved for Jessie.

"I wanted to see her," said Aldy, dragging her eyes from that emotionally charged gaze. "I came as soon as Julie told me what happened."

The elevator door opened at parking level C and Adam smiled his appreciation as he led Aldy to his car. He opened the passenger's side and helped her in.

Aldora stared down at her chalk-stained jeans. As Adam slid behind the wheel she said, "I'm really not dressed for dinner, Adam, I—"

He silenced her protest with a raised hand. "None of that. You look fine. . .lovely," he added, grinning when she blushed. "It won't be anything fancy." He pulled the Lincoln onto the exit ramp and adjusted the air vents as the car spiraled smoothly up to the street level.

"Do you like Chinese food?" he asked as the car merged into the traffic and headed west toward the ocean.

"I love it," Aldy said and watched Adam slip a tape into the dash. She grinned as John Denver's voice began to soar through the intricacies of his hit about a "natural" high.

"I can change it if—"

It was Aldy's turn to silence him with a wave of her hand. "I've painted some of my best pictures with John's vocal assistance." Aldy settled back against the soft leather seat.

They rode in silence, each enjoying the images Denver painted with his words. As John was thanking God for being a country boy, Adam pulled to the curb. He switched the key to accessory and left the tape on for Aldora. "I'll only be a minute," he said as he climbed out of the car.

Aldora watched him run up the steps of a Chinese carry-out restaurant.

What was he up to? Aldy grew more curious. Then she remembered that he'd told Jess he'd be back later. *That's it,* she thought. *We're taking this back to the hospital. It's a surprise picnic!* Aldy smiled and tapped her foot to the beat of the music as she thought about Jessie's reaction.

Adam came back with an armload of white bags. They gave off tantalizing aromas as he set them carefully on the seat next to Aldora. "Don't let this one tip," he said, handing her one of the bags.

Aldora cradled the package in her lap, feeling slightly uneasy as she discerned the tall, tapering bottle that rested coldly against her palm. Only the presence of two stacked containers that felt like coffee cups kept her from real discomfort. She remembered Grant pouring wine for everyone at the restaurant last Monday night. She recalled hoping that no one would notice that her glass never emptied.

Suddenly Aldora was aware that Adam was taking the long ramp that led down to the coast highway. This wasn't the way back to the hospital! Where were they going? Aldora was about to voice her question but Adam anticipated her.

"Just listen to the music," he said mysteriously. He smiled as he drove north on Highway 101.

Aldora's curiosity swelled until she was sure she couldn't remain silent another moment. Then Adam turned left into a deserted lot and parked by a beach café that was closed for the winter.

"You carry that one," Adam said, gathering the rest of the sacks in his arms and climbing from the car. He set the bags on the table and ran to get Aldy's door before she could collect her wits. "Your surf-side café," he said, bowing and helping her grandly to the picnic table.

Aldora was too amazed to speak. She set the bag on the table and took a seat.

"Voilà!" Adam said, swinging his long legs over the bench and sitting beside her. "Nothing fancy." He grinned and began opening bags and setting out the waxed cartons. He pulled out two paper plates and some plastic spoons and forks. "You start dishing up the food. I'll handle the beverages." He reached for the sack Aldy had been holding on her lap.

Aldora scooped sweet-and-sour pork onto a plate but watched Adam out of the corner of her eye. He took the tall bottle from the sack and twisted the plastic cap out of the way. Then he pried the metal cap off with a bottle opener. She couldn't conceal her look of surprise.

"Sparkling Apple," he said, pouring the bubbly, champagne-looking liquid into little plastic glasses. "And hot coffee," he added, patting the bag that still held the two stacked containers. He laughed as Aldora stood with her mouth open and the spoon dripping sweet-and-sour pork sauce onto the tabletop. "If I remember correctly, the lady doesn't drink." He smiled and began to help her with the plates.

Aldora took a hot butterfly shrimp from a little paper envelope and shook her head. "Pretty keen eye for a nonartist," she mumbled as she felt the color creeping into her cheeks.

Adam winked at her over a forkful of chop suey.

Aldora laughed and raised her glass. "To your sharp eye." She let the Sparkling Apple roll over her tongue and silently added, *And your kindness*.

"Eat before it gets cold." Adam touched his glass to hers.

Aldora followed Adam's example and tasted the chop suey.

"This is terrific." She savored the sweet-and-sour pork and crunched into a steaming shrimp.

Adam nodded, wiped his chin with his napkin. "The cook's a friend of mine."

As they ate, the sun settled lower over the water and flecks of gold danced on the waves like coins glittering at the bottom of a wishing pool.

When the meal was over, Adam pulled out the containers of hot coffee and a small bag with two fortune cookies. He stood up, opened the car door, and pushed a new tape into the player. The "Allemande" of Bach's Fifth French Suite rose on the evening air as Adam climbed back over the bench and sat just a bit closer to Aldora. "You first," he said, handing her a fortune cookie.

Aldora broke open the cookie and straightened the slip of paper.

"Well?"

"Who writes this stuff?" said Aldy, stalling for time.

"Later. Read."

"'The sea will bring you great happiness,'" Aldora read and her cheeks grew hot again.

Adam chuckled. "To answer your question, the cook."

"Your *friend*, the cook?"

Adam laughed. "The same."

"Now yours," Aldy said.

Adam shook his head. "No need."

Aldy started to protest.

Adam handed her his fortune cookie. "You read it."

Aldora turned the cookie over in her hand with suspicion. Breaking it open she smoothed the paper. Her eyes widened and she laughed delightedly, realizing that Adam *had* known the content. "He *does* write them!" she said, amazed at this stroke of creativity.

Adam joined in her laughter.

Aldy gathered the slips of paper. "I'm saving these," she said and tucked them into her purse.

"Glad you're a good sport, Aldy," Adam said, pulling his pipe from his jacket pocket.

Aldora sipped at her coffee. "Whoever heard of custom fortunes, tailored to fit the occasion in paired responses?"

"You just did," Adam teased as he packed tobacco into the bowl of his pipe and grinned. He lit the pipe and slipped his arm around Aldy's shoulders. "'The sea will bring you great happiness,'" he quoted.

Aldora leaned against his shoulder and quoted the slip that had been his fortune: "'Same to you, fella.'" She started laughing again as Adam hugged her tightly against his side and chuckled.

Aldora looked up at the rugged line of Adam's jaw, his eyes, sparkling with humor and warmth. And in that moment Adam looked down at her. Setting his pipe on the table, he placed his free hand under her chin and drew her face close to his own.

The last thing Aldora saw was the way Adam's lids dropped to half-conceal the passion burning in those green depths as his mouth came down on hers and she responded with a hunger that had thus far been left unsated by the romantic beach-side dinner.

Aldora's hands flattened against the hardness of Adam's chest and she let them roam up to rest on his shoulders and then fastened her fingers in the soft hair that curled at the nape of his neck. At this unspoken consent Adam's mouth grew insistent as he pressed her slim form against his body and wrapped his arms around her. His hands rubbed her shoulders and flowed down her spine to seek the curve at the small of her back. Cupping her hip in one hand, he pressed the full length of her firmly to him while continuing to stroke her shoulders and twine the other into the strands of her long black hair.

Aldy's senses flared to fever pitch as Adam's tongue flicked expertly at the corners of her mouth, begging entry. She parted her lips and his tongue probed eagerly, questing, inciting; her own answered the throbbing request.

When they drew slightly apart, Aldora was breathless with passion.

Adam's face held a dazed look and he shook his head as if to drive it away. "My God, woman, you could give a man a heart attack," he murmured as his lips sought hers once again.

This time the kiss was soft, sweet and lingering like a melody borne on a gentle spring breeze. And Aldora's heart fluttered in her breast as she felt Adam's hands cup her face, his fingertips tracing the line of her cheek in a fervent caress.

Adam shifted his position then and tucked Aldy close to his side. Cradling her against him, he looked out at the steadily darkening horizon.

Aldora snuggled deeper into the hollow of his shoulder and listened to the waves rushing up onto the sand and the soothing rattle of the rocks that were being dragged ever deeper into the sea.

At last Adam spoke. "I'm afraid we'd better be getting back," he said softly. "I promised Jess I'd look in."

Aldy nodded and together they began to clear away all evidence of the romantic picnic by the sea.

Aldora scattered the last of the fortune cookie crumbs for the gulls to find in the morning and climbed into the car.

Humming softly with the music on the tape, Adam drove slowly back to the hospital.

He parked the Lincoln and came around to help Aldy out. "Where's your car?" he asked.

Aldy pointed to the blue VW at the end of the row. "Down there."

Taking her hand in his, he walked her to her car, opened the door, rolled down the window, and handed her in behind the wheel.

"Thank you for a lovely evening, Adam," she said, smiling up at him.

He leaned down and his lips brushed hers. "The pleasure was *mine*," he said. Then he reached in and locked her door. He gave her an unreadable look. "Gotta keep you safe." He slid his hand slowly away from the lock button and smiled. Then he turned and headed for the elevators.

Aldora sat staring at the door lock. A lump formed in her throat as she watched Adam's broad shoulders disappear behind a pillar. She couldn't remember anyone ever taking the care to lock her into her car. It touched her in a deeply disturbing way. Lip service to caring she'd had before but a man who acted out his concern was a whole new sensation. Aldora started the engine and drove slowly out of the parking structure. As she took the winding road to her house, her emotions were in a state of definite disquiet. All the way home Aldy tried to convince herself that there was nothing all that unusual about a man locking her door like that. By the time she reached her driveway, she had reviewed all the reports of muggings and assaults that filled the news each day in an effort to show herself that Adam's locking her car was only common sense.

She pulled into the garage and grabbed the door handle. The door didn't open. As she lifted the lock button, she could see Adam's hand, the tapered fingers pushing the lock down, and she heard his deep, rich voice saying: "Gotta keep you safe." As she climbed the stairs, the lump was back in her throat.

Aldora heard her phone ringing as she unlocked the front door and set her purse on the kitchen counter.

"Just wanted to make sure you got home all right," said Adam when she picked up the receiver.

"I'm fine, thanks," she said. "And thank you again for that lovely dinner." Aldy really wanted to thank him for much more but she didn't know how. "And Jessie?" she prompted.

"She's sleeping and the fever's down."

"Terrific," Aldy said, glad to hear the relief in Adam's voice.

"Good night, Aldy."

"Good night, Adam." Aldora set the phone gently back on its hook and walked to the bedroom. Then she went back and got her purse off the counter. She took out the two slips of paper, and chuckling to herself, she set them on her nightstand and got ready for bed.

Chapter Eight

By Friday afternoon Aldora and her two helpers were busily mixing batches of color and looking forward to painting on Monday.

"Great. Eddy, a touch more of that sap green," Aldy directed. "Kate, more viridian." She stirred and watched the rich, leafy color deepen to an exact shade. "That's it."

Kate took a rubber mallet and tapped the lid rim down on the viridian while Eddy closed up the sap green with a well-positioned boot heel.

"What's our tally, Kate?" Aldy asked.

"Three gallons of dark green for shadow areas; three of the light green for sunlight; four of this," Kate answered.

"Sorry," Aldy said, pointing to the freshly sealed cans. "We'd better have one more of this color, then."

Kate and Eddy reopened the sap and viridian and began mixing.

"Ooops!" Eddy dropped his stirring stick, flinging drops of sap green into the air.

"Right," said Kate, wiping the drops from her eyebrow. "Some things never change." She looked at Aldy and giggled. "Oh, no! You, too!"

Aldora laughed and wiped at the splatters of green on her cheek.

"Are you two really muralists, or should I circle the wagons?"

"Grant!" said Aldy, rubbing the green into longer war-paint-like streaks. "I didn't hear your theme song."

"Naturally not, you're standing on the floor," he

joked logically. "It looks impressive." He squinted up at the tracings.

"Wait till Monday," Kate said. "We'll start putting on the paint."

"That'll impress the bosses," Eddy added.

"Only if they like green," said Aldy, smiling.

"Well, this 'boss' is knocking off early," Grant said. "You gonna need any special equipment for Monday?"

"Just luck," Aldy said. "Thanks anyway."

"A carload of rags?" Kate suggested as she elbowed Eddy.

Grant laughed, waving his hand as he headed out of the building.

"Kate, jot me a note. I've got those bundles of rags at home that we used to use for the classes," Aldy said.

Kate walked over and scribbled the note on Aldy's clipboard. "See you Monday," she said, linking arms with Eddy.

"Right, thanks." Aldora slid the mixed gallons of paint against the baseboard and gathered her things. She heard a step behind her and looked back.

Adam grinned down at her. "Thought you were going to paint the *wall*," he said chuckling at the green stripes across her face.

"That's on *Monday*," Aldy joked, brushing ineffectually at the streaks. "Eddy got carried away."

Adam pulled a handkerchief from his pocket. "Is he safe?" He wadded the handkerchief into a ball.

"Sure...he's just hyperactive."

"Stick out your tongue." Adam wet the hanky against the tip of Aldy's tongue and rubbed gently at the paint on her cheek. His brow furrowed with concentration.

"What's the matter?"

"Nothing," said Adam as he dabbed at her face. "I think I like you in green."

Aldora laughed. "How's Jessie?"

"She's coming home Monday." Adam put the handkerchief back in his pocket. "I'll bring her by here on her way out."

"Great. What time?"

"Probably after noon."

"We should have a bit of paint on by that time."

"On what?" Adam teased.

Aldy narrowed her brown eyes mischievously. "That depends," she said in her best Boris Karloff imitation.

"I'll be the one with the umbrella," Adam said, chuckling.

Aldy looked up at him. " 'Same to you, fella,' " she quoted.

Adam smiled. "How about dinner Saturday?"

"I'd love—" she began, then, "Oh, I'm sorry, Adam. I promised my friend Ellen that I'd come to her barbecue. She and her husband, Bill, are having a Saturday afternoon bash and I am to arrive bearing camping gear." Her voice rang with sincere remorse. She'd have liked nothing better than dinner with Adam.

"I've heard of some strange hostess gifts, but that takes it," said Adam, shaking his head in disbelief.

Aldy laughed. "It's a send-off for Bill's and Ellen's vacation. I'm loaning them my tent."

"Oh, okay," Adam said but disappointment showed in his tone.

"Thanks, though," Aldy said.

Adam turned back. "Aldy?"

"Yes."

"Hold next Saturday, all right?"

"Glad to. Dinner?"

"The whole day," Adam said.

Aldora looked up at him, waiting for an explanation.

"Just hold it open," he said. "More later." He walked off down the hall, smiling innocently.

Aldora stood, hands on hips, looking after him. "I really needed an enigma!" she muttered as she grabbed her clipboard and started for the elevators.

ALDORA pushed open the door to the spa and waved to Karen.

"Uh-oh," Karen said seriously. "This makes every night this week but two!"

Aldy shrugged. "It's those ladders." She went to the locker room and changed into a suit.

Lounging in the hot tub after her workout, Aldora wondered what Adam could possibly be planning for next Saturday. *He probably wants to take Jess somewhere if she's up to it,* Aldy decided climbing from the water. She dressed and drove home.

Saturday morning Aldora went up to her studio and uncovered her easel. She took the napkin off her corkboard and stared at the pen drawing she had done of Adam that day in the restaurant.

Squeezing yellow ocher onto her palette, she began to rough in Adam's portrait on the white canvas. Not having enough information on the napkin, she washed her brushes and gave up in favor of loading the tent into the VW. Then she came back up to the house and dressed for the barbecue.

ALDY tooted the horn as she pulled into Ellen's driveway. "Here's the gear," she said when Bill came to the car. She jumped out and pulled the seat forward.

"Thanks," Bill said, grabbing the tent and poles with one arm and slinging the bag of stakes over his shoulder. "Ellie's round the back." He nodded toward the gate as he lugged the camp equipment to the garage and loaded it into his pickup.

"Hi, Ellie!" Aldy called as she trotted across the lawn toward the patio.

"Aldy," Ellen said, grinning. "Did you bring the tent?"

"Bill's got it."

Ellen looked at Aldora. "You've been painting!" she said excitedly.

Aldora was puzzled. "How'd you—"

Ellen grabbed Aldy's elbow. "Is that or is that not yellow ocher oil paint?"

Aldora twisted to see the back of her arm. She grinned sheepishly. "Okay, Sherlock. I guess I missed some."

"What's it of?"

"Yellow ocher," Aldy teased.

"No! The subject!" Ellen waved her barbecue tongs threateningly.

"Okay," said Aldy, holding up her hands in defense. "It's a portrait. Adam Holcomb. Foundation director."

Ellen looked suspicious. "I thought you said he was married?"

Aldy blushed and shrugged. "I thought he was. I was wrong." She ignored Ellen's openmouthed surprise and poured herself a glass of punch. "Want some?" She held out a glass to Ellen.

"You don't get off that easy!" Ellie said firmly. "Tell more!"

Aldora laughed and sat on a folding chair and related the whole story while Ellen puttered with the charcoal and lighter fluid. When Aldora started describing the dinner at the beach, Ellen stopped puttering and gave all her attention to Aldora.

"Custom fortune cookies?" she said in amazement.

Aldy nodded and chuckled as she quoted the fortunes.

Ellen shook her head slowly. "Whew! This guy sounds fantastic!" She began to get that shoes-and-rice look again.

Aldora neglected to tell Ellie about the matter of the door lock, somehow she didn't want to confide that any more than she would have shared the details of their closeness as they had looked out at the water afterward.

"Called to see you got home safe?" Ellen said approvingly.

Aldora nodded.

"I almost wish we weren't going," Ellen said, grinning. "Keep me posted."

"There's nothing to 'post,'" Aldora said uneasily.

"Help me bring the chicken out here." For some reason Ellen wasn't pressing anymore.

Aldy sighed, relieved at the change of topic, she followed Ellen into the house.

"Think you'll have enough?" asked Aldy, staring at the two huge platters of marinated chicken sitting on the counter.

"I'm cooking extra for the trip."

Aldy lugged one of the platters out to the grill and Bill began placing the pieces on the grate.

"Mmm, smells good already," said Ellen, crossing the patio and setting the second platter on the picnic table.

While Bill manned the tongs, Ellie and Aldy kept him well supplied with punch and conversation.

Ellen got out a map and showed Aldy the itinerary. "Just us and the bears," Ellen said, pointing to the Yosemite Valley area. "Off-season this time of year." She winked at Aldy. "Bill doesn't know it's *me* he'll have to fend against."

"Who's gonna be fending?" Bill shrugged and gave Ellie a wicked grin.

"More punch?" Aldy offered. Somehow she wasn't comfortable with any sort of romantic topic right now.

When the first batch of chicken was ready, Bill set the rest of the pieces on the grill and cranked the grate higher from the coals. "Let's eat!"

Munching crisp chicken, potato salad, and cole slaw, Aldy worked the topics around to the mural, the new book, her triumph over the scaffolding. Any topic but

Adam Holcomb. She was grateful that Ellen did not plunge into a recap of what Aldy had told her of the "date" in her usual fashion. Ellen simply mentioned that Aldy was painting again and let it go at that.

When they had finished their coffee, Aldy helped Ellen with the dishes and then got ready to leave.

"You two have a great trip," she said, picking up her purse and hunting for her keys. "Thanks for the dinner."

"Thanks for the tent," said Bill as he stood in the doorway with Ellie and watched Aldy walk to her car.

"Don't bother to write." Aldy waved and backed the VW out of the drive.

As she drove toward home Aldy realized that she would miss Ellen's friendly support, her daily calls to make sure Aldy wasn't overdoing it. But she also realized that she wished she had someone to go camping with again. She had to admit that she'd been afraid to try it alone, afraid to risk a crippling muscle spasm far from home. It was this, more than the excuse of too much work, that held her back.

Aldora promised herself that she would take some time off for a vacation as soon as the mural was finished. She knew she needed to get away for a while. Cabin fever was definitely setting in—two and a half years worth!

Monday morning Aldy was already setting out the paint when Kate and Eddy arrived at eight thirty.

"She's starting without us!" Eddy said, grabbing a brush and racing to the nearest ladder.

"I wouldn't think of it," Aldy said, waving him over to her. "Forget something?" She held up a gallon of paint and a color copy of the composite.

Eddy grinned sheepishly and came to collect the supplies.

Kate laughed, shook her head, and took her equipment to the far end of the wall. "Can I start over here, where it's safe?" she asked, throwing Aldy a mock-plaintive look.

Aldy chuckled. "Anywhere. It's all gotta get painted."

The work went along smoothly. Aldora had to walk back and forth a lot to check the progress and color blends, to advise Kate and Eddy, but both her former students were bright and talented. They soon caught the rhythm of the work and moved with it.

Aldora was just walking back across the room from one of her overview checks when she heard an excited squeal.

"Take me closer!" Jessie cried as her father and an orderly wheeled her into the recreation room.

Aldora turned and trotted over to Jess. "Welcome!" she said. "What d'ya think?" She grinned at Jess and saluted.

"It's super!" Jess didn't even look at Aldy; her eyes scanned the huge wall eagerly. "When will it be finished?"

Aldora laughed and placed a hand against her forehead. "Supervisors!" she groaned and winked at Adam. "There's a long way to go, Jess."

Adam let the orderly take Jess on a tour of the mural. When Jessie was out of earshot, he leaned down to Aldy and whispered: "Saturday's on."

"What's the plan?" asked Aldy, assuming that it was only Jess he was keeping secrets from.

"A surprise."

Aldora looked at him. "Well..."

"If I tell you, it won't be a surprise." Adam smiled.

"Fine," Aldy said, throwing up her hands in exasperation. "I'll wear my jeans under my evening gown and bring an overcoat!"

Adam laughed. "Okay, okay. We'll be spending the day on the boat. But that's all you get out of me." He grinned at her look of astonishment. "You're not phobic about water, are you?"

Aldora grinned back at him. "No phobias at all," she said. Then added mischievously: "That show."

"Ah, woman of mystery; gonna beat me at my own game?"

Aldy laughed. "Maybe." She thought of the portrait on her easel. Perhaps she could bring her camera and get enough pictures Saturday to do that painting after all. That would be a big breakthrough. She hadn't painted since Ken....

"Be ready at eight. Jess and I will pick you up." Adam smiled and went to get Jessie.

"Come on, pumpkin. Let's get you home." He pushed the chair past Aldora. "Looks great," he said, waving an arm at the wall. "Later." He wheeled Jess toward the elevators.

Aldora waved and turned back to her work. *I was just promising me a day in the fresh air and sunshine,* she thought as she climbed to the second platform. She began laying in the light green of sunstruck leaves, but her mind was making out an equipment list for Saturday: Camera, lenses, color slide film, black-and-white film....

"Hey, lunchtime," Eddy called.

Aldora looked down and saw Kate holding up her brown bag. "He never learned to whistle," Kate joked.

THE WORK seemed to fly. The base coat colors for the entire wall were nearly completed by Friday at noon. Aldy and Kate stood back across the room waiting for Eddy to wash his brush and join them for lunch. In honor of the swift progress, Aldy was taking both to the cafeteria.

"Not the Ritz," she said as Eddy jogged over to them. "But at least they'll let us in!" She pointed at Eddy's paint-spattered jeans. "They used to be *blue* jeans, didn't they, Eddy?" she teased.

"You've no right to talk," he said, looking at Aldy's shirt.

"This," said Aldy holding the front of her work smock out gingerly, "is a whole week's worth." She unzipped the smock with a triumphant smile and hung it over a ladder. "And it comes off." She pointed smugly at the jeans. "*Those* were blue this morning!"

"They come off too!" said Eddy, wiggling his eyebrows and flicking an imaginary cigar like Groucho.

Kate grabbed Eddy's arm. "Don't let's press our luck!"

Aldora laughed and led the way to the cafeteria.

They were just setting their lunch trays on an empty table when Grant came over with a cup of coffee.

"Join us," Aldora said, pulling out the chair next to hers.

"Just saw the wall," Grant said. "It's fantastic!"

"And that's just the color blocking," Kate added between bites of omelet. "Wait'll we finish."

Aldora smiled at Kate's enthusiasm. "My new agent," she said, nodding her head at Kate.

Grant grinned. "Since you're obviously way ahead of schedule, why not knock off early? I heard you were crewing for Captain Bligh tomorrow." He looked at Aldora with pity.

"Really? Captain Bligh?" Aldy shuddered, feigning alarm.

"I've crewed for him before," Grant said. "Captain Bligh is a pantywaist compared to Adam."

"You crewing tomorrow?" Aldy asked.

"Wait and see." Grant gave her a cryptic grin, picked up his cup, and went off whistling "Yankee Doodle."

While they were finishing their lunch, Kate and Eddy convinced Aldora that Grant's idea had merit.

"Katie and I were gonna drive up the coast. We could get an early start," said Eddy hopefully.

"All right," Aldy said. They turned in their lunch trays and went back to the new wing to close up the paint cans and roll the canvas tarps.

Aldora watched Kate and Eddy stack the cans against the base of the wall. Her back was too tight for much stooping and bending. She helped arrange the rolled tarps into a protective barrier in front of the paint cans. "That's all," she said, smiling at them. "Have a good trip."

It's shaping up, she thought as she looked the mural over one last time. She smiled, picked up her workbasket, and walked to her car.

Chapter Nine

Saturday dawned crisp and clear. Aldora was up long before her alarm went off. Kids and circuses, she thought, letting herself float on excited anticipation.

She pulled on white denim pants and a blue-and-white striped shirt that hugged her flat stomach and accentuated the curve of her breasts. She plaited her hair Indian-style, weaving a thin blue ribbon through each braid. Then she padded out to the kitchen and plugged in the coffeepot. While the coffee dripped, she applied a minimum of makeup and dug her denim deck shoes out of the back of the closet.

She was just finishing her second cup of coffee and lacing up her sneakers when Adam appeared at the door.

Aldora hurriedly tied her shoes and ran to let him in. He was wearing much-washed blue jeans that hugged his lean hips and a white turtleneck pullover of a soft knitted fabric. White deck shoes and a navy wool seaman's cap completed the picture. This was the way Aldy wanted to paint him! She slid the door open. "What? A *seaman's* cap?" she teased.

Adam struck a lazy pose against the doorjamb. "*Everybody* works on my ship, lady." But he couldn't keep a straight face. He broke into happy laughter.

Aldy laughed too and ran to get her camera bag. "I'm going to immortalize you falling overboard."

"What a shame," he said, shaking his head in grief.

"How so?"

"Cameras don't do well in salt water." He leered at her. "If I go in," he slid an arm around her waist and squeezed, "you go in!" Adam didn't let go of her right away. He leaned down and his lips brushed hers with a lingering promise.

Aldora's senses, tingling at the mere touch of Adam's arm around her waist, recognized that the teasing kiss he'd dropped on her mouth was compounding her physical response to him in a most delightful way. She clung to him for a moment, looking up with a promise of her own shining in her dark eyes.

"You *are* an alluring siren for this Odysseus," Adam whispered holding her closer.

His intent unmistakable, Aldora braced him, slid her hands to encompass his biceps. "Hold that thought," she said playfully, "or Jessie'll get impatient."

ADAM parked the car in the boat owner's section of the Marina Club lot and led the way to the docks with Jessie squirming excitedly in his arms. "Not a word, mate," he growled in her ear. "You nearly gave it away once." He kissed her hard on the cheek.

Jess giggled her delight, her arms wrapped tightly around her father's neck.

Aldora was nearly left behind as she tried to follow and take pictures at the same time. She almost ran into Adam's broad back when he stopped abruptly in front of a thirty-two foot motor-sailor and beamed with pride.

"The other lady in my life, girls," he said and motioned to the gracefully bobbing vessel whose crisp black-on-white lettering proclaimed her to be the *Amara Alexandra*.

Jessie twisted in her father's arms, noticed Aldy's surprised expression. She pointed to the bow of the boat. "Her name means something in Greek," she said.

Aldora looked to Adam for a translation, but Jess protested. "Let me, Daddy, I know, I know!"

Adam smiled indulgently.

"*Alexandra* means 'helper of mankind,'" Jess began quickly. "And *Amara...*" she paused. "Don't tell me, Daddy." She wrinkled her small brow in concentration. "'Ever faithful!'" She looked to her father for approval.

"Almost, pumpkin," he said gently. "It's 'unfading,' but your explanation means the same thing."

Jessie glowed with pride. "My great-grandfather was from Greece." She held a small whistle to her father's lips. "Pipe us aboard, Daddy." Her little fingers moved as Adam puffed into the mouthpiece, changing the tone to make the familiar two-note boarding welcome.

Adam led the way up the gangplank. "Through there." He nodded toward the door of the cabin.

Aldora pulled it open, then caught her breath.

"Surprise!" yelled Grant and Julie springing to greet her.

Aldy was momentarily speechless. She stared at Grant. "What's going on?"

"It's the surprise!" Jessie squealed. "A party for your mural *and* Uncle Grant's engagement."

"Oh!" Aldora stepped over to Julie and hugged her. "Congratulations, Julie!"

Grant leaned over and gave Aldy a loud kiss on the cheek. "Congratulations, yourself."

"Yes," Julie added. "That mural is a winner!"

"Never mind the mural," Aldy insisted. "It's not half finished! When are you two getting married?" She grinned and held out her hand to Julie. "Let's see."

Julie showed off her emerald and diamond engagement ring. "I did the setting design," she murmured softly.

"Oh, Julie, it's gorgeous!" Aldy said, awed by this new facet of Julie's talent. "Now, when?"

"We haven't set a date yet," Grant answered. "Probably August."

Aldy did a quick calculation. "That's seven months!"

"Yes. Julie's mom and dad will be back east for the first part of the summer." Grant winced. "And this one"—he pointed accusingly at Julie—"has to have time to 'plan everything.'"

Aldora laughed. "How large of a wedding?" she asked, picking up Grant's meaning.

"Too large!" Grant said.

Julie gave him a gentle shove. "He's the one with all the relatives! Haven't made up the list yet, but you will come?" She looked pleadingly at Aldy.

"I wouldn't miss it."

"Get the glasses, Grant," said Adam, starting to uncork a bottle of champagne. The cork flew across the cabin. "And a towel!" he yelled as the foamy liquid shot up and over his shirtfront.

Adam poured and glasses were raised to Grant and Julie. Aldora sipped only enough of her champagne to validate the toast. She watched some of the clear liquid trickle down Jessie's chin. Jess made a funny face and handed her glass to her father. "Ugh!" she said, wrinkling her nose.

"Never mind," said Aldy quickly. "Me too!" She wrinkled back at Jessie and set her own glass on the table.

"Let's get this ship under sail!" Adam said, leading the way topside. Grant scooped up Jess; Aldy and Julie brought up the rear.

THE day was ideal. Aldy went through three rolls of black-and-white and two of color slides. She was sure that she had plenty of good shots to paint from. Snap, and she caught Jessie silhouetted against an incredibly blue sky, her face framed with a bit of rigging. Snap, and she froze Grant going overboard from Julie's playful push while the *Amara* lay at anchor in a quiet cove. Snap, and she had a lovely portrait of Adam at the wheel with the white sail billowing behind his dark head. There were so many prize shots, Aldy couldn't count them: Grant making a funny face and pretending to strangle Julie with a piece of line; Jessie trying to help him; Grant and Julie standing arm-in-arm by the bowsprit and smiling lovingly into each other's eyes.

"Hey," Adam's deep voice sounded close in Aldy's ear. "The *Amara* will be back in the slip and you won't know we were out." He lifted the strap gently from around her neck and placed the camera carefully in its case. "Help me steer."

Adam led Aldy to the helm. Laughing, he put his arms around her as she manned the wheel. "She's a natural!" he shouted. Grant grabbed her camera and snapped that picture for her.

"Picture-perfect day," Grant hooted while Julie grimaced at his pun.

Aldora was enjoying her turn at the wheel of this sleek, responsive boat. She had handled speedboats a number of times. Water-skiing had been a hobby of Ken's and they had gone out a lot before the accident. But this was Aldy's first time aboard a sailboat.

"It's so quiet!" she said as Adam helped her tack out of the cove.

"Wait'll you handle her on a long run." He grinned with pleasure as the boat cleared the sheltering arm of the cliff and the *Amara* began to run before the wind. "Take her."

Aldy put both hands on the wheel as Adam guided her firmly.

"Over that way," he said.

Aldy steered where Adam pointed and gasped as the *Amara* began to heel over.

Adam laughed. "Don't worry! She can take a lot more."

"But can I?" Aldora said, chuckling nervously.

Adam's eyes sparkled. He took the wheel. "The lady with no phobias? Sure you can!" He heeled the boat harder. When Aldora gasped and grabbed for a support, Adam was right there to hold her closely against him.

It was a good feeling, Aldy thought. The beauty of the ocean, the cool breeze, and Adam's warm arms around her, his lean hardness pressing against her body. She was beginning to wish that it would go on forever.

"Daddy!" Jessie cried. "Now me!" She held out her arms to her father.

"In a minute, pumpkin," said Adam, apparently as reluctant to release Aldy from his embrace as she was to have this moment end.

Jessie's eyes turned a cloudy green. "I haven't had a turn!" she said, a hint of ill-humor in her tone.

Grant came forward and took the wheel.

Adam, murmuring an I'm sorry, let go of Aldy. He walked over to Jess. "Hey," he said gently, "I thought you wanted Aldy to learn to sail the *Amara*."

Tears filled Jessie's eyes as she sensed the reproving tone in her father's voice. "*I* did," she quavered. "But *you're* showing her."

Adam rumpled her hair tenderly. "Okay, you do it." He carried Jess to the helm.

Grant slid out of the captain's chair and Adam placed Jess on the seat.

She stretched out her arms and grasped the wheel firmly. Grinning, she heeled the boat over like her father had done. "I'm not afraid," she challenged.

Aldora gasped again and nearly lost her footing.

Adam's hands left Jessie's shoulders and he reached to help Aldora. "Easy, Jess! You know better!"

Jessie straightened the boat but the set of her mouth made it clear that she would rather have done more daring maneuvers. "Sailors *have* to learn," she said stubbornly. "That's what you told Mommy."

Adam's jaw went tight. "This is different! Aldy's never sailed before. I expect your consideration."

"She can't learn unless you let me do some more." Jess was sparring now.

Aldora, seeing the child's jealousy where Adam was concerned, threw him a warning look and pushed his hands away. She moved closer to Jess. "You have a point, Jess," she said. "Let me know and I'll hang on better next time." She smiled and gripped the back of the captain's chair. "Do your worst!" She winked at Adam.

Adam, catching Aldy's drift, gave Jess a hug. "Put her through her paces, honey." He helped Jessie maneuver the large boat through the water as Aldora, white-knuckled, murmured appreciative words to the small skipper.

At last, Aldy begged for mercy. "You're too good a sailor for me, Jess," she said warmly. "How 'bout some lunch and a rest for your crew?"

Jess giggled happily at Aldy's suggestion. "Okay, take her, Daddy." She grinned and held out her arms to Aldora. "Me 'n' Miss Cassidy'll make lunch."

Aldy knew she shouldn't lift Jess, but she didn't dare hesitate. Jessie was beginning to accept her, trying to share the only way she knew how. Aldora slid one arm under Jessie's knees. "Hang on tight," she said, hoping the girl would take some of the weight with her own arms.

Aldy lifted.

She felt a definite twinge as she straightened, but thought Jessie couldn't be over sixty or seventy pounds.

"Better let me," said Grant, reaching for Jess.

"No!" Jessie cried. "I want Miss Cassidy!"

"She's not heavy," Aldy said, balancing Jessie's weight expertly. *As an artist,* she thought, *I've had to carry bulkier things than this small child.* Recalling Adam's remark about how sensitive Jess was about her condition, Aldy was not going to add to Jessie's embarrassment by handing her over like a sack of potatoes. "We'll holler when it's ready," she said over her shoulder. Then to Jess: "I think as skipper of this ship you could call me Aldy, don't you?"

Jess grinned and hugged Aldora's neck. "Right, Aldy," she said. "I'll get the door." She leaned forward eagerly, her hand outstretched to grab the latch.

Aldy tried hard not to flinch as the girl upset the carefully established balance of weight and pulled Aldora into the most painful of forward-leaning angles as they went through to the galley area. Aldora set Jess at the table.

"You can chop the celery," she said. She straightened and one hand strayed to rub her back. "Which drawer for knives?"

Jess pointed to the one by the sink. "There, Aldy." Pleased with the new familiarity Jess seemed determined to use the name at every occasion.

Aldy smiled and got out a knife and some stalks of celery. She rinsed them, gave them to Jessie and set a bowl on the table for her to use. Then she went to the sink and started chopping red onions, hard-boiled eggs, and parsley for the tuna salad.

Julie came below. "Need help?"

"Sure," said Aldy, tossing her a tomato. "Scoop out five of these for stuffing."

Julie moved to the sink and began preparing the tomatoes. "English muffins are down there in that bin, Aldy." Julie pointed with the tip of her knife.

Aldy started to lean forward, but her back muscles warned her that a deep-knee bend would be safer. She squatted down and pulled the plastic bag of muffins out of the locker. Aldy split them with a fork and set them under the broiler. Then she gathered up the chopped celery and added it to the tuna salad. "Looks great, Jess," she said. "You're hired."

Julie and Aldy spooned tuna salad into the tomato shells.

"You go call the men," Julie said. "I'll finish up."

Glad for a chance to walk around, Aldy went topside and called to Grant and Adam. "Chow's on!"

The men were deep in conversation so she called

again. They waved and began to secure the boat. Aldy waited and then followed them below.

Later that afternoon, Aldora took another turn at the helm. She was glad to see that Jess didn't seem to mind. It was worth it, she thought, as she glanced around to make sure no one noticed her rubbing at her cramping back muscles.

The *Amara* was back in her slip and being secured as the sun was sinking into the sea. Jessie had caught a small rock fish and Grant helped her to cut it up for the gulls.

"How are your sea legs?" Adam said, putting his arm around Aldy's shoulders and sprawling her against him.

"Fine," she answered, beginning to like his easy way with a look and a touch. "I love sailing!" She smiled up at him.

"Ready to go again?" he tested.

"Any time!"

Adam grinned. Aldora thought she saw a flicker of relief smooth Adam's forehead as he chuckled and gave her a squeeze.

Grant, tossing the last mooring line to Julie, looked over and winked at Adam. "Uh-oh, she's addicted!"

Adam laughed when Aldy nodded her head in vigorous agreement.

Julie and Grant waved from the dock. "Thanks," they called and walked up the ramp toward the parking lot.

Adam waved and carried Jess off the ship. "How about a seafood dinner?" he asked.

Aldy grinned.

"Oh, Daddy!" Jess cried. "The place with the whale, please!"

Chuckling at Aldy's startled expression, Adam explained: "Moby's Dock. They did a sculptural pair of flukes and put a restaurant under them."

Aldora smiled. "Santa Monica pier?"

"You know it!"

"You could say that," said Aldy mysteriously. She smiled to herself, wondering if the restaurant still had her seascape hanging in the bar. That had been one of her first commissions, done before Aldy had decided to hold such work off until after her one-woman show. By then she'd be able to ask a better price. The oils were painstaking and she didn't yet have enough of a name to command what they were really worth. That made the customary one-third down too small an amount to invest such a large block of time against, hoping that the finished picture would be approved and the balance paid.

Adam turned down the ramp to the pier. He placed the handicapped sign in the windshield and was waved out onto the wooden structure by an attendant.

"We'll probably have to wait in the bar," Adam said as he pushed Jessie's chair along the boardwalk. "No reservations."

"Can I have a Shirley Temple, Daddy?" Jessie asked craning her neck to look up at her father.

"You *both* can," he said, winking at Aldy.

Adam gave his name to the hostess and a busboy cleared a place for the wheelchair at a table in the bar.

Aldora looked at the wall in back of the table. The painting was still there! She wondered if Adam might notice it. Not likely, she decided. No one ever really looked at the paintings in restaurants any more than they ever really listened to the Muzak in shopping malls or elevators.

Adam held Aldy's chair, then took the one opposite the wall for himself. He ordered a Scotch and two Shirley Temples, then sat back to fill his pipe. "Changed much since you were here last?" he asked.

"No, not at all." Aldy was feeling mischievous. "I was never here for dinner, though." She chuckled at Adam's raised eyebrows. "Business," she said.

The waitress returned with the drinks and Adam handed her a bill. "Well," he said, folding his change into his wallet, "that must mean—" He stopped talking and his eyes looked immediately past Aldora to the wall behind her. He grinned and squinted at the lower left-hand corner. "And I thought our walls were the first," he said, caressing the painting with his glance. He let out a low whistle. "That's magnificent, Aldy." He continued to stare at the painting as only a man in love with the sea would do. "I didn't know you were in fine arts." He looked at Aldy.

"I started out in oils," she said softly. "I used to teach. Kate and Eddy were students of mine be—" She paused, recalling the joyful hours at her easel, the smell of linseed oil and turpentine.

"You mean you gave it up?" Adam looked shocked. "Why? You're fantastic!"

Aldora was still recovering from her near-slip. She had almost said "Kate and Eddy were students of mine before the accident." She looked up at Adam. "Oh, I got swamped with the books, illustrating, writing." She let her voice trail off, hoping Adam wouldn't press the issue.

Adam shook his head. "Any others?" he asked eagerly.

"A few," Aldy fibbed, thinking of the stacks of canvases in a studio closet that had been readied for her one-woman show. The mute evidence of a talent that had put the first wedge between her and Ken, and that now lay abandoned. No, she thought angrily, waiting!

As if reading her thoughts, Adam asked: "Why don't you show in a gallery?"

Aldora grew uneasy. She began to think that admitting to even knowing of Moby's Dock had been a mistake. "Oh, I don't have time." She fussed nervously with her glass. "You know...hacking in and out of galleries with a load of canvases and—"

"No need," Adam interrupted. "Julie! She knows the best in town. She'd love to act as agent."

Aldora felt the flush wash through her, sending red to

her cheeks and forcing beads of perspiration out on her brow. This very thing had nearly destroyed one relationship, she thought anxiously. Oh, why had she ever mixed business and pleasure? It couldn't work. "I couldn't...impose," she stammered. "Julie's so busy...the wedding...her job."

"She's got to see your work." Adam grinned at her. "She's always grumbling about the quality of work galleries offer." Adam was rolling; there was no reasoning with him. "I want a private showing after dinner." He looked at her. "Okay?"

Aldora was touched by his supportive praise. He was looking at her like a kid begging ice cream. "Okay," she said, smiling. "If it's not too late." She glanced at Jessie who was busily picking all the fruit out of her Shirley Temple.

"I wanna see!" Jess said, spearing a cherry with her straw. "I thought we saw everything on the tour." She glared accusingly at Aldy. "You held out!" Then she smiled and put her hands together in a prayerful attitude. "Say yes, please!"

Aldora laughed. As she agreed, the waitress came to call them to the dining room.

After dinner Adam drove to Aldora's and carried Jess upstairs. "No peeking until I get back," he said.

Aldy plugged in the coffeepot and sat on the sofa with Jess to wait for Adam to get the chair from the car.

"Did you really do that painting in the restaurant?" Jess asked.

"Yes." Aldy pointed to an unsigned painting by the stairwell. "That one too."

Jess looked at the landscape with the sagging old three-story Victorian that Aldy had done from a photograph she'd taken in Oregon. "Bet it has ghosts," Jess whispered.

"Boo!" said Adam, coming up behind her. He took the chair to the studio and came back for Jess. "Tour number two," he said, following Aldy up the stairs.

Aldora took her oils from the closet and, hands shaking slightly, placed them around the walls of the studio.

Adam was quiet for a long time. He just looked from picture to picture and paced back and forth in front of them.

At last he shook his head. "It's a waste! A pure waste," he said angrily. He turned to Aldora. "You should be ashamed," he scolded. "Hiding these in a closet." He walked over and put his arms around her, clicking his tongue against the roof of his mouth disdainfully. "I'm going to talk to Julie."

Aldora started to protest. Adam silenced her, his fingertips gentle on her lips. "No arguments." The way he looked at her made Aldy hold back.

She tried to suppress the swell of happy excitement, but it had been so long since anyone had cared. No one had ever offered the support of helping to arrange for others to see her work. That had been exclusively Aldora's job. It had been the time involved in making contacts, visiting galleries, and attending to every detail of the promotion work herself that had caused Ken to declare her fine art too time consuming to fit into their lives. Aldy's eyes brimmed with tears at Adam's gesture. She blinked them back. "Coffee's ready," she said, turning to the stairs to hide her emotion.

"And that apple stuff?" Jess asked. "I'm hungry."

"Again?" Adam carried her down to the kitchen. "Aldy'll think I only feed you in public!"

Jess laughed. "I can always eat dessert."

Aldora chuckled and set out cups and dished up three portions of the apple crumble. "All your milk though, promise?"

Jess nodded and stuffed a large spoonful of the sweet, apple dessert into her mouth.

The three of them sat in companionable silence, then Adam said, "Why aren't you in a gallery, Aldy?"

"Long, depressing story," she said. "It'd ruin a nice evening." She looked pointedly at Jessie.

Adam deftly changed the subject.

When Jess had finished her milk, Adam stood up. "It's getting late, pumpkin," he said.

"Thanks, Aldy," Jessie said as her father lifted her into his arms.

"Thank you, Jess. I had a wonderful sail."

Jessie grinned.

While Aldy waited for Adam to take Jess to the car, she realized that she'd been looking forward to the end of the evening almost as much as she'd looked forward to the start of today's adventure. She folded the wheelchair. Would Adam keep any part of the promise this morning's kiss had hinted, or would Jess, waiting below in the car, inhibit things too greatly?

Adam reappeared silently. He smiled at her and his eyes were tender as he spoke. "Another lovely evening, thanks to you."

She sensed the emotion in his voice and waited for him to come closer. She was suddenly light-headed with her own longing. She wanted him to hold her as he had on the boat, wanted him to kiss her. "Adam," she said softly, "I've never had such a perfect day."

"That's how I feel," he said, moving toward her. He seemed to be struggling with himself. "You will come out again?" he blurted. His eyes, distressed, searched hers. "Jess really did enjoy it; she just got a little jealous, she—" Adam floundered.

Aldy smiled. So, Adam had been concerned all along that Jess's temper display earlier would have put her off. "Don't mention it," she reassured, slipping her arm through his. "It's normal. You're her world."

Adam's face twisted with pain. "I'm sorry, Aldy," he murmured, fighting for control. "You don't know what—" He broke off and rubbed his eyes as if trying to wipe an ugly image from the lids. He took a deep breath. "Forget it." He smiled down at her. "Just so you'll come along again." His voice held a note of urgency that set Aldy's blood racing.

She looked at him, trying to understand the pain that had given way to such urgency.

Adam squeezed her hard against his body and tilted his head down to look into her eyes. "Next time," he whispered, "you'll show me the one on the easel."

Aldora, expecting to be kissed, reeled at the non sequitur. She groped madly for a reply. "Not until it's finished," she said firmly.

"Ah, you're a hard woman, Aldora Cassidy!" He sighed and gave her a mock scowl.

Aldora was sure that her feelings had betrayed her. Perhaps Adam's voice hadn't held restrained passion, his eyes hadn't been filled with desire. Maybe his eyes only reflected her own longing! She felt her embarrassment sending blood to her face as she tried to think of something light, friendly, in keeping with this mood Adam had set.

Suddenly Adam's face was very close to hers. His lips rested, featherlight, on her mouth and were gone almost before she knew she'd been kissed. Aldora looked up, amazed. Exasperated. He had left her standing at the starting gate!

Adam smiled, chuckling softly at her bewildered expression, he pulled her closer. Lifting her off the floor, he pressed his mouth against hers. No featherlight kiss, this time his lips sought hers hungrily. His hands caressed her back, telegraphing his passion, his need.

Aldora felt herself responding as her arms slid easily up around his neck and her mouth answered his desire with a need all her own.

Adam's mouth grew hot, a sparking brand that sent Aldora's head spinning. Then he pulled away, setting her firmly on the floor. He swallowed hard, his voice a ragged whisper when he spoke: "You *are* a hard woman."

She looked up, uncomprehending.

"Hard to leave alone." He grabbed the chair and vanished down the front stairs.

Aldora stood listening to his car pull away. Her heart pounded and the blood roared in her ears. Part of her still fought against the emotions this man fanned in her, fought to keep banked that which had been dormant so long. But the fragile woman inside cried out for all that Adam's kisses had promised, all his inquiring hands had implied. Aldy was used to walling out potential danger, steeling herself against hurt, but kindness was so much harder to resist.

Chapter Ten

Aldora slept poorly and woke early Sunday morning to a gray dawn. The gloom matched her own inner turmoil. She stared out at the fog-shrouded trees outside her window and thought about Adam's swift retreat... his parting comment. If not for the way he had bolted down the stairs, she could have considered it purely complimentary. And what had that remark to do with Adam's obvious pain when she had said that Jessie's jealousy had been a normal reaction to being forced to share the only person in her life who made her condition bearable? His answer implied that there was much more to it than a typical reaction to the sharing of a friendship.

Friendship? Aldora's pulse quickened as she remembered Adam's lips on hers, the strong hands caressing her, pressing her body hard against his own. She knew Adam had wanted her, needed her, and the way her own long-suppressed desire had kindled at his kiss, forced Aldy to admit that the safety she'd felt when she believed such feelings were dead was a false safety. Last night she'd wanted Adam as much as his caresses had said he'd wanted her; this was more than a friendship. She'd known it then; she knew it now.

Aldora rolled over to the edge of her bed and sat up. Her back felt tight and she reached for her cane. Pulling herself to her feet, she walked stiffly out to the kitchen and put on the kettle for tea. When she'd lifted Jessie, she'd known there would be a price. Dropping two slices of whole wheat bread into the toaster, she decided to work in her darkroom, take her mind off the tightness in her back. Aldy silently cursed the fact that the spa wasn't open on Sundays.

She finished her breakfast, dressed, and went to the garage. There, under the glow of the dim safe-light in the darkroom, Aldy eclipsed her pain with the joy of watching print after print emerge almost magically in the developing tray. The pictures were as good as she'd suspected, better than she'd dared hope.

As she watched the prints drop from the dryer, the whole glorious day was returned to her. The fun, the warm affection, the laughter. Aldy could hardly wait to get to her easel. Not only would she be able to do a portrait of Adam, but the shot of Grant and Julie by the bowsprit would make up into a lovely wedding present.

By three that afternoon Aldy was completing the rough of Adam's portrait. She had ignored lunch in favor of running the color film to the night drop at her camera store. The rolls would be picked up Monday morning and she would be able to collect them on her way home from work Tuesday night. These slides would provide the color references she'd need to refine the painting. If the weather cleared, the rough would be dry enough to proceed by the time she brought the slides home.

The phone rang and Aldy dipped her brushes into the turpentine and answered it.

"Aldy, it's Adam." His voice seemed all the closer for the portrait standing on her easel. "Just wanted to make sure Jessie's sailing hadn't done you in."

Aldy chuckled. "No, I was just looking at the pictures. 'Proof' positive of the fun we had," she joked.

Adam laughed and Aldora sensed a relief in his laughter that hinted more than her physical well-being had prompted Adam's call.

"Can't wait to see them," he prompted.

"Any time," Aldy offered. "You and Jessie will love them."

Adam hesitated. "Jess overdid a bit yesterday; she's

stuck with bed rest for a day or two. Is that invitation still good for one?"

"Of course," said Aldy. "Is Jess going to be okay?"

"I think so. I'll put her down early and Margaret will stay with her. How's seven thirty sound?"

"See you then."

"Right." Adam rang off and Aldy finished cleaning her brushes. She wondered what Adam's real motive was. Why had he sounded uneasy at first and then relieved once she'd cracked that joke about "proofs"? It almost seemed as if he'd been expecting Aldora to be angry. She covered the portrait and went down to take a shower.

Wrapped in a thick terry robe, Aldy prepared a light supper and waited for her freshly washed hair to dry a bit more before she opted for a nap in lieu of baking a batch of oatmeal cookies.

She set her alarm for six. It was early yet, maybe she'd have time to make the cookies before Adam arrived, but now she had to get her feet up. She'd spent too long standing on the cement floor of the darkroom, too much time on the stool in front of her easel, and her back was aching.

Reaching for her heating pad, Aldy eased it under her and set the control to medium. She raised her knees to press the small of her back against the warmth.

"Come on," she mumbled desperately, "loosen up! I just can't cancel out on Adam."

The warmth from the heating pad flowed into her back muscles and Aldy fought a mounting panic. Adam hadn't been too upset that first time she'd had to refuse a date because of that barbecue with Bill and Ellen, but refusing was bound to be different than canceling after plans were already set! Maybe Adam was more understanding than Ken had been, but maybe he was just putting his best foot forward because the relationship was so new.

Aldora shuddered as she recalled the fights she and

Ken used to have each time that work interfered with pleasure.

"Dammit, Aldora!" Ken had raged on one such occasion, "Why do you make me take a backseat to some overstuffed client?" His face contorted with anger and he waved a doubled fist at her as he spoke. "I suppose a lousy one-third down is adequate compensation entitling Mr. John Q. Customer to half our life!"

"Look, Ken," Aldy pleaded, "the art world runs on deadlines. You've known it from the start." She looked longingly at him, her eyes begged him to understand. "I never interfere with your clients or begrudge you your business dinners and parties." As soon as the words were out, Aldy regretted them. The mood change in Ken's features was frightening.

"That's right, Aldora," he said, his tone deadly, "you never do because you're always too busy to come to those 'business dinners,' too damn busy with your own work to come and help me advance mine!" He slammed out of the studio then and it was days before things were peaceful again.

That had been only one of any number of arguments over just such a conflict. Well, maybe Adam was different, but Aldy knew that she could definitely wait to find out. She pushed deeper into the warmth of the heating pad and tried to sleep.

WHEN Adam rapped on the glass, Aldy was just taking a tray of oatmeal cookies from the oven. She beckoned with her stove mitt, "It's open!"

"Mmm, smelled terrific all the way down the front stairs," said Adam, crossing to the kitchen, his nose pantomiming in overtime. He smiled and gave Aldy a quick hug. "What kind?"

"Hello to you too," she teased, returning his hug. "Molasses oatmeal."

Adam grinned. "Specters from my pampered

childhood!'' He filched a warm cookie and bit into it before Aldy could stop him.

"They're too hot," she protested. "It'll make you sick."

"That's what Margaret always says." He munched happily. "Never happened."

Aldora laughed at his expression of complete bliss. The facile way Adam's expressions changed delighted her artist's eyes. The loving, tender father, the stern director of the Edgely Foundation, the rugged man of the sea squinting at the horizon, and this boyish charm that transformed a man of forty-one into an overgrown kid that Aldy wanted to hug. She pushed the other two main categories of expression from her mind: Adam's face contorted with pain and the Adam that looked out at her when his eyes grew hungry with need, desire.

"Ah, Margaret, watchdog of my tender years," Adam said, stuffing the last of the cookie into his mouth. "She's been with our family for ages. Takes care of Jess now. These are as good as hers," he said, grabbing another cookie and waltzing lithely out of range as Aldy swung a potholder at him. "Where are the pictures?"

"The coffee table. Start in, I'll be right there."

Aldy took the last cookie sheet from the oven and undid her apron. "Tea okay?" she asked, turning the flame on low under the kettle. She crossed to the sofa, sat next to him.

Without taking his eyes from the photo of Jess, Adam nodded. "This is great," he said, pointing at the frame of rigging around Jessie's smiling face. "Would you mind making another print of..." he began awkwardly.

"Take that one," Aldy said quickly. Adam was obviously uncomfortable with asking favors. "I counted on it, made two of them."

Adam smiled. A wistfulness crept into his voice. "I don't have any pictures of Jess since the accident." His face turned solemn. "She's better now, but cameras used to make her nearly hysterical at first." He anticipated Aldy's questions. "Louise, Jessie's mother, was really phobic after the crash; Jess got it from her."

"You needn't go into it," Aldy said, placing a hand on his arm. "Julie told me about the accident." She was looking for a way to ease Adam's growing discomfort.

He took her hand in both of his, cradling it gently. "I didn't come about the pictures, Aldy," he fumbled. "I know I behaved badly last night, I wanted to apolog—"

"Don't, Adam," Aldy cut in. "There's no need."

Adam wouldn't stop. "I have to explain, want to," he said softly. "Did Julie tell you about Louise?"

Aldy could sense his need. "Only that she was driving, suffered cuts from the windshield." Aldy was aching for his pain.

"The cuts were minor," he said stiffly. "Jessie was the real victim, in so many ways." He leaned back against the sofa and pulled Aldy against him.

Leaning on Adam's shoulder, Aldy listened quietly while he poured it all out. Louise's initial guilt, the way that guilt had turned to resentment when Louise discovered Jess was crippled. The Foundation specialists had decreed the scar on her own white throat too modest to warrant surgery. She heard Adam's voice grow harsh, cold as he told of Louise's near breakdown at this news.

"My wife was a very beautiful woman," he said.

Aldy's heart ached to imagine Adam's double pain: a child crippled, a beloved wife's beauty marred. The edge in Adam's next statement caused Aldy to look up suddenly.

"Unfortunately, Louise believed that was her only asset. She began to blame Jess for her own loss."

Aldy listened, shocked that Adam didn't display more sympathy. "It must have been very difficult for her." Aldy's own sympathy for scarring ran deep. "I mean, for anyone, but to be so beautiful and lose—"

"Lose!" Adam spat the word into the middle of their

conversation. "Louise didn't lose anything! Her mind magnified it, pushed it out of proportion. The only scar that even showed she could hide with a half thimble of makeup!" Adam's eyes were narrowed, his jaw set, as he related Louise's part in causing Jessie's seemingly disproportionate fear and jealousy.

Aldora tried to be objective, realized Adam had a right to his anger as he told of Louise's hostility toward her own daughter, her resentment, her nervous collapse, her eventual abandonment of Jessie and Adam four years ago. But in spite of Louise's seeming cruelty, Aldy's growing affection for Adam Holcomb, Aldy could feel a sorrow for this unknown woman that she believed a man could never comprehend. Men bore scars as badges, symbols of their courage or strength; it was different for a woman. Aldy had never thought of herself as a beauty, but her own reluctance to admit the obvious imperfection that ran half the length of her spine was proof enough that someone as lovely as Louise must have been would suffer horribly.

"That's what I meant last night," Adam finished. "About you not knowing. Jess knows her mother left because of the disability; she's terrified of being abandoned again."

Aldy stared in disbelief. "Surely she can't think *you'd*...I mean, how could she suspect her mother of—" Aldy floundered.

Adam cut in harshly. "Suspect! God, Aldy! She *knows*! Louise's exit line to us was some trash about not wanting to spend her good years as a nurse to a cripple!" Adam's anger carried him to his feet and Aldy sat mutely watching him pace out his rage in long, restless strides.

"She said that?" Aldy's voice was thin and reedy and the words slipped out before she could stop them, tears beginning to run openly down her cheeks, also unchecked.

Adam looked at her. His face softened. He came to

her side, put his arms around her shoulders. "I'm sorry, Aldy," he soothed. "I shouldn't let my damn temper go like that." He held her, stroked her hair, while Aldy clung to him, recalling every hurtful remark strangers had hurled at her after her own surgery. At least the people who had walked out on her had been more tactful, offered excuses, all except Ken.

Adam brushed at her tears with his fingers. "Guess I'm not used to being anything but blunt anymore," he said awkwardly. "Nobody to practice on." He looked into her eyes. "Should have known you were too sensitive, finely strung, just from what you bring to your paintings." He cupped her face in his hands and gently kissed her forehead, her eyelids. Little, light kisses that stilled her tears but set her heart to rioting. "To be able to feel so much for another's pain—" He drew her close and tucked her head under his chin.

Aldy felt like a fraud. Unearned praise again, she thought bitterly. She almost longed to tell Adam that not all her tears were for Jessie. She pulled away from him and reached for the photos. "The pictures should help her to feel more secure," said Aldy, holding up two different shots of Adam and Jess on the *Amara*. She had to do something, turn his attention away from herself. "The love you have for her shows so clearly in these."

Adam seemed to respect her need to lighten up the conversation. "Thanks," he said, smiling. "What about that tea?"

"Oh." Aldy jumped up. "Must have all boiled away by now!" she said, rushing to the kitchen. She shook the kettle and only a soft slosh sounded. Running in more water, Aldy set out cups and arranged cookies on a plate. "Just take any of those you want. I can make more," she said, bringing the cookies to the coffee table.

"These two for sure," said Adam, setting out the photos Aldy had picked. He leafed through the shots again as he reached for a cookie. "If you ever tell Margaret that I said these were as good as hers," he growled, "I'll deny it."

Aldy laughed and went to pour the tea. She carried the steaming cups to the couch and helped Adam select more pictures. She jotted down the ones she'd have to reprint.

Adam fell silent. He was staring at one of the pictures. He looked at Aldy. "I—I'd really like to have this one," he said, holding out the photo Grant had taken of him and Aldy at the wheel.

Aldora started to smile, then she saw Adam's look of regret. "But I can't take it," he said, the words caught in his throat. "Jessie would—" He stammered and looked again at the picture. "God, I look so. . . contented," he murmured uneasily.

"I understand," Aldy said. She chuckled. "You're entitled, but I probably couldn't part with that shot anyway." She tried to make her voice sound light, airy. She nibbled at a cookie and reached for her teacup.

Adam smiled his gratitude. "It's getting late," he said, finishing the tea and collecting the photographs into a pile.

"Let me put those in an envelope," Aldy said. She took the photos up to the studio and dug a manila envelope out of the bottom drawer of her taboret. Her back caught painfully as she straightened up. She dropped the envelope on the drafting table and rubbed at her back muscles with both hands. Her right eyebrow pulled in as she realized that she would have to go in late tomorrow, stop at the spa on her way, and hope that she could ward off the spasm that was building in intensity.

When she came downstairs, Adam had carried the dishes in to the sink and run water in the cups. "Thank you," she said. "I'll do those later." She handed Adam the photographs and walked him to the door.

There was no misunderstanding his intentions;

Adam's purpose was clear as he slid his arms around her waist and leaned down.

Aldora raised herself on tiptoe and met his kiss willingly. She let her arms encircle his shoulders and ran her hands over the hard muscles of Adam's back as his lips stirred feelings that seared through her with raw desire.

Adam's kiss grew gentle and he trailed small, light kisses down her neck. "Six-five doesn't line up too well with a standing embrace," he said, chuckling at his own awkwardness. He lifted her as easily as he had Jessie and straightened to his full height. "Mmm, much better," he murmured as his lips found hers once again.

Aldora was about to protest, but Adam's mouth was hard on hers, his tongue searching. Aldy parted her lips and need coupled with her longing as his tongue sought hers with soft, flicking thrusts. The arm that supported her shoulders pressed her more closely to his chest while the hand beneath her knees caressed fire into her thighs. Aldy twined her fingers in Adam's thick hair and surrendered to the passions he ignited.

Hugging her closely, Adam walked slowly to the sofa, his mouth and hands working their magic like a slow-burning flame, a tenderness coming through that was so much more arousing than any overt assault on her senses. Adam nestled her against the cushions and settled beside her. His hands, stroking her gently, slid the loose neckline of her peasant blouse off one smooth shoulder.

Aldy dragged a fingertip along the line of his jaw and let her lips nip gently at his lobe, drawing in her breath as he nuzzled her neck and expertly found the sensitive place midway between her ear and shoulder before moving on to the warm hollow of her throat.

Reaching under the ribbed waist of his sweater, Aldy ran her hands along the smoothness of Adam's skin, felt the hard muscles of his back ripple with pleasure at her caress.

Adam's lips tracked the length of her single bared

shoulder and the point of his chin edged the neck of her blouse lower over the swell of her breasts.

Desire rose in Aldora like a spring floodwater and she sent her hand following the curve of his muscular neck, her fingers lacing their way through his hair as she pulled his head closer to its destination.

Cupping one white breast gently in his palm, a low moan escaped Adam's throat as his lips teased the nipple to a throbbing firmness. He raised his head, dragging his mouth from the pleasure of her body. Framing her face gently with his hands, he said hoarsely, "If I don't leave now, I'll be here Judgment Day." His mouth slowly claimed hers as Aldy responded with almost drugged insistence.

"Witch," he murmured as he tucked the shoulder of her blouse back into place and glanced reluctantly at the luminous glow of the clock on the end table.

Aldora stared in wonder at his face. Passion seemed to melt his features into a newfound softness; a tenderness almost like that he reserved for Jessie, but haunted with unrequited desire, crept into Adam's expression.

He pulled her to her feet. "That statement I made last night," he said, moving with her to the door. "I meant every word." He grinned, kissed her lightly on the top of the head, picked up the envelope, and stepped out the door.

"Adam," Aldy called after him.

He looked back, one eyebrow raised expectantly.

"I'm glad." She slid the door closed with an answering smile and raised her hand against the glass.

Aldy watched Adam run lightly down the stairs, then she switched off the lights and walked slowly to the bedroom. *Dear Lord,* she thought uneasily, *he's so easy to...love.* She shook her head. *I'm losing control, falling for him,* she admitted reluctantly. Aldora tried to force herself to recall the pain loving had always brought, the hurt, but as Adam's words, his kisses, caressed her in a memory much fresher than that pain, she knew she had never felt this way about anyone before. What Adam stirred in her made her almost grateful that Ken had left, glad she'd sealed herself off afterward, to wait until Adam Holcomb came into her life.

She climbed into bed and pulled the covers up under her chin. Maybe it could work, she thought as she turned on her side and drew one knee toward her chest. The twinge in her back was an angry denial. She pushed it away and drifted into happier dreams.

Chapter Eleven

Early Monday morning Aldora left a message at the hospital that she'd be in late and called Kate.

"It's Aldora, Kate," she said when the girl's groggy voice reached across the line. "Sorry to call you so early. Don't bother coming in until eleven."

"What's wrong?" said Kate, instantly alarmed.

"Gotta stop at the spa on my way in," Aldy said. "Guess I overdid it."

"Good Saturday, huh?" Kate teased.

"Kate!" said Aldy, laughing. "Oh, remember, not a word in front of anyone at the hospital. If they knew, we'd all be looking for work!" She had warned Kate and Eddy that the hospital's insurance would never permit a chronic back case to climb about on scaffolding, but she wanted to be sure Kate remembered.

"Mum's the word," Kate agreed. "Eddy and I'll do the high stuff."

"I'll be fine after my workout," Aldy said but she was touched by Kate's offer to cover for her. "See you at eleven."

Aldora grabbed up her cane and limped out to her car. She drove to the spa and was waiting when Karen unlocked the door at nine.

"Rough weekend?" Karen asked, looking anxiously at Aldy.

"Too much darkroom time on Sunday," Aldy said, heading for the lockers. "A cement floor."

Aldora climbed gingerly into the pool and started her laps. The exercise wasn't having its optimal effect on the tightness. She did a few extra laps and then went to relax in the hot tub. The pummeling of the Jacuzzi seemed to help more and Aldy was reluctant to get out when the clock showed ten thirty. *I should have allowed more time,* she thought as she stepped out of the tub and tested her weight on her left leg. A slight twinge, but she'd manage. She walked carefully to the lockers, dressed, and drove to the hospital.

Kate and Eddy were waiting for her.

"Okay?" Kate asked softly.

"Fine," Aldy fibbed. "Let's get to work."

At noon Grant stopped by to see them. "Got your message," he said, walking Aldy to the atrium bench. "Anything wrong?" He looked concerned.

"No," Aldy said quickly. "Just had some errands that couldn't wait."

Grant looked relieved. "I thought maybe Jess was too much for you," he said, smiling.

Aldora began to panic. Had Grant found out about her back? He *had* wanted to carry Jess for her. She took a deep breath.

"She was pretty rugged with all those fancy maneuvers at the helm," Grant went on.

Aldora let the breath out slowly. He didn't know. Just a case of her own paranoia forcing her to hasty conclusions. She smiled and shook her head. "No, I enjoyed it all." She pulled a sandwich out of her lunch sack. "How's Julie?"

"Feisty as ever." Grant grinned. "Sea air does things for her." He winked wickedly. "See you all later."

After lunch Aldy and her helpers worked steadily until three. Aldora climbed off a ladder and walked across to get a perspective on the waterfall. Her back had tightened unbearably and her stomach felt queasy with the pain.

"Kate!" she called and waved the girl over to her.

"What's up, boss?"

Aldy smiled. "I'm gonna have to quit for the day," she said quietly. "Maybe skip tomorrow. I'm gonna plead flu."

Kate's brown eyes clouded with concern. "Aldy, maybe—"

Aldora held up her hand. "Not another word. Time in the hot tub, a day off. It'll fix me right up."

Kate didn't look convinced.

"I'll call you tomorrow night," she promised. "Will you and Eddy close up?"

"Sure," said Kate. "But you call me if you need anything. I know Ellie's out of town."

Aldora smiled at Kate's willingness. "Thanks." She gave Kate a quick hug and went toward the elevators. She'd go tell Grant now. With her present nausea, flu wouldn't even seem far enough from the truth to make her blush.

Aldora entered the second-floor office and asked the girl at the desk to buzz Grant.

Grant smiled at her as she came into the conference room, but his smile faded as he noticed her blanched color. "What's wrong?" he said, jumping up and taking her arm.

"No problems," she said easily. "I just think I must be getting a touch of flu or something." She took the offered chair. "I wanted to tell you I might be out tomorrow if I don't feel better."

"Can I drive you home?" said Grant, looking closely at her. "You don't look like you should be—"

"No," Aldy interrupted him gently. "I just need the proverbial bed rest and fluids." She forced a laugh. "Thanks anyway, but I'm a real loner when I'm under par." She hoped the laughter and the bid for privacy would be something Grant wouldn't argue with.

"Okay," Grant said. "I want you to call if you need anything, though."

"What? And have to explain to Julie why she'd be coming down with flu!" Aldy teased.

The touch of humor worked wonderfully. Grant grinned at her and then chuckled. "You'll be fine."

Aldora said good-bye and went to her car. She eased

herself in under the steering wheel and tossed her purse on the backseat. She drove home by way of the spa.

Hurting too much to eat, Aldy sipped hot tea and stared dismally out at the gathering darkness. *You were a fool to think you could juggle a career, a romance, and a disability,* she thought miserably. She took two muscle relaxers and looked at the picture of herself and Adam. How contented would he look if he'd suspected he'd had *two* invalids on his hands? Aldora got up slowly, and leaning on her cane, she made her way down the hall to the bedroom. She stretched out on the heating pad and closed her eyes. The room spun crazily and she forced herself to fix on a point on the far wall. Even if she could manage to hide her cane, the sounds of throwing up from the pain would be pretty unmistakable to anyone who entered into a relationship with her, she thought bitterly. She pulled herself to her feet and hobbled to the bathroom. The only happy thought that crossed her mind as she hung over the john was that Adam wasn't there to see it.

By noon the following day Aldy had recovered enough to drag herself to the spa, but she knew she'd need another day. She notified Kate, then called Grant. She swore she was well on her way to recovery and said she'd be in Thursday for sure.

On Wednesday evening Adam called as Aldy was loading her workbasket for the following day.

"Yes, Adam," she assured him, "I'm fine and I'll be back to work tomorrow."

"I don't care about the job, Aldy. I just wish you'd let me know you were sick. I could have helped, gone to the store for you, something."

Aldy's heart pounded hard beneath her ribs. He was being so caring. It was all she could do not to weaken in her resolve to end this go-nowhere affair before things worsened, before Adam learned the truth about her sudden "flu attack." "I just need to be alone when I'm sick," she said firmly.

"Well, if you're really better," he said hopefully, "how about dinner Saturday evening, just the two of us?"

He sounded so eager, Aldora ached to say yes, but the thought of her humiliating evening hanging over the john made her seize on the most ready excuse. "I'm sorry, Adam, Bill and Ellen are due back and I have a date set with them for Saturday."

Adam's disappointed tone made Aldy flinch as she turned down an alternate offer for Sunday also. "I'd best not overdo so soon after the flu," she said. "Ellen's is a second home and I can just lie around on the sofa, but I don't feel up to going out anywhere yet."

Adam chuckled. "We could arrange for you to lie around on *your* sofa, if memory serves—" He waited.

Was he half-expecting a positive response to that? Aldy laughed. "I don't think that's what the doctor would order, Adam," she said as gently as she could. But memories of that evening wrapped in Adam's arms played havoc with her infant resolve. She feared Adam might press, but he turned the conversation. "Jess really loved the photographs you sent, Aldy. Thanks."

"Oh, glad she liked them. I can do her favorites in eleven-by-fourteen...for posting in her room," she offered.

"She'd paper the walls if I'd let her," Adam said, laughing. "Of course you can guess that she complained most bitterly about missing out on the oatmeal cookies."

"I should have sent some of those along with you," Aldy said quickly. "I could bring some to work tomorrow."

"That's okay, she's hounded Margaret into baking her a batch by now."

After Adam hung up, Aldora felt hollow inside. There was no prearranged prospect of a date with Adam in her immediate future. She lay on the bed in the dark and let the tears come.

THURSDAY Aldy was back on the scaffolding and her work was going well. Kate and Eddy were speeding production at a surprising rate. By next Tuesday, Aldy thought, she'd be able to give them time off until the start of the hall mural. The large wall would be far enough along by then to command only her finishing work, if her luck held.

As Aldy was walking out to her car that evening, she heard Julie call to her.

"Aldy." Julie ran down the parking aisle toward Aldy's car. "How are you?" she said, stopping by the VW and leaning on the car to catch her breath.

"I'm fine," Aldy said, smiling, glad to see Julie again.

"Adam told me about the paintings," she said excitedly, "could I come by and see them?"

Aldora was stunned. Adam had spoken to her already! He hadn't forgotten. She felt tears prick her eyelids as she thought of Adam taking time to pitch for her art, and the way she'd refused his company this weekend. This was all making it so much more difficult to resist him.

"Well?" Julie was looking at her.

"Oh...sure, Julie," Aldy said, tearing her thoughts away from Adam. "When would you have time?"

"Now? Tonight?" Julie said eagerly. "From what Adam said, I have some galleries all selected."

Aldy laughed. "Easy, bride-to-be, you may be biting off more than you can chew."

"Can't work on the wedding until Mom gets back," Julie said logically. "How about it?"

"Okay, I'll lead." Aldy started the engine and waited for Julie to get to her car. "Follow me," she called as Julie pulled alongside.

Julie nodded and nosed the yellow Mustang in behind Aldora's VW.

"The place is a mess," Aldy warned as she led Julie up the front stairs.

"I won't look at anything but the paintings," Julie promised, laughing.

Aldy unlocked the door and set the kettle on the stove. "Tea?"

"Thanks," said Julie, walking immediately to the painting of the old house that hung by the stairwell. "Is this one of them?" she asked, turning wide eyes on Aldora.

Aldy nodded. Julie turned back to stare at the picture. "This architectural landscape looks a lot like Andrew Weyth's work! Adam didn't say nearly enough," she said firmly.

Aldy turned the fire low under the teakettle and led Julie upstairs.

"Love the studio," Julie said.

"You promised not to look," Aldy teased, waving Julie over to a chair. She pulled the paintings from the closet and began placing them around the walls. Julie was very quiet.

Aldora stepped back after she had braced the last canvas and shrugged nervously. "That's it."

Julie got up and walked around the room, stooping before each painting and examining carefully. She shook her head and stood in the center of the room, gazing at the fifteen canvases in dazed silence. "They're... incredible!" she breathed, looking at last at Aldy. "Why aren't they in a gallery already?"

"I'll tell you over tea," said Aldy and started for the stairs.

Julie listened, her mouth agape, as Aldy fixed the tea and told of the wedge her painting had driven in her relationship with Ken. She didn't exactly say that it had been the only factor causing the breakup, but she didn't go into the rest.

"I'd have left him too," Julie said, sipping at her tea. "He actually wanted you to give up that incredible talent to party and play house?" Julie's face was etched with anger and disbelief. "Pardon me, Aldy, I don't usually comment on my friends' personal lives," she said as Aldy nodded a yes to her previous question, "but that guy must have been really *thick*!"

Aldora chuckled at Julie's effort at tact. "He was a bit insensitive," she said, smiling.

Julie laughed. "Pretty gift for understatement you have too," she said, catching Aldy's tone. "Seriously, Aldy, I do have a good gallery in mind. I gotta go now, but I'll work on it. I'll let you know soon." She gave Aldy a hug. "I'm gonna have a famous artist at my wedding!" she said as she grabbed her keys and started out the door.

"Well, thanks for the ego boost, anyway," Aldy said, walking her to her car.

"Those paintings deserve the best," said Julie, waving and pulling out of the driveway.

Aldy laughed and went back up to the house. She climbed to the studio and looked at the pictures a long time before she put them away. Maybe Julie was right, but Ken had had one valid point. You had to draw the line somewhere. Even if she could have juggled two careers and a relationship back then, she couldn't do it now. The books could work into her bread-and-butter eventually; she didn't make much on her solo works yet, but the illustrations she'd done for other writers helped and her reputation was building. The murals would certainly boost her demand and royalties from several different sources might make things a little easier. The hospital murals and the books could work together, play off each other like recordings and concerts, but the oils were a long shot. No matter how enthusiastic Julie and Adam were, they couldn't know how long it took for one to build enough of a name in fine arts to make a livable income. And royalties were nonexistent unless one got prominent enough to be offered reproduction rights. That meant an art sale was a one-shot sum that came all too few and far between.

Aldora went down to fix supper. She couldn't even think of what getting involved with Adam would do to

her time schedule. She'd be back in that same tight corner Ken had backed her into before she knew it. There
just weren't enough good hours left to her anymore, she
thought unhappily. If only she could work a full day,
every day, without buckling physically, maybe a man
like Adam Holcomb could be satisfied with the remainder. He had a time-consuming job, a daughter to
absorb his hours. He was busy enough himself that—
Stop it! Aldy slammed her fist on the counter. *Stop
playing "what if,"* she scolded. *You can't work like
that anymore. Forget it!*

Aldora stared at the salad she'd been fixing and
swallowed against the bitterness in her mouth. She set
the plate in the fridge and went to bed.

ON Saturday afternoon she drove over to Ellen's.

"Aldy!" Ellen squealed, running to meet her car.
"We had the most fantastic time!" She grabbed Aldy as
she stepped from the car and hugged her hard. "I can't
wait to get my pictures back."

Aldora returned the hug. "I sure missed you,"
she said, holding Ellie at arm's length and surveying
the sunburned nose, the eyes sparkling with happy
health.

"Missed you too," said Ellie, leading the way into the
house. "Bill's in the shower," she said. "He'll get the
tent in your car later." She poured Aldy a glass of soda
and plunked in ice cubes. "Well?" she said.

"Well, what?" Aldy asked, sipping at her drink.

"Oh!" Ellen said in exasperation. "Post me!" she
ordered and sat opposite Aldy at the kitchen table.
"What'd I miss?"

Aldora was suddenly, unaccountably tearful. She
poured out her story to Ellie's sympathetic ear between
sobs.

"So why are you crying?" Ellen asked when Aldy had
finished. "You're in love with the guy. He sounds like
he's in love with you." She looked at Aldy expectantly.

"Didn't you hear a single other word I said?" Aldy groaned.

"I heard that this guy is all for you *and* your art," Ellen said firmly. "I heard you say he's even trying to set up a show. I *didn't* hear how all that equals a catastrophe!"

Aldy smiled a little and chuckled nervously. Ellen had a gift for cutting to the heart of things, stripping away all but the bare bones. "I know it sounds great," she said, "but Adam doesn't have any idea what he's dealing with."

Ellen looked confused. "Dealing with? He's dealing with a terrifically talented woman and seems bright enough to recognize it," said Ellen, leaning across to take Aldy's hand. "Unlike some others you've known."

Aldy squeezed Ellen's hand. "That's not it," she said softly. "He doesn't know I'm—" The word wouldn't come. "He has no idea I can't—"

"For God's sake!" Ellen cried. "He doesn't know you have good and bad days like everyone else in the world!"

"Dammit, Ellen, you know it's more than that!" Aldy was hurting. Her voice was angrier than Ellie deserved but she couldn't seem to stop. "He has enough with Jessie! He can't take care of *two cripples* for the rest of his life!" Her own words stunned her to silence. Ellen's arms went around her and she cried into Ellie's comforting embrace.

"You're wrong," Ellen said gently when Aldy's tears slowed. "Love isn't like that. Disability isn't a deterrent; you can learn to make more of the good days." Ellen patted Aldy's shoulders. "Don't hang Ken's crime on Adam."

"You don't understand," Aldy said quietly. "I'm afraid it *wouldn't* matter to Adam, and he doesn't need that."

Ellen let go of Aldy and stared at her. "Right! The noble act. Give him up for his own good." She glared at her friend. "My God, Aldy, you talk as if you're hardly ever on your feet! You've lost all perspective. Is it your back that's damaged or your brain?"

Aldy started to speak but Ellen waved her into silence. "Don't you think Adam has a right to make his own choice? Your noble gesture is playing God, Aldy, nothing else." Ellen took hold of Aldy's hand. "If you really believe he'd accept your condition, be honest with him!"

"No!" The cry tore from Aldora's throat. "I can't. . .couldn't ever tell him!"

"You're scared he'll walk out," Ellen accused. "He must be pretty slimy if you believe that in your heart. Forget him!" Ellen stood up and walked to the sink.

"He's not slimy!" Aldy shouted at Ellen's back. "He's. . .wonderful." Aldora watched her friend turn slowly to face her. Ellen had a knowing grin on her face as she came to hug Aldy.

"Sure glad we got that straight," she said slyly.

Aldy chuckled. "You tricked me, Ellen Hardesty. You—" She shook her fist in mock anger.

Ellen laughed. "Getting *you* to admit that was the first step. Now deal with it."

"I'll think about it," Aldy said. "Give me time."

"Take all you want, honey," Ellen said gently. "It's a new feeling for you." She turned back to the sink and began tearing lettuce for the salad.

"Can a guy get a drink in here?" said Bill, poking his head around the kitchen door and scrubbing at his wet hair with a towel.

"Sure," said Aldy, wiping at her cheeks and stepping to the refrigerator. "What'd you like?"

"A beer," Bill mumbled from under his towel.

"Coming up." Aldora pulled the top and poured the foamy liquid slowly down the side of a glass.

Bill tossed his towel on a chair and took the beer, squinting appreciatively. "No head. Pours pretty good for a teetotaler," he said, grinning at her. He wrapped one arm around her and gave her a warm hug. "Good to see you again."

"Thanks," Aldy said. She took the salad bowl from Ellen and carried it to the table. "I'll set," she said, grabbing plates off the shelf, silverware from the drawer.

"Okay, we're out of napkins though," Ellen muttered as she reached into the oven for a bubbly casserole. "Macaroni and cheese," she said. "I haven't been to the store yet."

"Ask me if I care," said Aldy, spooning a generous portion of the casserole onto each plate.

Ellen smiled and plopped salad tongs into the bowl as she sat down at her place.

Aldora savored the gooey cheese and listened to Bill's elaborate reconstruction of the vacation. He embroidered the event of the bear chase until Aldy's sides ached from laughing.

"Don't believe a word," Ellen said, chuckling. "It wasn't Bill's hollering and thrashing that scared it off, it was my beating on that pan with a metal spoon!"

Bill looked wounded. "Ya had to tell her, eh?" He glared at his wife in an hilarious imitation of her "fierce look." "How am I gonna keep my hero standing with you around?"

"It's all right, Bill. The next time I'm bothered by a bear I promise I'll call," Aldy said solemnly. Then she broke into new laughter.

After coffee and cake in the living room Aldora helped with the dishes and chatted with Ellen under the cover of Bill's television noise.

"I promise I'll think about it," she said to Ellen's prodding. "Now I'd better get on home. Work and 'flu' can be wearing."

"That's okay," said Ellen, grinning and tossing the dishcloth aside, "you're going to be giving up that kind of 'flu.'"

Bill pulled himself away from the news long enough

to load the tent into Aldy's car and called a hasty thanks as he rushed back into the house.

"You'd think he'd be glad to miss reports like they've been giving," said Ellie. She shrugged and waited until Aldy backed her car out of the drive. Then she waved and went back to the house.

Alone on the drive home, Aldy felt her Ellen-inspired confidence ebbing away. There was time, she thought anxiously; she didn't have to tell Adam immediately.

As Aldy pulled her nightgown over her head she wondered if Ellen might be right about playing God. If only Adam had known what he was getting into from the first, then maybe.... Aldy's head throbbed with indecision. She pushed the unanswerable from her mind and sank gratefully into bed.

ALDY was right on schedule with the mural. By Tuesday afternoon she gave Kate and Eddy bonus checks, a leave of absence, and was looking forward to starting the meticulous finishing work on Wednesday. She was collecting her clipboard and purse when Grant came up whistling "Yankee Doodle" and grinning.

"I'm not on the scaffold," she said, smiling at him.

"Habit," he said, staring up at the wall. "That really looks fine." Putting an arm around her, he gave her a big kiss. "That's 'hello' from Adam," Grant explained as she looked at him in surprise. "The man misses you!"

"Nonsense!" said Aldy lightly. "He has enough to do with Jess and this place to miss meals, not me!" A part of Aldy was jubilant that Adam had sent such a message; another part, more cowardly, realized that only honesty on her side could make accepting this from Adam more comfortable. And that was the part of her that thought it might be wise to start "easing" things, via Grant. If word of her casualness reached Adam, he could feel free to back off, maybe even stop dating her altogether. The jubilant part ached at that idea.

Grant interrupted her train of thought. "Speaking of meals," he said. "Julie and I are taking you to lunch tomorrow."

"What's the occasion?" said Aldy, raising one eyebrow.

Grant waved at the mural. "That. *And* Julie's news."

Aldora looked stricken. "Oh, Grant," she teased, "when will you get it straight? *First* the wedding, *then* the children!"

Grant laughed and took her arm. "Joke if you want but I'm not telling! Julie'd kill me!" He walked her to the elevators. "We'll collect you at eleven thirty." He steered her through the waiting doors and trotted off down the hall.

"Sure is a rough crowd for the curious," Aldy shouted as the elevator doors closed. She pressed the button for her parking level and wondered what Julie could have to announce. The mural was almost finished, maybe the sofas and benches were ready early. It would be great if they were moved in to play against the mural by the time Aldy proclaimed it complete. With any luck, that should be Friday, Monday at the latest.

Aldy went to her car and stopped at the spa on her way home. The rigid campaign she'd been waging with her workouts and medication seemed to be holding most of her pain at bay.

At eleven thirty the next day Aldora heard the strains of "Yankee Doodle" call her from the scaffold. She looked down and saw Julie waving up at her.

"It's fantastic!" Julie said, motioning to the mural. "It's nearly finished!"

Aldora climbed down and took off her smock. "I hope this is come-as-you-are," she said, looking at Julie's tidy appearance.

"Definitely," Grant said. "Julie's presentable 'cause she had a hot date with the floor covering man." He gave Julie a mock scowl.

"Some hot date," she replied, rolling her eyes and groaning.

Grant laughed and put his arms around her. "The guy's trying to beat my time! I hope you flashed him your ring twice for every pass he made."

"Three times," Julie yelped and held her oath-taking hand aloft.

"Good," Grant said casually, " 'cause I've got Aldy waiting in the wings if you get cute!"

The three of them laughed and started down the hall arm in arm.

"I'd be worried to death," Julie said, "if I didn't know that Adam would have a lot to say about that."

Grant seconded that notion heartily.

"Quit, you two," Aldy protested. "I've barely met the man." She chalked up another point for her hermit campaign, but noticed that Grant and Julie looked at each other mysteriously.

Seated in a cozy booth at the deli where she had first met Adam, Aldy chatted with her two companions and munched pastrami on rye.

"Got to start planning the big unveiling bash," said Grant between bites.

"Right," Julie mumbled around her roast beef. "What's the projected completion date for the hall?"

Aldora chewed thoughtfully for a few moments and ran some figures through her interior, deadline computer. "If the hall goes as well as the recreation room," she said slowly, "and if Kate and Eddy keep up the pace, maybe another three weeks."

"Great," said Julie, "just in time for the holiday weekend."

"What holiday?" asked Aldy startled. "Palm Sunday?"

"Don't be ridiculous. Memorial Day," said Julie waving her forkful of cole slaw.

"That's at the end of May!" said Aldy. "Two months plus!"

"Right. Gotta allow time for everyone to fly in from wherever." Julie took another bite of sandwich.

Trying not to be excluded, Grant nearly choked on a bite of pickle. "No way," he garbled at them. "A holiday is out. Plane reservations are too tricky."

Julie nodded. "I didn't think of that."

Aldora was confused. "What are you two talking about?" she said. "An unveiling or the launching of the *Lusitania*?" Such an affair as they seemed to be discussing made Aldy a little nervous.

"The *Lusitania*!" Grant and Julie answered in unison.

"Might as well be," said Grant. "The big money that supported this new wing conception could afford to raise her. They wouldn't miss the unveiling. Prestige." He winked at Aldy. "You know, come to America, be squired around, wined and dined, then see 'your' hospital and the handcrafted murals by a prominent American artist, and *meet* that artist!" He grinned and pointed at Aldora.

She was blushing at the thought of such nonsense. Then she saw that Julie was confirming every word with eager nods of her head. "Good grief!" she gasped. "I had no idea!" Her research, it appeared, hadn't revealed all the details of the Edgely Foundation.

"So many foreign parents are so grateful for the miracles the Foundation has given their children," Grant said seriously. "Most of them insisted on giving huge donations to aid the building of the new wing so that no child would have to be refused for lack of facilities."

"Yes," Julie said, "Adam's grandmother was more than wealthy enough to get it off the ground in first-class style, but even the Edgelys can't do it all!"

"Adam's grandmother!" Aldora felt as if someone had just dropped a brick on her foot.

"You didn't know?" said Grant in surprise. "Edgely was the family name on his mother's side." He grinned wickedly. "Lord," he gasped and slapped his forehead, "she's not after his money after all!" he said to Julie and jerked his head in Aldora's direction.

Aldora blushed a deep red feeling her temper mount. "I'm not *after* anyone!" she snapped. But she realized she was overreacting when Grant and Julie both looked instantly contrite.

"She's right, honey," Julie said quietly. "Keep teasing and you'll ruin a good thing before it's begun."

Aldora watched numbly as Grant shrugged an apology. These two were really convinced that she and Adam were an item! What gave them that impression? As far as they knew, she'd only seen Adam three times! Certainly they hadn't got the notion from Adam. Had they? She felt perspiration bead on her brow.

Her discomfort must have been obvious. Grant patted her hand affectionately. "I'm sorry, Aldy," he said. "It's just that you're the first woman Adam's opened up to since Louise walked out four years ago."

"Guess we're just relieved to see him making a stab at normality," Julie added. "He's a great guy." Julie's voice was full of emotion and Grant was apparently in complete agreement with this diagnosis for their behavior.

Aldora looked at their serious expressions and moved uneasily in her seat. Four years was a long time to keep your friends in a state of anxiety, she thought. Maybe Adam was just testing the water before jumping into serious dating. Aldy couldn't quite convince herself that Adam was really breaking ground for a madcap whirl at middle-age crazy. . . starting with her! And would she be any more comfortable with the idea that she might soon be one of the many? The thought made her shudder involuntarily. She was glad when Grant changed the subject. The funny pain such an idea brought was frightening.

"Get on with your news," he said to Julie.

"I nearly forgot," Julie said excitedly.

"Swell," Grant joked. "'Matchmaker forgets raison d'être, film at eleven!'"

Julie grabbed his hand. "You should talk!" She smiled at Aldy. "Good news. I'll pick up your paintings Thursday morning." She sat waiting for Aldy's reaction.

Aldora was awestruck. "My paintings?" she said weakly.

Julie nodded excitedly. "I've got a terrific gallery all lined up. They want to see the work as soon as possible."

Aldy gulped. So fast? Just like that and Julie had a prospect? She couldn't believe it. Her abandoned show had taken months to arrange. Weeks of soliciting before she had made the right contacts. "How?" she gagged at Julie.

Julie's eyes sparkled. "Connections," she said with feigned sophistication. Then she laughed. "Dad knows *everybody* in the art world," she explained. "I've been in and out of galleries since I could be lifted from my cradle." She looked at Aldy expectantly.

Plainly Julie seemed to think Aldora should be understanding a lot more than what had just been stated. Aldy gaped.

"Give her a hint," said Grant. "She's in shock."

"Frank Edwin Shore," said Julie, smiling.

Now Aldy's mouth refused all commands to close. "Frank Shore? Your father?" Her mind boggled helplessly. Frank Shore was one of the foremost art appraisers in the world of fine arts. "I never made a connection," she said numbly. "I mean—" Words failed her.

"That's why Adam suggested Julie," Grant explained. "He knew Julie would be the best judge of the potential as well as the possibilities." He grinned proudly and leaned to hug Julie.

"You mean you'd really agent for me?" said Aldy, overwhelmed with emotion.

"For those paintings," Julie said firmly, "I'd quit my job with Grant and promote you." She grinned and reached across the table to Aldora.

Grant punched her softly in the arm. "Quit me?"

"Just the short-term contract, darling," Julie said quickly. "You're stuck with the long-term one!" She flashed her engagement ring at him playfully.

As Aldora took Julie's hand she brushed tears away with her napkin.

"Now, would you care to retract your self-demeaning comments regarding your work?"

"I'm sorry, Julie," Aldy said contritely. "I had no idea, I thought you were just—"

"Being nice?" Julie finished. "Not where the family business is involved," she said sternly. "Dad's got a reputation to uphold." She grinned at Aldy. "And you'll uphold it."

Aldora couldn't believe it. With backing like this, maybe she did have a chance. Maybe. . . her mind raced to thoughts of Adam and her impossible schedule. She looked at Julie. "What time do you want them?"

"Nine," Julie said. "You can go in late. Adam won't break your contract." She laughed and got up to hug Aldy while Grant paid the check.

During the drive back to the hospital Julie outlined the campaign. She had appointments with two posh galleries and she'd play one against the other to wangle the best percentages. "Most want fifty percent for a one-woman show," said Julie, "but if I can find a compatible, would you go for forty percent and sharing a show?"

Aldora was awed. "*Those* galleries?" she said when Julie mentioned the names. "If they want to hang me in effigy, I'll accept!"

"Okay," Julie said, laughing, "but I'm sure they'd rather hang the paintings."

Following Grant and Julie into the elevators, Aldy felt shaky. *My legs will never get me up a ladder now,* she thought.

"Need any of them framed for this?" she asked Julie.

"Nope." Julie shook her head. "These guys do all their own. They'd rather see the work without for first impressions."

Aldy got out on the main floor. "Thank you, Julie," she said and gave her a quick hug.

"Tomorrow at nine," Julie called as the doors slid shut.

Aldora walked to the new wing and stared up at the mural. "You sure turned my luck around," she whispered to the giant wall. "I owe you." She put on her smock and grabbed her brushes. Then she climbed carefully to the third tier and started working.

At six thirty Aldy climbed down, cleaned her equipment, and headed for the spa. Lounging in the hot water of the Jacuzzi, she let happy, hopeful thoughts rush in. If she could get a good purchase on her fine-art career, maybe she could afford to turn down some of her commercial work. If she could do that, it might buy her enough time for a "relationship" after all! She sighed contentedly and wondered what Adam was doing tonight.

Her phone was ringing when she came in the door. She hurried to pick it up.

"Aldy?" Adam's voice, eager, excited, reached out to her.

"Adam," she said happily. "I was just thinking about you."

"Julie told you?" he asked quickly. "I didn't call before. I knew I'd spoil her surprise." He paused for breath.

"She told me," Aldy said. "I nearly fainted!"

Adam laughed. "When you didn't pick up on her name, I figured I'd keep quiet till she made the move."

"I'll never be able to thank her," Aldy said. "Or you."

"Oh, I promise I'll think of something," Adam said, chuckling suggestively.

"Whatever are you implying?" Aldy teased in her best simper.

"Well, it's not more oatmeal cookies," he joked. "How about dinner on Sunday?"

"I'd love to." Aldy added: "Sorry you don't like the cookies."

"Bring 'em along. I'll pick you up at seven thirty."

Aldora had just hung up when the phone rang again. It was her publisher.

"All right, Miriam," Aldy said. "I'll see what I can arrange." She drew her hand across her forehead and dropped the phone back on its hook. Damn! The artwork for two pages, double spreads in the new book, had been damaged by a roof leak. She'd have to redo them, take them to San Francisco *and* stay through the Monday press run. Some problem with the color separations and the new printer.

Aldora fixed a light supper and thought gloomily of canceling her date with Adam, of the holdup on the mural work. If she tried to do all the illustrations on Saturday, she'd cripple herself. She couldn't press like that anymore. She knew she'd have to spread the work over Saturday and Sunday. Maybe she could catch the red-eye late Sunday night? No, leaning over a drafting table all day, dinner with Adam, and then traveling all night would never leave her enough steam to supervise the Monday press run, especially if there were corrections to do.

As Aldy flopped exhaustedly into bed, she wondered how Adam would take the bad news. At least, she thought dismally, this would tell her all she needed to know of the future. If Adam blew up over this sort of career-related inconvenience, if he even looked like he'd react as Ken always had, she might as well forget any thought of a relationship. It could only get worse! She snapped off the light and tossed uneasily trying to get comfortable; comfort wasn't possible.

JULIE arrived promptly at nine and Aldy helped her load the canvases into the car. She told Julie of the emergency trip to San Francisco and made her promise to call collect if there was any news about the show.

"Call to the hospital or here?" Julie asked, then grinned at Aldy's look of astonishment. "I'll have our choices outlined by this afternoon. Tonight, at the latest."

"You're incredible!"

"You can think about it while you're away," said Julie, starting the car and holding up her hand with the first finger and thumb touching.

Aldy gave her a thumbs-up and climbed into her own car.

At the hospital Aldy took the south elevator up to the eighth floor of the new wing. She had never been to Adam's office, never been up to see the rest of the new wing.

As she stepped from the elevator the sights of a working hospital assailed her and she was grateful that the recreation room held no such memory-jogging activity. She followed the signs to Room 810 and opened the door. Giving her name to the receptionist, she tugged nervously at the hem of her jacket and took a deep breath when the girl told her to go right in.

Adam was on the phone, but he smiled at her and motioned to a chair. Aldy sat on the front edge of the deep, soft chair that could have been designed by a ghoul who had it in for back patients. Staring at Adam's strong profile, she hoped fervently that he'd take the news with grace; the idea of losing him permanently caused her eyes to blur with ready tears. She turned her gaze to the office furnishings, trying to collect herself. The room seemed to reflect its tenant: bold, graceful, dynamic. It was unlikely that Julie had had anything to do with this interior. The reed-textured wall covering that blended so nicely with the earth-tone carpet, the glass display case that held a dramatic sculpture of a leaping gazelle and some smaller pewter figures of children playing a circle game, all bespoke a personal involvement between owner and decorator. Aldy smiled to see the wooden troll, typical of Danish folk art crouched on the bottom shelf, and next to it, a child's clay hand-print ashtray. Aldora didn't have to read the name painted cross the palm indentation to know it was Jessie's. She felt a lump fill her throat and pulled her eyes away, directed them to the serigraph of a sailing ship on the far wall.

"Aldy." Adam's voice brought her attention back to the uncomfortable task before her. "What a nice surprise." Adam came around the desk and dropped a kiss on her cheek.

"You may not think so," said Aldy hesitantly.

Adam looked at her. "What's wrong, sweetheart?" His face was lined with concern and his use of the endearment made Aldy's heart lurch.

"I have to cancel our date," she blurted. "I'm sorry, Adam. Trouble with the book. I have to fly to San Francisco Sunday." She looked up at him and saw the disappointment in his eyes. She explained the whole problem, rushing on in fits and starts of nervous chatter.

"Oh, honey," said Adam, sitting on the arm of her chair and hugging her to him with one strong arm. "That's awful."

Here it comes, Aldy thought, *the wheedling, the protest.*

"Do you need the sketch you gave Jess?" he asked. "She'll understand."

Aldy shook her head and looked at him in amazement. No anger? No denial? Just offers of help?

"What's the matter, Aldy?"

"I—I thought you'd be. . .angry," she stammered. "I—"

Adam laughed and hugged her harder. "I won't say I'm not very disappointed. But *you're* the one with the extra work load."

"But your plans. . .our date?"

"Honey, it can't be helped. That's fun; this is business." He smiled down at her. "Only one real problem," he said, looking solemn. "Jess. She was just getting used to letting me out on my own occasionally. She'll be spoiled rotten by the time you get back."

Aldy laughed. "Are you always this reasonable?" she asked, mentally crossing her fingers.

Adam looked serious. "This *is* my best foot, Aldy. But it's usually well forward!" He grinned. "Now, will you need a lift to the airport?"

"My plane leaves in the afternoon," she hesitated, "unless I catch the red-eye," she offered.

"No way!" said Adam firmly. "I won't have you tramping around San Francisco in the dead of night all alone!"

There he was, taking care of her again. Aldy felt tears threaten at his kindness.

"What time's your flight?"

"I should be at the airport by three," she said. "But I'd better take my car. I don't know for sure when I'll be getting back."

Adam looked concerned.

"The press run," Aldy explained. "I may have to stay longer if there are corrections."

"Oh." He nodded. "Well, I won't push. Do what's best for you."

Aldy stood up. "Thanks for understanding, Adam. I really am sorry for the scramble."

He took her in his arms. "Call me when you get there. Call me when you get back." He kissed her.

The touch of him was making Aldy's pulse race and his after-shave was a heady stimulus to her already budding desire. She wrapped her arms around his neck and felt him lift her slightly free of the floor. When he set her down again, he scribbled his home number on a slip of paper. "Call me," he repeated. "Now, get out of here, woman. I've got work to do; you're a definite distraction." He scowled at her, but the passion that still blazed in his eyes left no margin for doubting the real meaning of the term *distraction*.

Aldy folded the piece of paper into her purse and stepped through the doorway.

Out in the hall Aldy's knees were watery and she felt weak all over. He hadn't been angry at all. He'd understood. And his good-bye kiss told her it was no act; there was no hidden hostility to flare later, surface in a future misunderstanding, hurled in anger and geared to hurt. Aldy smiled as she got into the elevator, but she wondered how Adam would have taken it if he'd known about her incapacity. Would he have been as understanding if he'd known a healthy woman could have easily done the mural Saturday, all the illustrations Sunday, kept her date Sunday evening, and caught the red-eye to San Francisco late Sunday night? She'd done that often enough to pacify Ken. She'd stayed up all night to push and meet deadlines for grumpy editors or art clients. Most people expected you to press, pour it on now and then, especially in the art field. Aldy pulled her smock over her blouse and directed all her attention to the mural.

By five she still had no word from Julie so she left for the spa. If she got there early, she could get home in plenty of time to hear from Julie at the house.

Chapter Twelve

San Francisco was only a business success for Aldora. The breezy city with its cheerful cable cars and steep inclines rushing down to the sea failed to have its customary uplifting effect on her spirits. She spent a few hours wandering through Chinatown's shops and snapping pictures for her morgue, but her heart wasn't in this town. She did see a lovely silk kimono in white, with floral sprays in pink and lavender, and thought instantly of Jessie's blond curls and green eyes. Impulsively she bought the kimono and had it wrapped in white tissue paper.

The press run had dragged on an extra day and Aldy couldn't get a return flight until late Wednesday afternoon. She had called Adam, of course, and he had been so sympathetic and understanding. He said the mural could wait, so could he... if he had to! Aldora couldn't quite believe in anyone who could be *that* rational; maybe he just didn't care as much as he pretended. Aldy's only experience with love had been Ken's sort of demanding, jealous possessiveness. She packed for her flight and laid the package for Jess carefully on the top of her luggage. Well, she'd know when she got home, she thought; it was always better when you could look into someone's eyes for the unspoken answers. She hailed a cab and rode to the airport.

On the plane trip home Aldora was seated next to an ebullient business-type who chattered endlessly and made numerous passes interspersed with very bad jokes. *Just my luck,* Aldy thought. Dating, searching, hoping: all a royal pain!

Lulled into reflection by her traveling companion's

incessant droning, Aldy let her thoughts drift back to her meeting with Ken on just such a commuter flight. Then the business-type next to her breathed his "complimentary first-class drinks" breath at her and she was catapulted into the middle of that rowdy party Ken had insisted on attending. The one party that had changed her life forever.

Once a year Ken's boss threw a lavish get-together at his home in the hills. The main yard and natural-rock-bordered swimming pool looked out over the San Fernando Valley, while the gazebo, garden, and firepit faced on the sparkling lights of most of downtown Los Angeles. This mountain retreat was the perfect setting for Ken to show off his "jewel" of a bride-to-be and he was making the most of it.

It was typical of most of the parties Aldy had grown to hate. Loud music, overindulged guests and a liquor bill that would shame the national debt! Aldora was thinking that she was glad she didn't have to pay it, when a commotion in which Ken's voice figured prominently drew her attention.

"Oh, Lord," she cried as she ran across the flagstone patio toward the firepit. In the flickering light from the flames she could see Ken teetering on the low block wall that surrounded the property. The far side of the wall was nothing but steep cliff and the sort of brush that gave the Los Angeles Fire Department nightmares in the summer season. "Ken, please," she said as she approached, "get off of there." She glanced, embarrassed, at the other guests. They seemed to see nothing wrong with Ken's behavior. Aldy started to reach for her fiancé when a hand caught at her dress.

"Let go!" she cried as she grabbed a handful of her skirt material and tugged.

The man at the other end of that piece of material was huge, drunk, and Aldy had been avoiding him for most of the evening.

"C'mon, Abby," he slobbered at her, "let ol' Kenny

have some fun before you lead 'im to slaughter." He laughed, hiccuped, and took a firmer grip on the side of Aldy's skirt.

She yanked.

He yanked back. "Tug o' war," he singsonged at her and the bystanders began to laugh and applaud him.

Aldora's face felt hot; seething with humiliation and anger, she glanced up at Ken tripping his light fantastic on the wall's edge. "Ken, please!" she shouted, close to tears.

"Now, now," he said, wagging a finger at her. "Worried about me, baby?" he taunted, bleary from more than one-too-many. He tried to applaud her concern and seemed to have a deal of trouble making his hands come together in front of his body. He swayed dangerously.

"Ken!" Aldy gasped, and wrenching herself free of her heckler, she lunged closer to the wall.

"S'all right," Ken said, weaving as he held up a cautionary hand.

"Yeah," slurred the bully blundering after Aldora. "He's a'right, honey, leave 'im alone!" The man grabbed her shoulder and Aldora flinched from the pressure. She tried vainly to twist away.

"Hey!" said Ken, seeing the large man's hands on his fiancée. "Leggo of my girl!" He careened along the wall toward Aldora.

Aldy felt the back of her knees against the edge of the wall and pried at the fingers that dug into her shoulder. Then she knew nothing but the sound of her own scream as she went backward over the wall; she felt only the sharp pain in her left hip as she rolled to a stop against a tree stump that jutted from the hillside to break her fall...and her lower spine!

Ken came to the hospital a lot at first, pledged allegiance and love, promised married bliss. He quit drinking. But after the doctors decreed that only major surgery could help Aldy out of a hospital bed, Ken came less often. The night before her surgery Aldora looked up from the hazy warmth the night medication had surrounded her with and saw Ken walking in the door of her room.

"Hi, honey," he said, sitting carefully on the chair by her bed. He reached over and patted her hand. "So, tomorrow's the big day, huh?" He grinned at her.

Aldy nodded sleepily and smiled at him. "Thanks for coming," she mumbled. She licked at her dry lips and swallowed. "Some water, please," she said, reaching out her hand toward the bedtable.

Ken swiveled in his chair and grabbed at the water carafe. He sloshed some water into the cup and wiped ineffectually at the chipped ice and water he'd spilled. "Damn!" he muttered as he thrust the cup at her unsteadily.

"What's the matter, Ken?" Aldy asked, wrapping her fingers around his as she tried to manage the cup.

"Nothing, just an accident. Spilled some water." He leaned forward to help her and tipped the cup at a dangerous angle. Trying to recover, Ken sloshed half the contents across her arm and up her sleeve.

"Ken!" Aldy said, drawing a sharp breath as the iced water made her jump. The medication was loosening its hold in response to the icy dousing. "This isn't like you; what's wrong?"

Suddenly hostile toward her, Ken blotted awkwardly at the droplets of water on the sheet and covers. "I said nothing, and I mean it. Drop it!" He glared at her.

Aldora looked hard at him. "You've been drinking, Ken." Her eyes lowered and she twisted nervously at the covers with shaky fingers. "You're drunk!" Hot tears of betrayal ran unbidden down her cheeks.

"The hell I am!" Ken shouted. He flung the towel at the far wall and swayed unsteadily with the follow-through of the action.

"Look at you," Aldy cried as he caught himself on the arm of the chair. "Tonight of all nights," she said brokenly. "I needed you, your support." She shook her head.

"I am *not* drunk!" Ken said slowly and he swayed toward her. "See." He leaned forward and balanced the now empty water cup on the end of his index finger. It stayed momentarily then toppled to the bed.

Aldora glared at him. "Drinking's bad enough, but lying about it...." She couldn't see him very well from the mandatory flat position, but she wasn't sure she wanted to. She let her head roll to one side and looked away from him as tears blurred her vision again. She bit into her lower lip and willed the hurt to subside.

"Aldora, baby, I *needed* a little something to face your op—" he floundered and tried again, "operation." He grinned and leaned to kiss her wetly on the cheek.

The smell of liquor on his breath sent Aldy's mind reeling to the party, the fall down the mountain. She felt nausea engulfing her. Pushing him away with one hand, she clapped the other tightly over her mouth. She pinched her nostrils together and swallowed hard several times in succession.

Ken pushed her restraining hand away from him roughly and swore. "The hell with you, then," he slurred and slammed out of the room.

In the wake of his treachery, Aldora's nausea gave way to sobs that were stilled only when she surrendered her own iron control to the powers of the medication the nurse had administered an hour before.

Later, after her surgery, Ken had come to beg her forgiveness. He swore he'd quit drinking for good, promised to do better by her.

Aldy wanted to believe him, needed to. But in the days after her operation Ken came to visit less and less. The first day Aldy was allowed to stand up only Ellen and Bill were present to encourage her efforts.

The flight attendant's voice over the loudspeaker announced the plane's arrival at Los Angeles Airport and

Aldora fumbled with the buckle of her seat belt. She realized that her eyes were blurred with the memory of all the tears she'd cried in that hospital room. Blinking them back angrily, she threaded the seat belt across her lap and gripped the arms of the chair.

A damp, pudgy hand covered hers and she glared at the business-type with open malice.

"A little flight fright?" he drooled at her, closing his fingers around hers.

Aldora jerked her hand away. "Don't touch me," she said through clenched teeth.

"Take it easy, honey," he said. "I was just trying to help."

"You can't even help yourself!" Aldy snapped and indicated the miniature liquor bottle the man still clutched, unopened in his other hand.

He grinned sheepishly at her and dropped the little bottle into his briefcase. "Little souvenir for the wife," he slurred and pretended to focus on something outside the window.

Aldora shook her head. It figured, she thought, "the wife," and after the way he was coming on. Drunk *and* deceitful; they seemed to be inseparable.

As the wheels of the plane touched the runway, Aldora breathed a sigh of infinite relief.

WHEN Aldora got home, she phoned Julie before she even unpacked. She had mulled over the options Julie had given her before the trip and made her choice. She'd wanted to decide immediately, pick a gallery Friday before she left, but as both choices were good, Julie insisted that Aldy think on it. Better to let the gallery folk sweat a little, anyway, Julie had coached.

"Julie?"

"Aldy! You're back! How was the trip?" Julie's voice, warm and welcoming, made Aldy feel good, wiped away the gloom of the return trip.

"Fine," she said, dismissing her journey with a single syllable. "I've decided."

"Well?"

"I'll follow your judgment, of course, but I thought I'd go with the one-woman show. It may cost me a few percent, but the prestige *and* that gallery are worth it." She waited, trying to imagine Julie's expression, guess her reaction.

"I hoped you'd say that!" Julie said. "I didn't know if you could afford to go that route, but I'm sure glad you picked my favorite."

Aldora listened while Julie babbled excitedly about setting it all up and arranging a meeting with Aldy and the owner, the contracts, the invitations for the showing, the refreshments. It all seemed too overwhelming.

"My Lord, Julie," Aldy said when Julie ran down a bit, "is all of that customary?"

"It is for *this* gallery," she said proudly. "First class all the way."

"It sounds like a lot of work. You don't have the time for such involvement in my—"

Julie cut her off. "Stop! Most of it's arranged by the gallery anyway. I'll get together with you and we'll divide the detail work."

Aldy started to protest again.

"Not one word," Julie threatened. "I love this sort of thing. I cut my teeth on it; it's a snap!"

Aldy laughed. "I don't believe you," she said, "but you have my undying gratitude!"

Julie chuckled. "Just wait. The bill will come due when I fall behind on my wedding arrangements."

"You've got it, Julie," Aldy promised. She said good-bye and then phoned to let Adam know she was back. He was out so she left a message with the secretary.

Aldora puttered around the house, unpacking, straightening, fixing supper, denying that she was really just waiting for Adam to return her call. She denied this so firmly that when the phone did ring at nearly eight thirty, she froze midstride and stared stupidly at it for three full rings.

"Aldy?"

"Oh, hello, Grant," said Aldora, her heart sinking as she recognized the voice.

"How was the trip?"

"Just fine," Aldy said, fighting to keep her tone cheery despite her disappointment that it wasn't Adam, angry that her emotions were allowing her to mar one situation with another. "The book's all ready to go and the first press run after the corrections came out wonderfully."

"Good," Grant said. Then teasing: "The whole staff has been driving me crazy at the hospital."

"Oh?"

"Yeah, they keep asking after the lady tightrope walker who used to perform from eight to five!"

Aldora chuckled. Grant's warmth and humor had restored her perspective. She talked excitedly with him about the gallery decision, and when he asked her out to a combination celebration and welcome-home dinner for the next night, Aldy didn't have to think twice. "I'd love to," she said.

"Great. Bring a change of sneakers to work; we'll take you some place special."

Aldy said good-bye and went to her closet. "Special," Grant had said. She stared at her wardrobe, rubbed her aching back as she tried to decide. *Probably wouldn't have warned me if it wasn't going to be dressy,* she thought. She took a soft, floor-length halter dress, in a lilac jersey, from the back of the closet. *A great color, won't wrinkle. I can leave it in the car all day and it'll look none the worse by evening,* Aldy thought as she tried it on. It fit perfectly over her slim figure, clung and draped alluringly over her long legs. And it could be considered dressy, especially in southern California where anything that wasn't made of denim was practically formal! She reached back to unzip and her muscles spasmed painfully. *Damn! Not again, please,* she thought as she slowly worked the zipper down by degrees and looked at the clock. Nearly nine! Aldy tossed the dress on the bed and dialed Karen at the spa.

"It's Aldora, Karen," she said, pausing to allow Karen her customary enthusiasm. "Yes, the trip was fine. I've got a problem, though." Aldora crossed her fingers. "Could you possibly hold the door for me?"

"Well, how long?" Karen hadn't said no, but the hesitation was there.

"I hate to ask; not long. I just need the Jacuzzi and a few laps. That plane trip, the aggravation...." Aldy waited hopefully. She wouldn't be able to go tomorrow after work. She'd never have accepted Grant's invitation if she'd realized she was close to a major spasm.

"Sure," said Karen, apparently sensing the urgency. "I guess I could do a little work on the books. Come on over."

"Thanks, Karen, you're a lifesaver. See you soon."

Aldy hung up and grabbed her tote bag off the chair. She threw in a big terry towel and pulled a cotton shift over her panties. After slipping into her sandals she hurried to her car. She'd ward off the back pain for now, worry about missing her workout tomorrow when the time came.

Aldora tapped on the back door of the spa. Only ten after nine; she wouldn't have to keep Karen too late after all.

"Hi, Aldy," said Karen, pushing open the door and waving Aldy through the locker room. "Take your time," she said as she shot the bolt on the back door. "I decided to let you do me a favor."

"Anything." Aldy looked thankfully at her.

"This is it. If I do the books now, I can leave early on Saturday," Karen said, smiling. "Hot date with Mr. Right." She grinned at Aldora.

"Who's Mr. Right this time, Karen?" Aldy asked

laughing. The vivacious redhead had seized upon a new Mr. Right at least once a month since Aldy had started coming to the spa. Her constant complaint was that all her choices had no real ambition, no passion for anything but their own well-muscled bodies.

Karen feigned an injured look. "Aldy! Chuck Willis, naturally." She watched Aldy for a reaction.

"Chuck-with-the-brains-as-well-as-brawn Willis?" said Aldy in surprise as Karen nodded excitedly. "Chuck with the new health club and gym in Santa Monica?"

"Right where the sand meets the surf," Karen answered happily.

"How long has this been going on?" Aldy teased as she slid her sandals under the bench and started to undress.

"Since the health club convention last October."

"Last October?" Aldy said, pulling the shift off over her head. "But I thought—"

Karen laughed. "That's when *I* fell for *him*," she explained. "I didn't hear anything for a while and began to think it just wasn't mutual."

Aldy's stomach tightened as Karen described her unrequited passion for her muscleman. The ones you felt you could go for never seemed to feel the same way about you, she mused, thinking of the unanswered message she'd left with Adam's secretary.

"Then," Karen was saying, "when he got back from the publicity tour with those bodybuilders from the new club, he called. We've been going out ever since." Karen smiled triumphantly. "He said he didn't want to tie me up until he could be in town a lot and free to give me reasons for liking it." She winked at Aldora.

"Well?"

"I *like* it!" Karen flipped on only the overheads in the pool area. "Just holler if you need more than skinny-dip lighting." She headed down the hall to her office.

"Thanks," Aldy called after her. She wrapped her

towel around her and walked to the edge of the pool. Slipping into the still water, Aldy tried to relax, relish the silky feel of it against her bare skin, the freedom of movement without her muscles having to bear her body weight or fight the resistance of constricting clothing; the water caressing her body only made her think of Adam, his caresses.

As she swam Aldy wondered what it would be like to have Adam next to her in the water. She sat on a pool step to catch her breath and the silken waters became his firm, insistent hands.

In her mind Adam fitted his palm against her bare waist and let it follow the natural lines of Aldy's body as he drew her against him.

Aldy felt her body conforming, molding against his even as she tried to protest, her hands pushing ineffectually against the wet mat of hair that clung to his chest. She could feel the lean hardness of him and surrendered to the delight of his warm flesh chasing the chill from the blue water. The droplets stood shining against his tanned shoulders like diamonds set into nature's most exquisite cloth. She brushed at them with her fingers, trailing caresses down his strong arms, sliding her hands into the curve of his waist as she wrapped herself tightly around him and pressed her face against his chest.

Adam encircled the back of her knees with one long leg and held the full length of her close against his body, then his lips traced a line down her neck as one hand brushed the heavy wetness of her long hair aside and he lowered his head to let his mouth taste the salty droplets of pool water that clung impudently to the tips of her firm white breasts.

Aldora felt a moan of pleasure escape her throat as Adam caressed her, worked a magic with his mouth and hands.

Wrenching herself out of fantasy, Aldy struck out across the pool in angry strokes. "He hasn't even returned your call!" she muttered at the sloshing wavelets as she slammed her feet against the side of the pool and turned to swim another long, stretching lap. When she reached the shallow water and climbed out, not all of the water that trickled down her cheeks as she walked to the hot tub was from the swim.

At about ten o'clock Karen came to the Jacuzzi. "Aldy?"

"Mmm?"

"You okay? I'm nearly ready to go, unless you're—"

"No," Aldy said quickly, seeing Karen's gray eyes fill with concern. "I'm fine now. Much better." She climbed, dripping, from the steamy water and took the towel Karen offered. "I can't begin to thank you," she said, blotting the water drops from her hips and thighs.

Karen grinned. "Chuck should thank *you*," she teased. "He was hoping for an early start Saturday. Now one of the girls can lock up for me." Karen smiled. "We're gonna drive to Santa Barbara, stay over, loll around, maybe fish. I've got Monday off."

Aldora grinned at her. "Enjoy," she said, dropping her towel over her arm and starting for the lockers.

"You know," Karen said, "you should get one of those French-cut bikinis, you've great legs for it."

Aldy looked back and smiled. "Sure, and a scar to go with it." Aldora had given up on two-piece suits after the surgery. "Thanks, anyway." She pulled her shift from her locker and began to dress.

Karen peeked around the corner. "Dumb!"

Aldy looked up.

"That thin white line barely shows," said Karen and trotted off down the hall.

By ten fifteen Karen and Aldy had locked up the spa and were headed across the parking lot.

"Thanks again, Karen," Aldy said, unlocking her VW. "You saved my life."

Karen grinned at her. "Any time," she said waving and pulling past Aldy's car to the driveway.

Aldora watched her leave. She hoped the girl's expectations for Santa Barbara would repay her for her kindness.

ALDORA turned on the lamp by her bed and glanced at the clock. Ten thirty-five. Certainly Adam wouldn't call anymore tonight. She sighed and pulled off her clothes. Adam Holcomb was apparently out for the evening! She slipped in between the cool, sun-dried sheets and tried to let their crispness rub the angry, prickly feeling from her bare skin. *You've got no right to be upset,* she thought gloomily, *you can't offer him much.* Ken went from hot, to cool, to gone also. But Ken had *known,* she thought desperately, Adam thinks— Oh, who the hell knew what he thought! Aldy slammed at her pillow in angry frustration. She switched off the lamp and tossed over on her side.

AT five on Thursday Grant came to the base of the scaffold and whistled his now-famous tune. He showed Aldy to the new nurses' lounge in an alcove off the main hall and pointed out the shower and linens. "First class," he said. "See you in about twenty minutes out front, unless you're typical."

Aldy looked puzzled.

"Julie's never on time," he said. "But it's always worth the wait."

Aldora nipped in and out of the shower and touched up her makeup in the lounge mirror. She loosened her braid and shook her dark hair into waves down her back. Braiding it freshly washed had caused it to ripple its way to her waist like a midnight waterfall. She brushed it vigorously, then slipped on her long dress. She noted that the pink-purple color played up the high, natural color in her cheeks and emphasized her dark features. She slid her feet into low-heeled, open sandals. Very effective, she decided as she left the lounge and made her way to the front of the building. It was apparent that several people Aldy passed in the hall agreed with her.

Grant was waiting in his beloved MG. He leaped over the driver's door and let out a long, low whistle. "Wow!" he breathed. "If Julie didn't already love you, I'd be in trouble!"

Aldora grinned at him. "Thanks. Where is Julie?"

"Oh, she went ahead to help Adam with Jessie," said Grant, sliding the MG into traffic between two commuter buses. "They'll meet us at the restaurant."

Aldora's heart began to thump wildly. "Adam and Jess?" she said softly.

"Well, this is your welcome-home party," Grant said, smiling. "Besides, Jess has had a rough week. You'll be just what this doctor ordered." He paused, noticing Aldy's look of apprehension. "What's wrong?"

"I...nothing. I got Jess something in San Francisco. I'd have brought it along if I'd known."

"No problem, pretty lady," Grant said, turning the car toward the foothills. "We'll swing by and get it. You navigate."

Grant parked in Aldy's driveway and waited while she ran up to the house. So Adam had been busy with Jessie, Aldy thought, grabbing up the package and hurrying back down her stairs. *I should have called him again.* Her step was light, joyous; Adam hadn't ignored her call intentionally! She slid into the MG, held up the present. "Okay." She couldn't wait to see Adam, now.

"Good Lord!" said Aldy when Grant pulled up in front of a swank-looking Beverly Hills restaurant and turned the MG over to the parking attendant. "You weren't kidding!" She walked into the foyer with Jessie's package clutched to her chest, as if its presence could shield her heart from pounding right out of her body.

Grant gave Adam's name to the maître d' and they were escorted to a secluded alcove, dimly lit by dainty hurricane lamps. Aldora heard a gleeful squeal and saw Jessie's blond head bobbing over the back of her chair. Julie waved a hello and Adam stood up.

Aldora called a general greeting to all and zeroed in on Jessie. She hugged her and set the package in her lap. "All the way from San Francisco," she said. Then she turned her attention to Adam. If she had thought him handsome in street dress, Adam in evening dress made her catch her breath. She smiled up at him. Even in her heels she barely reached to his shoulder.

Adam's eyes were traveling the full length of her. He was staring, almost slack-jawed, and he had a look in his eyes that verged on hostility! Aldora was off balance, couldn't understand why his eyes devoured her one moment and glowered at her the next.

"That dress is terrific," Julie said, breaking the awkward silence as Adam pulled out Aldy's chair for her.

"Thanks, Julie," she said, sliding into her seat. "Thank you, Adam." She glanced up and smiled.

"San Francisco must have agreed with you," he said.

"Mostly slave labor, I'm afraid." Was that a hint of bitterness she detected in his smile? What was going on? Aldy tried to recall if she'd done anything to warrant the chill in his manner; she looked over to see if Julie had noticed.

"Your publisher must be brother to Attila the Hun," said Julie, laughing. Apparently, Julie hadn't sensed the frost on Adam's words.

"Who's Attila the Hun?" Jessie asked.

Aldy leaned closer to her. "He was the *original* bad guy!"

Jess giggled happily. "Can I open this?"

Aldy nodded and thought she saw Adam's face soften a bit at her last comment. She watched the thin fingers rip eagerly at the tissue.

"Oh," Jessie breathed as the paper revealed its silky

contents. "It's beautiful, pink-lavender, just like your dress."

As everyone expressed their appreciation Jess held the kimono out to her father. "Help me, please, Daddy."

Adam smiled. He pulled the kimono over her arms and Aldy noted the tenderness in his touch as he tucked the lapels across his daughter's chest. "You look ravishing," he declared and hugged her.

"Like Aldy?" Jessie asked.

Aldy blushed and thought she saw Adam's smile waver. "Of course," he said, keeping his eyes on Jess.

Dinner was a marvelous affair and Adam seemed to relax a little by the time the orchestra began to play soft dance music.

"Do you like to dance?" Jess asked.

"I'm afraid I'm not very good at it, Jess," Aldy answered, smiling at Adam.

"Daddy used to let me dance on his feet when I was little," Jessie said.

"That's the only place you were safe!" Adam teased. But Aldy saw a flicker of pain in his eyes as he leaned back and rummaged for his pipe. "Ungainliest thing on feet," he said, pointing a thumb at his chest as he spoke.

Aldy saw Jessie watching Grant and Julie move across the dance floor and swallowed hard as she thought of Jess waltzing around on her father's shoe-tops. She knew how Jess's innocent remark had jabbed Adam's heart. She longed to hold him, caress away his pain. Retreating from this thought, Aldy grabbed her bag and pulled out a pen and notebook. Sketching rapidly, the drawing swam before her eyes for a moment. She fought for control as she completed a dainty caricature of Jess, looking like an Oriental princess on a throne, and held it out to the child.

"It's me!" Jessie said and thrust the paper at her father.

He smiled and looked at Aldora. "Good, and so fast! Ever work a carny circuit?"

Aldy laughed, but Adam had placed a strange emphasis on the word *carny*. "No, just an occasional church bazaar," she answered.

"Could you teach me to draw like that?" Jess asked hopefully.

"Well, not all at once, but I could work you into my roster of students." Aldy smiled at her.

"Oh, boy! Promise, Aldy? Can I, Daddy?" Jess looked expectantly from one to the other.

"We'll see, pumpkin," said Adam. His face was unreadable. Standing up, he took Aldy's hand. "Let's try," he said, nodding at the dance floor.

Aldora was about to refuse, but the pressure Adam put on her wrist silenced her and she rose and followed him.

Adam swept her into his arms and smiled. "What the hell are you trying to do to me?" he whispered stiffly.

Aldy, just beginning to relish the closeness of him, the warmth of his arms, felt as if he'd hit her. "What?" she said, eyes wide with shock.

"Don't play innocent," Adam snarled through lips that still outwardly smiled at her.

Aldora, temper flaring, tried to wrench herself free from his grasp. He pulled her closer, pinning her against his body.

"Oh, no," he said. His laugh had a hard edge that bit into Aldy's heart as his fingers did her wrist. "No fool like an old fool, eh? *I* don't care, but, dammit, leave my daughter out of your flirtations!"

Aldora was stunned. "Flirtations?"

He maneuvered them through the pulsating bodies toward the doors to the open patio. "I guess I deserve it," he muttered as he half-dragged Aldy through the courtyard to a secluded arbor. "But I trusted you not to hurt Jess! She's had enough of *leaving*!" He pushed her down onto the stone bench and sat beside her in the darkness, still gripping her wrist tightly.

"You're hurting me!" Aldy cried, trying to pry his fingers from her flesh.

"And you're hurting Jessie!" He spoke harshly. "I was a fool to think you could care; don't take it out on her."

Aldy was shaking all over. Between the rage at this unprovoked attack, and the fear that coursed through her as she faced Adam's wrath, she could barely breathe. She gulped for air, forced it deep into her lungs. "Stop it!" she cried, swinging hard at Adam's face with her free hand.

He saw it coming, caught her arm. He held her like that, his face a mask of anger and pain.

Aldora felt tears of humiliation and hurt welling up, spilling down her cheeks. She was crying but no sound came from her throat. Slowly Adam's grip eased a little.

"Tears?" he said, his voice edged with mock amazement.

Aldy felt broken inside, beaten. "I'd never hurt Jess," she said, meeting Adam's eyes with hers. "Never!"

"But *I'm* fair game?"

"You?" Aldy floundered. What did he mean? "How?" she whispered.

Adam looked at her. "You really don't know?" he said, his face humorless. "I actually missed you! I was glad you called me as soon as you got home," he said softly. "But when I didn't return your call right away, you couldn't get out of that house fast enough!" He spat out a laugh in a harsh, lonely syllable. "Is one night at home alone too much for your delicate ego to stand?"

Aldy couldn't believe what she was hearing. "If that's what you think," she said, "I shouldn't bother to explain!" She glared at him, raised her chin.

Adam's face altered slightly. Some of the harshness fled and was replaced with questioning.

"Oh, any other reason hadn't occurred to you?" she asked, not waiting for an answer. "This is for *Jessie*!" She paused to be sure that he understood that she would never bother to excuse herself to him. "I was home almost all evening. Ask Grant. He called about eight thirty. I *had* hoped it was you." She pulled her wrist free and his fingers didn't protest. "Lord knows why," she added.

Adam searched her eyes, uncomprehending. "But I called. The line was busy," he stumbled on, "so I just stopped by the house. You were already gone . . . I . . ."

"Jumped to a hasty conclusion?" she suggested.

"Aldy." Adam's voice was soft, breaking with emotion. "I'm sorry for that," he murmured, putting his face in his hands, his shoulders slumped as he rested his elbows on his knees. "I'm so sorry." His words caught painfully, dragged at Aldy's anger.

She stared at him. He looked so tortured. She reached out her hand and her fingers closed on his arm. "If you felt that way," she said softly, "why did you come tonight?"

He looked up at her. "Jessie." The name fell from his lips like a stone. "She was looking forward to this, to seeing you. She has so little joy." He struggled to control his voice, his face a mask of discipline. "I thought I could handle it, thought I could see you again even knowing you didn't care." He looked at the ground, drew a deep, shaky breath. "Then you came in looking so damn beautiful." The last word was a whisper tearing from his throat.

Aldora closed her eyes. "Didn't care . . ." His words rang in her head, echoed hollowly. She'd let him tear at her defenses with his kindness, batter down her wall with his words, ignite her carefully banked passions with his kisses, and he knew she *didn't care*? She opened her eyes and looked at his anguish in disbelief. "What did you say?"

He drew a ragged breath. "You're so damn beautiful," he whispered, taking her hand.

Aldora stared at him, at her hand, so small in his. "No," she began, "not that part." But his fingers squeezed her silent.

"Don't tell me it wasn't intentional!" he said stiffly. "That dress, your hair, loose, shining, a black river a man could drown in." He let go of her hand, turned his face away from her.

Aldy looked at him. What was he babbling about? Why? "You said I didn't care," she repeated the words almost without knowing she'd spoken.

Adam looked at her strangely. "What?"

His lack of comprehension made Aldy aware that she really had said the words, and in so doing, refuted them.

"Aldy?" Adam's one questioning word told her he'd heard the denial too. His arms went around her and she melted bonelessly against him, relief flooding through her as he murmured love words and stroked her hair.

"Don't, sweetheart," he whispered cradling her face in his palm and using his thumb to brush at her tears.

Aldora was overwhelmed. Her mind spun as she clung to him. She loved him. Loved him more than she'd thought it possible to love anyone. And her great love had nearly been thrown away for a misunderstanding, for pride. "I went to the health club," she babbled helplessly.

Adam held her away from him and looked at her. "What?"

"The health club," she repeated, amazed he hadn't heard.

Adam laughed. He hugged her to him and laughed uncontrollably.

Aldora couldn't absorb it. She huddled against him, hiding in the security of the strong arms wrapped tightly around her shoulders, pressing her to him, and listened to that laughter, made more sonorous by the closeness of her ear to his chest.

"Oh, Aldy," he said softly, rocking her, running her hands tenderly over her trembling body, and shaking his head. "The health club." He started to laugh again. "I have such a"—he groped for words—"stupid temper," he finished lamely.

Aldora looked up at the underside of his jaw.

He bent his head and placed his mouth gently on hers. The sweetness of his kiss sent desire flaming through her with raw vibrancy. Her own passion welled and his mouth grew hard, urgent, drawing her love into him, making her quiver. And when their lips parted, it was she who was breathless, aching with need.

Adam drew a deep, shuddering breath. "I think we'd better go in," he said haltingly.

Aldy's hands flew to her face. "Oh!" she gasped. "I must look awful!"

Adam pulled out a handkerchief and handed it to her.

She took it, stared at it a moment, and giggled. "It's going to take cold water, I think," she said, imagining how red her eyes must be and feeling flushed.

Adam grinned, lowered his gaze. "I'll meet you back at the table," he said. He kissed her lightly, stood, and walked purposefully back into the dining room.

Aldy took a deep breath and headed for the ladies' room.

It was all too much. The fight, the tension of the previous night, the grueling trip. Aldy pushed blindly through the swinging door and rushed to splash water on her hot cheeks, her reddened eyes. As she leaned over the basin, her back tightened and the pain shot down her left leg. Supporting her weight with one hand, she continued to douse her face with cold water.

"Aldy?" Julie's soft voice sounded at her side. "Adam said you were in here."

Aldy turned to face her.

"My God!" Julie's arm went around her. "What happened?" she asked. "Are you ill?"

"No," Aldy whispered. "It's okay." She straightened and took her purse from Julie's hand. Julie led her to a chair.

"What happened?"

"Adam and I had a misunderstanding," she said.

Then, seeing Julie's frightened stare: "We straightened it out."

"You and Adam?" Julie gaped at Aldy. "But—"

"It's fine now."

Julie looked uneasy.

"What's wrong, Julie?"

Julie patted Aldy's shoulder. "It's Jessie. You two were gone quite a long time. But Adam can handle her."

Aldy's mind raced. *Poor Adam,* she thought, *all this tension, now Jessie, hurt by us after all.* She looked at Julie. "I'm sorry. We lost track of—"

"Time?" Julie said, grinning at her. "What else is new?"

Aldora could see the humor, needed it. She hugged Julie and started to laugh, but the tears came too. She couldn't control them.

Julie looked alarmed. "Aldy. Stop." She shook her gently. Then, more firmly, "Aldy!"

Aldora held up her hand. "I'm all right," she gasped. "It's so ironic; we were fighting about *not* hurting Jessie." She felt hysteria welling again and gripped the arm of the chair until her fingers ached.

"Don't explain," Julie said quickly, obviously eager to divert Aldy's direction of thought. "Let's pull you together." She got wet towels and bathed Aldy's face. "Breathe!" she commanded.

Aldy breathed.

"Deeper."

It was working. Aldy stood slowly, took her purse to the lounge mirror. She patted her eyes with the towels and tried to cover the ravages of emotion with fresh makeup.

"Much better," Julie coached. "Plead illness."

"Right," Aldy said, walking to the door.

The girls moved through the dancers to the table.

Aldora forced a feeble smile. "Sorry, everyone," she said softly. "I guess my trip caught up with me."

Jessie looked at her sullenly. Her cheeks were flushed, tear-streaked.

"I'm sorry, Jessie." Aldy saw the look soften a little. "I didn't mean to spoil your lovely party."

Jessie's eyes cleared a little. "I'm sorry you were sick," she said stiffly.

Aldora could see the indecision on her face. "I knew I could count on you to understand, honey," she said, her eyes pleading with the girl.

Jess rose to the occasion. "I get sick too," she offered. "Daddy says I overdo."

Relief was almost tangible to Aldora as she nodded. "Right. My trip, work, this lovely surprise you planned, I overdid it."

Jess seemed to accept this. She smiled a little. "Do we have to go right now?" She looked hesitant.

Aldy glanced at Adam. "I'll sit for a minute, maybe if I have some coffee."

Jessie watched as her father called a waiter.

"Two coffees," he said, then looked at Jess. "Go on." He nodded at Aldora.

Aldy's hands twisted the napkin in her lap. What was Adam doing?

Jess looked uncomfortable. She stared at her water glass, then turned an embarrassed green gaze on Aldora. "I'm sorry, Aldy," she said in a strained voice. She looked at her father. "I didn't know she was sick, honest!"

Aldora's heart ached for Jessie, for her own deception. "It's all right, Jess." She patted Jessie's hand.

Jess smiled, but some of the resistance still lingered.

Adam didn't look satisfied. "Come on, Jess, I'll show you the patio." He wheeled her from the table.

The waiter brought the coffee and Aldy sipped nervously.

Grant and Julie stopped dancing and came to sit with Aldora.

"Adam made her apologize," Aldy said. "She didn't have to, it was my fault."

Grant looked stern. "Yes, she did."

Aldy stared at him.

"She's got to learn," he said solemnly. "She used to pull the same thing with me when I started including Julie in get-togethers."

Aldy was uneasy. "But she's only a child."

"We all have feelings, needs," Julie said. "She's got to learn she's *not* alone in that."

Aldora nodded.

"You'll catch on," said Grant gently. "We all coddled her at first."

Julie got up from the table. "I'll go make myself available," she said, heading for the patio.

Aldy looked after her anxiously.

"Don't worry," Grant said, "Julie will whisk Jess to the powder room so we can talk to Adam." He reached across the table and took her hand.

"Thanks," Aldy said. She smiled at him then reached for her coffee.

Adam came to the table. He looked at Aldy. "She's okay, but I'd better get her home now." He looked at Grant. "Would you mind if—" He stopped, looked down at Aldy. "If Grant took you home?"

Aldy could see he hated to ask this of them. "That's fine, Adam. I don't mind." She smiled encouragement.

He glanced nervously over his shoulder and leaned down, gave her a hasty kiss on the cheek. "I'd rather take you myself—"

"Adam," Aldy cut in, "I understand. Jessie needs you."

He squeezed her shoulder gratefully. "Aldy, I'll—" He didn't get any farther. Julie and Jess came up to the table. He gave her shoulder a last squeeze. "Ready, Jess?"

Jess smiled at her father. "Yes, Daddy. Good night, everyone." She looked at Aldora. "Thank you for my present, Aldy," she said shyly. "I hope you feel better."

"You're welcome, Jess. I will." Aldy waved to her as Adam wheeled her from the restaurant.

Grant waited until they were well out of earshot. "You handled Jess very well, Aldy," he said. Then he looked at both his ladies. "Would you two like to have more coffee, or shall we go?"

"Work tomorrow," Julie said, looking at Aldora.

"Yes," she agreed. "Tomorrow should be the big day."

"You'll finish it?" Julie looked hopeful.

"I figure I'll be signing my name in the corner about noon."

Grant smiled. "That I gotta see." He escorted the girls to the front of the restaurant and handed the attendant his claim ticket.

When the man brought up the MG, Julie must have noticed Aldy's look of alarm. "We've managed before," she said, laughing.

Grant grinned at her. "Real cozy," he said, sliding the passenger seat all the way forward.

Aldora started to protest, sure that calling a cab was the better part of valor, but Julie held up her hand and climbed nimbly into the cramped baggage area. "No problem," she said. "It's sorta like college: stuffing all sorts of kids into a phone booth." She laughed.

Grant helped Aldy shoehorn herself into the front. Her back objected strenuously. The seat, too low in the first place, was now uncomfortably close to the dash. Aldy was bent nearly double. She watched Grant slide in behind the wheel and prayed for a quick trip home.

"If only Jess would have that surgery," Julie said as Grant pulled out onto the boulevard. "She'd be able to walk more, feel secure, less dependent."

Aldy was stunned. "Walk more?" she said, twisting in her seat to see Julie's mouth. The open car made lipreading a necessity.

"She can only walk in therapy now," Julie explained. "It's mostly just for muscle tone. Adam keeps praying we'll all talk her into the surgery someday."

Aldy nodded. She remembered that Julie had started to tell her about this surgery the day they had visited Jess at the hospital. Meeting Adam at the elevator had put an end to that discussion. If Jess was being helped to avoid a total deterioration of muscle in her legs, she certainly must be considered an operable case. "Why won't she have the surgery?" Aldy asked.

"Louise," Julie said. "Louise was so disfigurement-crazed after the crash that she convinced Jess the operation would only add insult to her injury."

Aldy brushed her hair from her eyes and twisted farther around. "What?"

"They used to have great loud fights about it: Adam listing the Foundation's success stories quietly and Louise accusing him loudly of using her 'baby' as a guinea pig." Julie leaned closer to the front as she spoke to compete with the noise of the traffic.

Grant glanced over at Aldy. "Louise was a great little grandstander," he said, turning the car onto the winding road that led to Aldora's. "High drama: She hung all over the poor kid hollering about risks, hideous scarring, disfigurement, that sort of thing."

"Especially after the Foundation surgeon wouldn't agree to further surgery for Louise's own scar," Julie added. "She made such a scene, bad-mouthing the doctors, that Jess is terrified, the worst possible surgical risk."

"Why couldn't they help Louise?" Aldy asked.

"Louise didn't have a scar worth the bother," Grant said harshly as he pulled into Aldy's driveway and killed the engine.

Aldy looked at him. What could he know about a woman's feelings? She looked at Julie. "Men don't understand," she began. "It's different for a woman, especially a beautiful woman."

Julie shook her head. "He's right, Aldy. After the initial surgery and some dermabrasion, Louise had nothing but a fast-fading scar on her neck. That was hairline," Julie said quietly. "You could hardly see it, even without makeup. Louise was *obsessed* with perfection, for herself *and* Jessie."

Grant turned to face Aldy. "For Louise," he said solemnly, "there were only two possibilities: Jess in a wheelchair, or Jess with ugly scar tissue. Since there are no guarantees with spinal surgery, Louise chose to believe that Jess would be the victim of both."

Aldy shook her head. She knew all about guarantees.

Grant got out and came around to help Aldora. "Don't worry," he said, misunderstanding her silence, "Jess'll come around one day." He opened the door and offered his hand.

"Sure," Julie said.

Aldy took hold of Grant's hand and steeled herself for the pain she knew was coming. "Maybe," she said, swinging her legs out of the car and clamping her jaw as she used Grant's assistance. The pain stabbed so forcefully that she nearly fell.

"What happened?" said Grant, catching her.

Aldy leaned on his arm, pretending to look down at her shoes in amazement. "I must have caught my heel in the hem," she said as she continued to lean on Grant and waited for the pain to subside. "Long dresses," she said, trying to make it casual.

"I do it all the time," Julie put in as she jumped from the back and took Aldy's place in the front seat. "Thanks for being such a love about Jess and all." She smiled up at Aldy.

"I understand how she must feel," said Aldy with a great deal more conviction than Julie and Grant would ever know she had reason for.

"See you tomorrow," Julie called as Grant helped Aldy to her door.

"Thanks, Grant," Aldy said, taking her key back from him.

He slid the door aside. "The foot all right?"

"Fine."

Aldy waved until they were out on the road, then limped inside and grabbed her cane.

Maybe Jessie should have the surgery, she thought as she undressed for bed, but she'd never be able to endorse it with a straight face.

Chapter Thirteen

The next morning Aldora could barely move. She knew she'd have to call in sick; it would take her a couple of days to reach her front door, let alone make it to work! She called Grant's office, wondering frantically what excuse she could give this time. She'd just had the "flu."

As Grant answered, inspiration struck. "I'm afraid I can't get in today," she said, trying to sound matter-of-fact. "I guess I must have tweaked my ankle harder than I thought last night."

"Have you seen a doctor?" Grant asked, sympathy and concern evident in his tone.

"It's not that bad," Aldy insisted. Then, recalling that humor usually derailed him: "My left foot just looks a little like a python digesting a cantaloupe." She chuckled.

Grant tried to sound anxious, but Aldy's visualization was too much for him. "Good grief, woman," he said, laughing, "I never—"

"I never did either," Aldy interrupted. "Anyway, sorry about the delay. I'll be fine by Monday."

"Oh, no," said Grant, sobering. "No scaffolds for you and your fat ankle."

Dear Lord, Aldy thought, for a sprain? What if he knew the truth? "All the finish work is on ground level," she said, grateful now she'd worked the mural from the top down. "You can pull that scaffold any time."

Grant sounded relieved. "I'll break it down tomorrow," he said. "It'll give everyone a clear view of the mural and won't be in your way when you get back."

"Great," Aldy said. "See you Monday." She placed a finger on the disconnect button before he could argue. Then she dialed Ellen. If Ellie could run her over to the spa, she would make it back by Monday.

MONDAY morning Aldy wrapped her ankle in an Ace bandage and drove to work. She still needed her cane and the sprain was a perfect excuse.

She leaned on the carved cedar stick, looked challengingly at the mural. "You're not gonna beat me," she muttered as she started assembling her equipment.

"Grandma Moses, I presume?"

Aldy turned to see Grant staring at her wrapped ankle. She laughed. "Adam's very words when he called Sunday," she said lightly.

"Maybe you ought to have X ray look at it."

"No!" Aldy nearly shouted the word and Grant gave her an odd look.

"Easy," he soothed, "I said X ray, not amputation."

Aldy chuckled. "Sorry." She struck a melodramatic pose and lowered her voice to confidential decibels. "I have a confession," she whispered.

Grant leaned forward, no doubt expecting her to disclose some scandalous tidbit.

Aldy looked around nervously, leaned nearer his ear and said: "I *hate* hospitals!"

Grant threw back his head and laughed heartily. "You are too much, Miss Moses," he said, indicating her environ for the past few weeks and many yet to come. He gave her a hug. "Carry on." Saluting, he marched off across the room.

Aldora arranged her paints and brushes and lowered herself gingerly to her knees. Then she sat on her good hip and began painting. Her back already ached, but if she could swap off sitting and standing she'd be able to manage. Only a half a day's work and she could sign her name. The next stage was all preparation. The cartoons for the hall mural could be done at home in her studio, at her own pace. Clinging to that thought, Aldy worked steadily, changing her position often and sitting whenever she could.

"What the devil do you think you're doing?" Adam's words reached down to her as his arms jerked her up off the floor and supported her firmly by his side. His face was a mask of anger, his jaw set, his green eyes nearly black with emotion. "I wouldn't have imagined you'd be so stupid!" he shouted.

Deep in concentration just prior to this unwarranted attack on both her body and brains, Aldy was startled into crying out. She felt anger and hurt welling up inside as Adam held her on her feet and hurled his opinions at her.

"Now, you get that ankle checked and go home!" he rasped.

Aldy's dark eyes narrowed as she winced with pain and fury. "Stupid?" she cried. "My work is *my* business, not yours!" Her back hurt terribly and the nausea that went with it threatened to embarrass her publicly. She tried to pull away from Adam and gasped as the pain shot through her body. She doubled over.

"Oh, God, Aldy!" Adam was instantly contrite. He lifted her gently and started for the nearest bench. "I'm sorry," he whispered. "I saw you working, saw your pain. I guess I just lost control." His eyes were tender now, as if he were looking at Jessie. He pressed her close against him for a moment then lowered her carefully onto a low, concrete planter-rim.

Aldy hurt so much, felt so ill. She wanted desperately to lean on Adam, let him care for her as he took care of Jess. She longed to blurt out all her deceptions, have Adam cradle her in his arms, tell her it didn't matter. That nothing mattered. That he loved her. She looked into his face, saw only tenderness, caring. Maybe? No! She was too frightened of the past; she couldn't bear to see that horror and revulsion ravage Adam's handsome features. "Just hand me my cane and let me get to the lounge," she said coldly.

Adam looked as if she'd slapped him hard. "I said I was sorry, Aldy. Let me take you home."

His kindness was ripping her apart. "That won't be necessary," she said, but she couldn't put any chill to her words this time. Her lips trembled and she couldn't look at him. She put a fist to her mouth and pressed her lips hard against her teeth, trying to blot out one pain with another.

Adam took her face in his hands. He cradled her cheeks in his palms and looked into her eyes. "You're hurting, Aldy," he soothed. "You'll feel better when I get you home."

This had to stop; Adam was everything she'd ever dreamed of and he knew just how to get to her. The tenderness, the hands on her face, the desire bridled only by his respect for her. She longed to let go; her need for him became a physical ache. But she knew the relationship was a foolish dream, she couldn't possibly hide her condition forever, couldn't ask him to accept her as she was. He became so incensed when he saw her in pain! Her mind framed the hurtful sentences that she knew would send him away, put an end to it all. But when he looked at her like this, she couldn't force herself to voice them. Instead she said, "Get me to the lounge, Adam, please!"

He lifted her as easily as he'd carried Jessie and strode quickly down the hall. He started to carry her into the lounge.

"No!" she cried. "Put me down. I'll be right out."

Adam set her carefully on her feet and pressed the handle of her cane into her palm. "You sure?" he asked.

"Positive." She lurched through the door, hobbled to a stall, and was violently ill.

At last, she came out and splashed water on her face, rinsed her mouth. The face in the mirror revealed a total stranger; inside and out, she was a wreck. She sat on the bench, put her face on her arms, and wept silently.

Minutes later, strong arms were around her shoulders. "It's all right, Aldy. It's gonna be fine, honey." Adam was holding her, crooning softly into her hair.

Aldora turned against his body. "I'm sorry, Adam," she whispered as her resolve withered.

"Let's get you home," he said gently.

SITTING on her bed with her perfectly good foot elevated on two pillows, Aldora felt like the worst sort of cheat. Adam had brought a water carafe and glass to her bedside and jotted his home number and the words: "Call Me!" on a pad he'd propped by the phone on the night table. It had been all Aldy could do to convince him the ankle was too sore to be a break. No X rays. He had apologized for leaving. Jessie had a therapy appointment and he had to go along; he'd promised to talk with the therapist, try to pitch surgery again.

Awash with guilt, Aldy dialed Ellen's number and began to sob. She told Ellen the whole dismal story from start to finish and then waited.

"You're a fool, Aldy Cassidy, and that's not strong enough," said Ellen evenly. "The man follows you into the ladies' room: he's in *love*!"

"You don't understand," Aldy protested. "He thinks it's a sprain!" Fresh tears pelted the front of her blouse. "That's why he's being so kind, so caring."

"Pain is pain," Ellen cut in. "He offered to help."

"Ellen, a sprain doesn't last a lifetime! What's really wrong with me does!" Aldy was nearly hysterical.

"*You* don't understand. He's obviously in love with you, the rest doesn't matter."

Aldora felt denial spring to her throat. "No, he may be, but it's false pretenses; he didn't know about my disability. He has enough with Jess. This has to stop."

Ellen said only two more words: "You're wrong."

Later that afternoon Adam and Jess stopped by on the way back from her therapy appointment.

"I'm sorry about your foot," Jess said. She giggled. "You should have been with me; we could have looked funny together."

Aldy's heart went out to Jess for her gallant attempt to console by drawing attention to her own disability. "I bet I'd look funnier," Aldy said, grinning at Jess. "You sit there graceful as a princess, and I'm all bent over like a granny." She did her best to look as ungainly as possible and thumped her cane soundly on the floor as she took a few limping steps.

Jess broke into fitful giggles and Adam had that tender look on his face again as he watched them both.

Then Aldy suggested that Jess go up to the studio and practice for her art lessons with some of Aldy's "professional equipment." Adam took her up and then came back to have coffee with Aldora.

"You're just great with her." He punctuated his praise, raising his cup to her. "Your grandma routine even had me chuckling," he said softly.

"She's easy to be great with," Aldy said and rushed on to crowd out the thought that Adam probably wouldn't think a permanent "grandma routine" too funny. "I can't wait to get well and start her lessons."

Adam reached for her hand, held it gently. "She's eager; she really likes you. But don't rush yourself. Sprains can be worse than a break." He drew her against his shoulder, stroked her hair. "Jessie's home tutors only cover so much, the essentials: three R's. The art will be so good for her. You're so good for her...."

The emotion in his voice told Aldy he was about to add something about himself to that statement. "It's easy," she said quickly. "She's a delight."

A hard expression invaded Adam's eyes as he looked down at her. "Not everyone would think so," he said. He went up to check on Jess.

Adam came down with his daughter in his arms.

"We'd better go," he said and carried her to the car. He came back for the chair. "Therapy wears her down so," he apologized. "I wish I could stay with you." He kissed her quickly on the mouth and drew away. "You call me," he murmured. He turned a haunted gaze toward the open door and left without saying more.

Tears filled Aldy's eyes as she watched him go. He was so obviously torn. Two people he loved, two who needed him. Aldy knew Jessie's pain, ached for the child. She could only imagine Adam's. How could she bear to *double* that pain?

Chapter Fourteen

By Wednesday afternoon Aldy's spa treatments and the easing of tensions with Adam and Jessie had helped remarkably. She could move quite normally and breathed a sigh of relief as she set up the smaller drafting table for Jessie's lesson.

The sample sketches that Aldora had had Jess do Monday indicated a definite flair, a feel for line and color that was amazing considering Jessie's lack of opportunity and instruction. Aldy couldn't wait to help this talent emerge.

There was a rapid tapping at the door as the bell was rung. Aldy ran down to see Jess knocking excitedly at the glass while Adam tried to keep her from wriggling out of his arms.

"Hi, Jess," said Aldy, throwing back the door and taking the tote bag from Adam's hand. "Hello, Adam."

"I'm ready," Jessie chirped. Her eyes sparkled with anticipation as Adam left to retrieve the chair. "What do I learn first?"

"To relax," said Aldy, laughing. She winked at Jessie. "Gotta let those lines *flow*."

Adam came back lugging a large drawing board and other oddments. "I think you're in for it, sweetheart," he said as he took the things up to the studio.

He came back and carried Jessie up, got her settled. "I'll see you two in about two hours," he said.

"Okay, Daddy," Jess called after him.

Aldora and Jess worked diligently. Aldy set up lights and some plaster molds of basic shapes and showed Jessie how shadows, properly handled, could turn a two-dimensional work into the illusion of three dimensions.

Jess was quick and eager to please. Aldora watched her carefully for signs of fatigue; she didn't want Jess to fall into her own worst habit: get engrossed and end up hurting. By the time Adam came quietly back up the stairs, both Aldy and Jess were laughing and on the way to an easy student-teacher rapport.

"How you doing?" Adam said, coming over to Jess and looking at her drawing board.

"Great, Daddy, look." Jess leafed through her shadow studies while Adam made appropriate sounds of appreciation.

"She's really doing fine work," Aldy said, smiling at Jess. "Takes direction so well I may hire her for the hall mural." She winked at Jessie.

Adam chuckled. "Thanks, Aldy. We'd better get you home, pumpkin," he said to Jess.

"Oh, just a few more minutes," Jessie pleaded.

Aldy looked at her. "Jess, you can finish that for your homework, honey. You don't want to overdo."

"Okay, Aldy," said Jess, starting to clear away her supplies. She looked a bit gloomy.

"You want to be able to make it back Friday, right?" Aldy encouraged.

"Right," Jess said, brightening.

Adam took Jessie's things to the car. "How about dinner Friday?" Adam asked after he'd put Jess in the car.

"I'd love to, Adam."

Adam slipped his arms around her and kissed her lightly. Then he called for an instant replay of that with stronger direction. He drew forcefully away. "If Jessie weren't down in that car, lady—" He left the sentence unfinished. But Aldy had no doubts about how he would have ended it. "Friday, then," he said and blew her another kiss as he went down the stairs.

ALDORA finished the mural Thursday morning and went home to start the cartoons for the hall. She worked until about six and then drove to the spa. She promised herself she'd adhere to her workouts faithfully; there was no room in her schedule for another spasm.

By Friday evening Aldy was ready to take a break, enjoy Adam's company. When he picked her up at seven thirty, she was waiting for him.

"Hello, sweetheart," Adam said, stepping into the living room and dropping a kiss on her forehead. "Ready?"

"Yes," Aldy said, taking her wrap from the kitchen chair.

They drove to a quiet restaurant by the beach. As they sat eating lobster and sipping coffee, they watched the waves through the window and Aldy recalled the evening picnic courtesy of the Chinese carry-out. "Is your friend still writing fortune cookie slips?" Aldy asked as a waiter took her plate and refilled her coffee cup.

Adam chuckled. "As far as I know." He took out his pipe and packed it. "Jess was really excited after her lesson this afternoon," Adam said. His eyes were happy, contented. "She tried to wangle an invitation tonight," he said, smiling.

"Oh, Adam. I wouldn't have minded."

Adam laughed. "I would." He grinned at Aldora. "Told her she'd cornered enough of your time, it was my turn."

Aldy smiled. "I love teaching her. She's doing well." She sobered a moment. "She wasn't feeling really jealous again, was she?"

Adam drew on his pipe. "She was a bit, but I explained things." He smiled mischievously. "I told her sometimes men and women like being alone with each other. I think she understood."

Aldy blushed. "Let's go easy with her, Adam. She's so vulnerable."

Adam reached across, took her hand. "So am I." He

gave her hand a squeeze. "But you're right, sweetheart, we will have to be careful." His eyes narrowed a bit. "I wish—" He stopped, looking at Aldy.

"What?" she asked softly.

"That we were down on that beach instead of in here," he said, smiling and calling for the check.

Aldy smiled back but she had the distinct impression that that hadn't been what Adam was originally going to say.

They climbed down the path to the shore and Aldy took off her shoes. Adam tucked them into his coat pockets and took her arm through his as they walked along the wet, packed sand near the water's edge. They came to a lifeguard kiosk, sat on the ramp holding hands and listening to the waves pounding the shore.

"Cold?" said Adam, putting his arm around her shoulders.

"Not now," she said, snuggling against him. He sighed happily as she wrapped an arm around his waist. "Adam," she began slowly, "what were you really going to tell me you wished back there in the restaurant?"

He shifted a little, cleared his throat. "I guess I'm not quite the selfless parent I pretend," he said uneasily. "I was going to wish that Jess didn't stand between us so much." He looked at the water and Aldy saw a tightness in his jaw as he haltingly confessed his breach of discipline.

"Don't, Adam," Aldy whispered as she placed her palm against his cheek and turned his face toward her again. "You're wonderful with Jessie, but you have needs too. It's not disloyal to express them."

Adam looked down at her. He smiled an almost sad smile as he lowered his mouth to meet hers.

Aldora could sense his pain, his great need as his lips moved on hers. He leaned her back against the ramp and his hands explored her body tenderly. He kissed her throat and trailed small, breathy kisses down the neckline of her dress to the swell of her breast. He brought one hand up to cup the fullness of that breast and as Aldy drew in her breath in pleasure, he returned his lips to her mouth with staggering passion.

Aldora ran her hands up under his jacket and over the knotted muscles of his back as his tongue sought hers, making her nearly faint with desire. She longed to give herself over to passion, surrender completely. His hands found new pleasure points and fired her longings expertly. She moaned softly as Adam pulled his shirt free of his belt and guided her hand up against his bare skin. She fingered the soft mat of springy hair, felt his nipples, erect with desire under her touch.

"God, Aldy," he whispered, burying his face in her neck. "I need you." He rolled reluctantly to one side and sat up. "Sorry, darling," he said, wiping at his forehead with his palm. "I—"

Aldora reached for him, pulling him back down. "It's all right, Adam. I understand," she whispered, her own passions making her bold, shameless. "I need you too." She twined her fingers in his dark hair and her eyes searched his for a long moment.

Adam ran his fingertips lightly along her cheek. His eyes smoldered, jade with desire. "Not like this, sweetheart," he said softly. The passion in his look changed subtly, suffused with tenderness. "You're not a passing night of pleasure, you're a lifetime of love." His face was deeply shadowed but Aldora could sense the emotion throbbing in his voice. "I don't have that lifetime to offer yet," he said. He kissed her again, softly, sweetly. A lingering kiss that supported his words. "I love you, Aldy."

"I love you too," Aldy whispered as he took her head and tucked it into the hollow of his throat, stroked her shoulders, her hair.

They lay against the incline of the wooden ramp for a long time, not speaking, listening to the surf. Finally Adam got to his feet, tucked in his shirt, and helped Aldy up. He walked her to the car and they drove slowly home. He kissed her at the door. "I won't *ask* more until I can *offer* more," he said solemnly and went down the stairs.

Aldora went in and got ready for bed. She sank into sleep and dreamed of a loving, gentle man and a little girl with green eyes.

THE weeks flew by. Aldora completed the sketches for the hall and called Kate and Eddy to help with the tracing. She went home early each Tuesday and Friday and gave Jess her art lessons. She stuck to her regimen of exercise at the spa as rigidly as she could and was happy that her disability interfered very little with the state of things. Not climbing scaffolding every day was a definite boon.

As the second mural neared completion Aldora was beginning to believe that her life had settled, that she just might be able to juggle her two careers and her blossoming relationship with Adam. She pushed her promise to Ellen firmly into the background. Each weekend she worked feverishly on the portrait. She wanted to have it ready for the show. Jessie had seen it and it was their secret. Sometimes Aldy would work on it in the afternoons while Jess had her lesson; she'd stop periodically, to check Jessie's progress.

On the day Aldy gave Kate and Eddy their final instructions and prepared to send them off so that she could begin the finish work, her heart was light and she felt as if nothing could send clouds to her horizon.

"You call us the instant it's finished," Kate said firmly.

"We want to witness the signing," Eddy added.

"It's a promise." Aldy waved as she watched them leave. That promise helped to stave off her job-windup depression. She closed the cans of paint and rolled sketches and wondered how it would feel to get up each morning and *not* come to this place and work among her friends. She sighed and turned her thoughts to her

list of potential work at home. Books she had outlined,
wanted to get started on again, paintings to ready for
her show in May, the unveiling gala for these murals.
She straightened up from washing the last brush.
"Monday you're on your own," she mumbled as she
reached for her workbasket.

"What was that?" said a familiar voice from in back
of her. "Can I quote you?"

"Ellie!" Aldy turned around quickly and saw Ellen
grinning at her. "What are you doing here?" she said in
surprise.

"Gee, super welcome you give," said Ellen jokingly.

"You know there's no one I'd rather be surprised
by," Aldy soothed. "What brings you over here?"

"The murals," she said. "I want my guided tour!"

"You got it." Aldora took Ellen's arm and led her to
the recreation room. "Ta-da!" she trumpeted and made
an expansive gesture at the painted wall with both arms.

Ellen's face spoke volumes. Her eyes glowed as she
scanned every inch and her grin grew wider and wider
until Aldy thought sure she'd sprain a cheek muscle.
That was one of Ellen's greatest features; she didn't
need words, she had one of the most expressive faces
Aldy had ever seen in action.

"I love it," she breathed at last. "It's magnificent!"

"You can't be too amazed," Aldy said, "you've seen
every sketch along the way."

"But it looks so much..." Ellen searched for the
word and failed. "Bigger," she finished inadequately.

Aldora laughed. "Yes, twenty-two six by thirty-two
feet bigger!" she quoted.

Ellen looked up at the wall. "Boy, I sure wish I'd
come by and seen you up there!" Ellen murmured. "It
looks a lot taller from down here than it sounded."

"It looked taller from up there too," Aldy said.

"But you did it!" Ellen beamed with pride. "And the
hall's nearly finished too."

"By the end of next week," Aldy agreed.

"Let's celebrate," Ellen said. "I'll order a pizza and we can stuff ourselves silly."

"Sounds good," Aldy said. She gathered up her basket and met Ellen by the parking structure entrance. "I'll follow you," she shouted out the car window. Ellen waved and pulled out onto the street.

Ellen carried the huge pizza box into her kitchen and called to Bill. "Come and get it," she said as Aldy took plates out of the cupboard and set out the beer mugs for Bill and Ellie.

"Not fair," Bill said as he sat down at the table. "I didn't get to see what we're celebrating."

"Someone has to work for my living," Ellen joked as she served thick slices of the mushroom and pepperoni pizza.

"I'll give you a private showing," Aldy promised.

"Really private?" said Bill, leering at her in fun.

"You bet, Bill," Aldy answered with a provocative purr. "Just you and me, and the record-breaking crowds that have taken to wandering by since I finished the big mural."

Bill laughed. "From what Ellie says, you're lucky they aren't thronging your front porch for autographs."

"Spare me!" Aldy said.

"You won't have a spare moment after that unveiling," Ellen said seriously. "You'll be swamped with work."

"I hope so," Aldy replied. Less time to think about missing everybody, she thought to herself.

Chapter Fifteen

When Aldy put the last stroke to the hall mural and signed her name near a corner mushroom, she had a very select audience.

It was a replay of the engagement party except that Kate and Eddy were there and the *Amara Alexandra* was absent. Adam poured champagne and Jessie proposed a toast she had written all by herself. Aldora didn't even try to prevent the tears from rolling down her cheeks. "That was lovely, honey," she said and embraced Jess and kissed her fondly.

"I can't top that," Grant said.

"I wouldn't even try," Adam added.

Jessie was nearly bursting with pride, but she still made a face over her champagne glass.

"Let's go," said Adam.

Aldy looked at him in surprise. "What's the rush?" She was completely unwilling for this part of her life to close.

"Dinner's getting cold," he said and nodded at Grant.

Aldora realized her two favorite enigmas were at it again.

"You'll ride with me, Aldy. Julie, you know what to do."

Julie gave Grant a salute and left with Adam and Jess.

· On the way to the car Aldora began to feel uneasy. She had never had much experience with mysteries and this particular bunch of people stirred up some lulus. "Confidentially," Aldy said as Grant pulled onto the freeway, "I'm not hot on surprises. Guess it stems from a maiden aunt who used to pop out of closets and yell 'Boo!' ' "

"Ah," said Grant, stroking an imaginary, psychiatric beard, "product of a *scared* childhood." He flashed her a grin with the pun. "You could have confessed earlier. You might have saved me from being labeled the Yankee Doodle of the Edgely Foundation."

Aldora chuckled. "You're not! Are you?"

Grant nodded sheepishly. " 'Fraid so," he said turning off Sunset Boulevard into the arched gates of Bel-Air.

"Where are we going?" Aldy asked, staring at the mammoth homes that lined the street.

"Don't tell me. You're the sort of Puritan who'd deny a doomed man his last fling," Grant teased. "I'm kidnapping you and holding you over for my bachelor party."

Aldora laughed and shook her head. "You don't give an inch."

Grant turned into a driveway that led to the most magnificent home Aldy had ever seen. All tall, sloping rooflines and herringbone brick, with half-timbering and large mullioned windows of leaded glass. The entrance was lit with amber floods and the front door stood open. As Grant pulled to a stop Aldy could see the drop-crystal chandelier in the entry hall. "Adam's?" she murmured and looked at Grant in wonderment.

He grinned and came around to help her out of the MG.

"Sort of looks like him, doesn't it?"

"Only an architect would claim people could look like their homes," quipped Aldy. But she could see what Grant meant. There was a feeling about that house that gave her the same warm glow that Adam's presence kindled.

Grant took her arm and escorted her into the house.

"Surprise!" Jessie yelled and other voices joined in.

Adam and Julie, of course. Kate and Eddy. But Aldy

was totally unprepared to hear Ellie and Bill join the chorus. Her mouth dropped open and she turned a bewildered gaze on Grant. "How? When...?" She couldn't find words, let alone phrase whole questions.

Grant laughed at her disoriented expression. "I met Ellen when she came to see the mural last week," he explained.

"He was the first person I stumbled into," Ellen said. "I asked him how to find the resident muralist."

"Stumbled is right. She was so busy looking for you that she never saw me at all." Grant gave Ellen a friendly grin. "When she explained she was a good friend of yours, I asked her to stop by my office and briefed her on the plan."

"You knew?"

Ellen gave Grant a conspiratorial wink. "All the time."

Aldy was still trying to take all this in when Adam's housekeeper summoned them to dinner.

All the men took their ladies' arms and Aldy stepped forward to help Adam push Jess in tandem.

"You take Aldy, Daddy," said Jess firmly and began to wheel herself expertly toward the dining room.

Adam made a small bow and slid his arm around Aldora's shoulders.

Matchmakers come in all sizes, she thought. But it was wonderful to feel Adam by her side and not worry that Jess might feel left out. So wonderful that she didn't even blush when Grant looked over his shoulder and smiled and nudged Julie.

There was no other word for the dining room but elegant. Candles flickered on the table and sideboard and more flames danced in a breathtaking candelabra-chandelier that hung from the center of the high, open-beam ceiling. All across one wall the Jacobean wallpaper design was obscured with a huge banner that draped to the waist-high wainscoting. "WE LOVE YOU, ALDY," it proclaimed in pink poster paint. And underneath, "Congratulations" in lavender letters. Aldora didn't have to guess who the artist was. The color scheme was a giveaway. Everyone had taken a brush and signed the banner in black India ink.

"Oh, Jessie," said Aldora, "that's a beautiful banner!"

Jessie beamed. "Told you, Daddy. I said she'd guess." She looked at Aldy. "You get to have the banner later."

"I'll keep it forever and ever," Aldy said, giving Jess a huge kiss. "Thank you all," she said, looking around the room. "I—" Her voice broke and she couldn't continue.

Ellen and Bill covered the lapse by starting a round of applause.

They all took their seats and Adam tapped his glass for attention. He stood by his chair and held up his wineglass. "My turn," he said. "A toast: To the lady who has brightened our walls"—he paused and looked directly into Aldora's eyes—"and our lives."

There were shouts of approval and glasses clinked all around. If Aldora hadn't ever guessed that it was possible to blush and cry at the same time, she knew it now. She could feel the color in her cheeks and wondered that her tears didn't sizzle as they rolled down her face. She couldn't take her eyes off Adam. "That was lovely," she said softly. "Thank you, Adam."

The dinner was fantastic. Prime rib and fresh steamed vegetable dishes with a chocolate mousse for dessert. Aldy suspected that Ellen had provided the information on all her favorites.

The conversation centered around the plans for the official unveiling. Aldy learned that Grant and Julie had underplayed the scope by a good margin at that afternoon lunch.

By the time the evening was winding down, the date had been fixed and everyone knew just what to expect from the occasion. Ellen and Bill were to be special

guests of the artist and Kate and Eddy would be heralded as "those without whom the job would not have been
possible." Adam assured Jessie that she would be allowed to stay for the entire party, although she would
have to agree to sleep in late that day and catch an afternoon nap to compensate.

When everyone had gone home, the housekeeper
served coffee to Adam and Aldy in the library and
brought a milk shake for Jess. She made a face.

"Don't you like milk shakes?" Aldy asked.

"Not this kind," she said.

"Come on," her father insisted. "Doctor's orders.
Builds you up, makes you even more beautiful."

Adam lit the fire and the three of them sat around
watching the flames while Jess told a ghost story.

Adam used every spooky phrase to hug Aldy to his
shoulder and his hand was a constant caress on her bare
arm. By the time Jess reached her big finish, Aldora was
brimming with desire.

"Let's tuck you in, pumpkin," said Adam, taking his
arm from around Aldora and standing up.

At Jessie's request Aldy came along to help.

Aldora watched as Adam lovingly settled Jess into
bed and pulled the covers gently over her. He had to
bend almost double to drop a tender kiss on her cheek.
There was so much gentleness in this giant of a man.
Aldora felt a tightness in her throat as she gave his
daughter a good-night kiss and let Adam guide her out
into the hall.

"I'll drive you home the long way," Adam said, smiling at her as they descended the sweeping staircase. He
paused one tread below her and took her face in his
hands.

Aldora, with the aid of the stair, was almost even with
his brow. She heard the implication in his words, felt
herself grow giddy as she read the message in his eyes.
She felt his arms encircle her and she leaned into his embrace. His lips touched hers so lightly. "Aldy," he mur-

mured. He tilted her chin up with his fingertips and grazed her mouth again with his own.

Aldora could hardly believe the effect his teasing kisses were having on her whole body. She wanted him to go on tantalizing her in this delicious manner forever, but another, savage part of her wished he'd press his mouth on hers with brutal, demanding force. Moments later she got her second wish.

Adam's mouth sought hers, expressing those demands in that age-old, wordless language.

Aldora answered his quest with a desire all her own and felt that she could have stood on that staircase with Adam cradling her in his arms through all eternity.

Gradually Adam's kiss became gentle again and he moved his hands across her back in tender caresses. He kissed her eyes, her cheeks and trailed small, light kisses down the side of her neck. Aldy felt her passion flare anew.

At last he lifted her onto the stair tread next to him and began to guide her down to the landing. He seemed to sense what Aldora knew. If he had left her unsupported for an instant, she would have crumpled onto the carpet. His kisses had dissolved her bones, leaving her helpless to perform even the basic function of standing and walking. Neither of them spoke. They moved as if in a trance, a tuneless melody measured their pace as they walked to the car.

When Adam finally pulled into Aldy's driveway, he turned off the engine but didn't get out of the car. He pulled her close, held her against his chest, and his fingers combed through the heavy length of her hair. When he did speak, his voice was a ragged whisper. "I guess you know," he said slowly, "I never expected this to happen, Aldy." He pressed her hard against him and continued. "I thought we could go on seeing each other, enjoying a loving friendship, but I've opened a door I can't close." He paused and Aldy could feel his heart beating strongly beneath his shirt. "I need you, Aldy," he said softly. "Jessie's coming around. Eventually she'll accept this." Adam stumbled and then went on. "I—I want to marry you," he blurted. "We can't tell Jess yet, but I want you always."

"Oh, Adam," Aldy gasped and clung to him as conflicted emotions whirled around her. She wanted him more than anything in the world, but he didn't know; she still hadn't told him he'd be getting a new burden in her. She ached to be honest with him, but the thought of losing him was too painful right now.

"You'll think about it?" Adam said, holding her gently.

"Oh, yes, Adam, I'll think about it." She kissed him then, pouring all her love and feeling into him and rejoicing as he responded eagerly, meeting her passion and taking it for unspoken assent to his question.

Adam walked Aldy up to her door. He kissed her again and when they drew apart, he was breathing heavily with undisguised desire. He lifted her and carried her inside to the sofa. Settling her, he held her in his arms. "I swore I wouldn't ask you again until I could offer you—"

"You don't have to ask, Adam," Aldy cut in, emboldened by his urgency, her own longing.

"That's not why I mentioned marriage," he whispered and Aldy could feel him smiling against her neck. Then, he tensed, pulled back, fighting for control: "Damn! If Jess would only have that lamifusion she'd be better, we could tell her, *make* her understand." Adam drew a hand across his eyes and didn't see how the word *lamifusion* had galvanized Aldora.

"Maybe now, that she's so fond of you, maybe you could—"

"Adam!" Aldy gasped. "I can't...couldn't ever ask her to face that for our own pleasure!" Her mind reeled at the thought of Jess and of her own undisclosed secret, her own lamifusion—none too successfully achieved.

Adam looked as if he'd been struck. His eyes were

hurt, disbelieving. "My, God, Aldy, is it asking so much for you to try?"

"Yes!" The word leaped from her lips and as quickly, she ached to call it back.

Adam, looking bewildered at the sudden sharpness of her reply, and obviously smarting from his own guilt as well as Aldy's seeming reprimand, thrust her away from him and strode to the door. "You *are* a hard woman," he spat from between clenched teeth. He wheeled and bolted out the door.

"Adam!" Aldora's strangled cry reached out into the night and dropped off into the darkness unanswered. She heard the engine roar to life and heard the tires grind the gravel of her drive and spit it viciously against the garage wall. Her nails made crescent wounds in her palms and she bit the inside of her bottom lip until the salt taste in her mouth made her feel ill. She ran for the bathroom as her stomach churned and she dove for the lid of the toilet. Her back muscles spasmed as her stomach tried to purge her soul of its shock. All she could think of was that she had been ready to surrender herself to this man totally, heart, mind, body, accept scraps and never ask more. He had flung her romantic offerings at her, plainly stating that it wasn't enough!

By the time the first rays of dawn crept through the window, Aldora was lying on the floor with her cheek pressed against the cold tile. She had neither the strength nor will enough to drag herself to her knees and crawl to the shelter of her bed. She drifted on the waves of her pain and only moved when the harsh ringing of the phone tore through the stillness several hours later. Struggling to her knees, she scrabbled into the hall and knocked the phone to the floor. Clutching the receiver to her ear, she cried: "Adam?"

"Sorry to disappoint you." Ellen's cheery greeting reached out across the wires. "I just—"

Aldora burst into hysterical sobs, let the receiver slip from her fingers.

"Aldy?" The voice came blindly into the room as Aldora stared mutely at the mouthpiece lying on the carpet.

THE receiver-off-the-hook signal was oscillating through the silence when Ellen came anxiously through the front door. "Aldy!" she cried and knelt to slip her arms around her friend's trembling body. "What happened?"

Aldora couldn't speak. She allowed Ellen to get her into bed, sipped hot tea, stared blankly while Ellen soothed and fussed.

"I can't believe it!" said Ellen after she'd coaxed the story from Aldy in bits and pieces. "You practically swore to me that you'd tell him!" Ellen's jaw was set but her blue eyes swam with compassion. "All or nothing is right," she said levelly. "He offered *all*, you took *nothing*! You could help Jessie, *more* than he ever suspected!" Ellen's face showed her distress and anger. "For God's sake, call him!"

"No!" Aldy's eyes blazed with fear.

"You think about it," said Ellen, walking to the door of the bedroom. "'Hard woman' wasn't strong enough. I'll be back later." She left Aldy staring after her.

Chapter Sixteen

During the next few days Aldora's shock ebbed to a stony depression. Ellen came daily to supervise her recovery, to urge Aldy to call Adam.

Aldora was barely able to walk. Her once humorous imitation of a decrepit granny that had brought delighted giggles from Jessie's throat was a harsh reality.

"Let me take you to the orthopedist," Ellen pleaded. "You need professional help with this one!"

"No!" Aldora was vehement. She almost relished the pain. She thought it was the only thing that could rival what she was feeling in her anguished heart; she preferred the familiar, physical stabbing to the searing agony of Adam's rejection. "My God, Ellie! You know what he'd suggest!" She stared at Ellen for a moment in amazement. "More surgery; fuse what didn't fuse the first time. No way!" Her voice was strident with emotion, denial.

Ellen sighed defeatedly. Aldy knew she was recalling how poorly Aldora had fared in surgery the first time, knew that Ellen wouldn't press her.

"Sorry, Aldy," she said. "Forget it." She placed a thick brown package on the kitchen table. "This was at your post office box."

Aldora looked at it. "Galleys," she mumbled. "I'll do them later."

"Want some help?"

Aldy shook her head. "No, thanks. It'll do me good to work."

Ellen shrugged and slipped out the door, pushing it closed behind her.

Aldora heaved to her feet and lugged the package to

the couch. She settled herself awkwardly and ripped the paper from the galleys of her newest book.

She worked steadily for two hours, then put her head back and dozed.

Hearing the door bang forcefully, Aldora started awake as Grant came angrily into the room.

"I just had to see for myself!" he yelled. "I couldn't believe it when Adam told me you *refused* to help Jess." He came toward her, eyes blazing. "I had to look into your face and hear you refuse to try."

Aldora grabbed her cane and lurched violently to her feet. "Shut up!" she screamed. She tried to move around the coffee table but her foot caught the skirt of the sofa. She doubled up as razor-sharp pain shot down her leg.

Grant's anger dissipated as he reached to catch her with a bewildered expression on his face.

Aldy pushed his hands away and glared spitefully. "I couldn't possibly tell Jess to have that operation," she rasped. "As you can see, it's hardly fail safe!" She stood breathing heavily, appraising the look on Grant's face as comprehension pushed him away from her. He sank into a chair and his jaw sagged. No sound came from his open mouth.

"What you see is what Adam would get, maybe times *two*!" she said bitterly. "I was never sick; no flu, no sprained ankle. I'm a fraud! I had a lamifusion two and a half years ago. It didn't work!" Angry tears ran down her face and she felt her knees give way as she sank onto the sofa, spent, humiliated.

"I'm sorry, Aldy." Grant's statement was a shocked whisper as he fought to take it all in.

Aldy saw the pity and confusion contort his features and she knew that she'd see another expression soon. Ken's face swam before her and she covered her eyes with her hands. "Just get out!" she yelled. "I can't help Jess; I can't help Adam; I can't even help myself! My big commitment is to trying to crawl out of bed every morning!'' Aldora heard Grant rise and cross the room. She didn't look up until she heard him slide the door shut.

Aldora sat watching the darkness creep into the evening sky. A strange sense of relief had washed over her after Grant had gone. She'd finally torn away her web of deception and she was still breathing. Unevenly, raggedly, but she was still breathing. The agony of her loss still twisted her inside, but the crushing humiliation and shame were lifting. She hobbled to the kitchen and put on water for tea.

Reaching woodenly for the cups, she stood absorbed, watching her own hands performing the simple actions as if they belonged to someone else. She poured boiling water over the tea bag and watched the water turn dark, rust-red, as the tea steeped.

Aldy reached for another cup when she heard the door slide in its tracks. ''Tea, Ellie?'' she called over her shoulder.

''Look again.'' The voice that reached her caused Aldy to stiffen. She tried to turn, look at Adam, clutching frantically for the edge of the counter; she tottered unsteadily as she tried to maintain her footing. ''What are *you* doing here?'' she gasped as she saw Adam's eyes narrowed in anger.

''What am I doing here?'' repeated Adam harshly. ''Grant said you had something to tell me. He insisted I had to come right away.'' Adam stood quietly. One hand on the bar, he waited and stared at her. ''Well?''

Aldora's mind raced wildly. Grant hadn't told him? Adam still *didn't* know!

''I had hoped it was an apology, Aldora.'' Adam's face was an unfathomable mask.

''Apology?'' Aldy said blankly.

''For the other night,'' Adam prompted. ''Jessie?''

Anger surged through her. She slid her hand along the counter and started to step toward Adam, but the folds of her robe caught the cane that had been balanced against the cabinets. It clattered to the floor and Aldy stared at it as if it were a viper.

Adam's eyes were riveted on the cane as he stooped to retrieve it. "What in the hell's going on here?" he said, holding the cane out to Aldora.

Aldora held out her hand for the cane, set it against the floor, and leaned on it. "I'm afraid Grant's sent you on a fool's errand," she said quietly. "He could have told you why I'd never apologize for not recommending this surgery to Jessie." She lifted her head and stood straight as she could in spite of the pain in her spine.

Adam's face seemed to crumble as he stared at her. "*This* surgery?" he whispered as his eyes widened with comprehension. He took a step toward her, reached for her shoulders. "Aldy, what are you saying?" His hands trembled slightly as he placed them firmly around her upper arms.

"I believe you heard me," Aldy said, fighting tears and nausea. "Lamifusions don't always work out." She looked down at the floor, unable to face Adam, afraid of what she would see in his expression.

"My God, Aldy," Adam breathed as he released her arm and placed strong fingers under her chin, tilted her face up to look into her eyes. "Why didn't you tell me before?" His voice was insistent, pleading.

Aldy opened her eyes, blinking tears back, and saw hurt on his face, heard it in his tone. "I . . . you had enough . . ." she stammered disjointedly. She closed her eyes again and felt the hot tears burn trails across her cheeks as they flowed silently from beneath her lids.

Adam brushed them away gently. "You couldn't think much of me if you thought my knowing would change my feeling for you," he said sadly.

Aldy looked at him again, saw the sadness in him, and felt a twisting pain in her chest as she realized the magnitude of her injustice. "I'm sorry, Adam," she said feebly. "I only wanted to—" She stopped. There was no excuse she could make. Ellen had been right. She *had* vested Adam with Ken's crimes; he'd a right to his hurt, a right to walk out of her life forever. Aldy bit her lower lip and struggled against a pain more vicious than any her surgery had produced.

Adam lifted her, carried her to the couch. Placing her carefully against the cushions, he took her hand. "I'm hardly an example of a trusting nature, myself," he admitted, smiling tenderly at her. Aldora knew he was referring to the argument they'd had at the restaurant. "Now, let's have it," he said firmly. "All of it."

Aldora felt her throat constrict as she realized his eyes displayed only concern, caring in his probing gaze. How could she admit that she'd mistrusted him because of another man's treachery? "You don't understand," she began, "there's so many things I can't do now. I can't run two careers and participate in a relationship as well." She'd said it. She stared at the pattern in the sofa cushions until it blurred before her eyes.

"So, who asked you to?" Adam said angrily.

Aldy's heart wrenched. Here it was again. All or nothing at all. Her temper flared. "I thought *you* had, once." She clenched her eyelids tightly. "I take it this is a retraction of your proposal," she said numbly.

Adam grabbed her shoulders. "I've retracted nothing!" he said harshly. "*You* never gave me an answer!"

Aldy opened her eyes. "How could I? When I started to say that I couldn't tell Jess to have surgery, you ran out of here like a madman!"

"Dammit, Aldy! Be fair! I didn't know your reasons."

"Fair? That's what I was being," she cried. "I don't have the stamina to care for a house, a man, a child, unless I abandon everything else. I won't do that again!" She averted her face, felt him let go of her.

Adam was silent for a long moment. When he spoke

again, his voice was hard. "I'm not buying a used car, Aldora. I can manage a house, Jessie, all of it on my own. Dammit, Aldy, I never wanted to *employ* you, just love you!" This last phrase was a choked whisper.

Aldy looked up. She could see lines of pain around his eyes, tightness around his mouth. "Oh, Adam, I want to love you too." She paused, unsure for a moment if his statement extended into the future or was frozen in that awful past tense.

"But?" Adam straightened up, braced as if expecting new pain.

"It's not enough. I can't give you enough."

"Isn't that *my* choice?" Adam cut in.

"And can you choose, now that you know? Can you choose a woman who can't care for you, tend your daughter, give you more children?" Her voice shook as she listed this last flaw. She waited for Adam's ultimate denial, his rejection.

Adam took her face in his hands, drew a long breath. "We'd have Jessie. You'd have your talent, your art. You have a lot of good days. Isn't that enough for you, Aldy?"

Hot blood rushed to her face as the words sank in. He was all but accusing her of being greedy, wanting it all. And he was right! Aldora wanted to scream, cry out against her own narrowness. Instead, she heard her own voice say: "It could be more than enough."

Adam smiled. "Don't answer now," he said gently. "I can't repeat my offer of marriage until Jess is better. She's very ill again. I have to go back to her." He rose and kissed her forehead tenderly. "You think about it. I know my feelings."

Aldora was stunned. "Adam," she blurted. "Take me with you." She struggled to stand.

Adam reached for her. Held her close. "You can't, Aldy," he said urgently. "You're hurting."

It was Aldy's turn to silence him. "I want to. I *can* help," she said firmly. "I know I can."

ADAM carried Aldy up the curving staircase to the bed-room door. He set her gently on her feet and took her arm.

Grant looked up in wonder as Aldora limped awk-wardly to the side of Jessie's bed.

Gazing down at the sleeping child, Aldy knelt on the floor and leaned to brush Jessie's hot cheek with her lips.

Jess stirred, opened her eyes. "Aldy?" she mur-mured. She tried to lift her head.

"Yes, honey, don't try to move," Aldy said. "I heard you weren't feeling well. I wanted to be with you."

Adam helped her up and Grant pulled a chair over for her.

Leaning on her cane and Adam's arm, she lowered herself carefully to the seat.

Jess looked confused. "Are you joking again, Aldy?" she asked, obviously recalling Aldora's granny routine. She smiled uncertainly.

"No, honey," Aldy answered. "Not this time. I have an injured spine too. It's acting up."

Jessie's eyes grew wide; she looked at her father.

Adam nodded. "It's true, pumpkin," he said. "Aldy had the same operation they want you to have."

Jess stared at Aldora. "But you painted the murals," she said haltingly. "You even went on the boat, sailed the *Amara*." Jess broke off, suspicion flooded her face. "You're lying!" she cried. "Uncle Grant and Daddy told you to say that!" Tears welled in her eyes. "I thought you were my friend!" she accused.

Aldora's heart thudded in her chest and she couldn't seem to get enough air. She slid painfully to her knees and leaned over Jessie's bed again. "I *am* your friend," she insisted gently. "I can do all those things *because* I had that operation, and I'm very grateful for all the good days I have now." Tears coursed down her own cheeks and her voice faltered as she recognized the truth in her words.

Jess looked at her. "Really?" she quavered. "You're not just saying that?"

Aldora looked up at Adam, put out her hand for help. He lifted her off the floor and she sat on the edge of Jessie's bed and turned her back to the child. Her fingers fumbled at the waist of her slacks as she pulled her shirttails free and raised the soft fabric over her own spine. "Would I ever lie to you?" she said lightly and felt soft fingers trace the narrow white scar that she knew disappeared below the waistband of her jeans.

"It's tiny," Jess breathed. "You can't hardly tell," she said in amazement.

"That's how all scars are, Jess," her father murmured. "When you care about someone, you don't even see them."

"But Mommy said—" she floundered. Adam's words seemed to hang in the air as Jess struggled to grasp them fully.

"That was a very long time ago, pumpkin," said Adam gently. "Mommy just couldn't believe in that kind of love."

Aldora saw the hesitation, a hint of fear in Jessie's questioning look. Anxious to divert the topic to a less threatening degree of emotional content, Aldy pulled herself up and leaned over her cane in an all-too-real rendition of her one-time joke. "Look at me, Jess," she said, thumping her cane imperiously. "I'm a wreck right now, but you still care for me." She grinned at Jess. "Well, don't you?"

Jessie held out her arms. "Oh, yes, Aldy, I do!"

Aldora reached out, grabbed both Jessie's hands in her free one. "Hang on, honey," she kidded, "I'll get there." She allowed Adam to help her back down on the bed and wrapped her arms warmly around Jess, hugging her hard. Then Aldy stiffened as Jess directed a question to her father over Aldy's shoulder.

"Do *you* still like Aldy, Daddy?"

Adam leaned down and hugged them both. "More

than ever, pumpkin.'' Tears ran unashamedly down Adam's rugged face but only Grant saw them and his own eyes were wet as he slipped soundlessly out of the room.

Chapter Seventeen

Aldora smiled as she opened the package of advance copies from her publisher. She turned to the dedication page and inscribed a copy for Jess. It had taken some clever persuasion to convince her editor to have the dedication reset, but when Aldy explained to Miriam about the approaching operation, her publisher had relented. It now read: For Jessie Holcomb, whose love and courage have all my admiration.

Aldora tucked the book into her tote bag and went to her car. As she drove to Adam's she could still see the whirling lights and hear the orchestra that had played at the gala unveiling the night before. Jess had sat excitedly in her chair as Adam had coaxed Aldy onto the dance floor. Then, later, Adam had lifted his daughter and waltzed with her too. Aldora had had tears in her eyes as she watched. She hoped fervently that once Jessie's operation was over, the little girl would be able to dance on her own two feet again, or at least on Adam's.

Aldora pulled into the circular drive and mounted the front stairs. Margaret answered the bell and showed Aldy up to Jessie's room.

"Hi, there," Aldy said brightly as she crossed to the bed.

Jess was sitting up and her color looked good. The party, Aldy's optimistic coaching, Margaret's milk shakes, all were beginning to have the desired effect on Jessie's readiness for surgery.

"Hi, Aldy," Jessie chirped. Her eyes went to the tote bag. "Did it come?"

Aldora didn't answer. She pulled the book from her bag and handed it to Jess.

"Oh, Aldy!" Jess shrilled, grabbing the book and holding it to her heart.

"Look inside," Aldy said. "Dedication page." She watched Jess read and saw her eyes widen in disbelief.

"It has my name *printed* in it!" she said.

"In all the copies, Jess. That's your own personal dedication."

Aldora was unprepared for the delighted tears of thanks that welled up in Jessie's eyes and spilled onto her yellow nightdress. She held Jess close and stroked her blond curls.

"Has Daddy seen it?"

"Not yet. I thought you'd surprise him."

"I'll call." Jess reached for the phone by her bed.

"He's not in his office, Jess. He's talking to your doctors about Friday." At the mention of her surgery date Jess sobered.

"Hey," Aldy said, "none of that. I'll be with you every step of the way. And Adam and your Uncle Grant, Julie too."

Jess tried to smile.

"You want to be Julie's flower girl, don't you?"

At that reminder, Jessie's smile grew wide. "And you want to be co-flower girl!" she said happily.

"You bet." Aldora and Julie had worked out a strong incentive to help carry Jess through the postoperative pain and therapy. Aldora and Jessie were to be co-flower girls. Aldy would help Jess down the aisle by carrying the basket of petals while Jess maneuvered in her back brace and cane, scattering blossoms with her free hand.

"I'm still scared," Jess whispered.

"I was too, honey, but I'll work out with you every day. I promise. I know all the tricks." She grinned and confidently thumped her chest with her fist.

Jess laughed and hugged Aldy tightly.

On Friday morning a groggy Jess was wheeled down the long hospital corridor with a bevy of supportive fans at her side-rails. Although anxiety had tightened Aldy's own back to near-spasm, she leaned on her cane and held Jessie's hand all the way to the surgery doors. Adam, Grant, Julie, all kissed Jess and whispered encouragement before the nurse rolled the gurney with its small white-draped form silently into the OR.

The surgery doors swung shut and Aldora looked at Adam. She could see fear etched into every fiber of his concerned expression and his body was taut with tension. She slipped her arm around his waist. "She'll be fine."

Adam clung to her as they walked to the waiting room.

"THIS is the longest six hours of my life," said Grant as he lit another cigarette and paced across the floor for perhaps the millionth time.

"You and Adam will force me to meet with the floorcoverings man again," Julie said, striving to lift tension with levity.

Adam smiled and sank exhaustedly onto a bench. He reached for Aldora and pulled her close to his side. Grant sat by Julie and tried to calm himself with deep, noisy inhalations.

"You'll hyperventilate, pass out, and miss the good news when the doctor comes to say Jess is fine," Aldy cautioned.

Grant smiled at her, leaned back in his chair.

An hour later they were all still sitting around anxiously; Aldora felt Adam start violently and his arm jerked free of her shoulders. She heard the scrape of Grant's chair and followed his gaze toward the waiting room doors. Instead of the expected green-garbed surgeon, Aldora found herself looking directly into the hazel eyes of the most breathtaking woman she had ever seen. Aldy sat, stunned, noting the naked rage on Adam's face as he glared at this elegant newcomer.

She looked at Julie but found no explanation in the decorator's shocked stare. All three of her friends were looking with open hostility at this stunning honey-blonde.

Aldora turned her gaze back to the doors and saw the sinuous ripple of the woman's black jersey sheath as she glided smoothly toward Adam. The dress flowed over the statuesque form and clung to every voluptuous curve of that tall, lithe body. Bitter resentment glittered in those hazel eyes as she moved.

Her lips parted, revealing small, perfect white teeth that glinted from between the red lips as she spoke. "Well, Adam, I hear you forced that ugly operation on our daughter after all."

Aldora caught her breath and felt her own jaw ache with clenching as she saw Adam rise to face Louise in one panther-swift motion. "What are you doing here?" His face was a mask of unrestrained anger as he fought to suppress violent impulses.

The woman laughed. "You offer our Jessica as a sacrifice on the altar of your precious surgical faith and you ask?" Her expression softened slightly. "I *am* the child's mother!" She let her eyes travel around the room while she waited for the declaration to take its full effect. As her eyes rested on Aldora, she let them sweep haughtily over Aldy's slight frame before resuming her disdainful scrutiny of Adam.

"No one would have guessed that four years ago!" Adam clenched his hands and his words erupted from between grinding teeth.

Nearly as tall as Adam, Louise stood quietly, her very pose a challenge. "I've kept in touch," she said evenly. "I did have all that horrid, reconstructive surgery to weather. I didn't notice you hovering in *my* waiting room!" She turned slowly from Adam and moved to the leather bench. "Lord knows how I managed all alone," she said, eyes narrowing with self-pity. One graceful hand reached to toss the heavy sheaf of blond hair away from her shoulder. "I *did* manage, though. It no longer shows."

Aldy looked hard at the creamy expanse of bare throat Louise revealed. Certainly nothing marred the beauty now. Aldora tried to visualize how this woman would have looked, how she would have felt, if a long, red line still crossed that flawless skin, but the woman's lovely features, her classic profile made it impossible for Aldy to imagine her otherwise. Perhaps such beauty *was* worth protecting, she thought, but at what cost?

"You didn't *need* that surgery, Louise," said Adam tightly. He was breathing heavily and his knuckles showed white with tension.

"*You* didn't have to look in my mirror each morning!" Louise said, lifting her chin defiantly.

"That scar was barely noticeable. It certainly didn't affect your ability to turn and run!" He hurled this last at her with a force so violent that the tendons on his muscular neck stood out tautly beneath the skin.

Aldora saw Grant move quietly to Adam's side.

"Get out, Louise! Jess doesn't need a postcard parent!"

Louise's eyes grew wide with hurt. "I'm going to stay right here," she said firmly. "Someone has to help Jessica cope with the hideous scarring *your* selfish decision will cause!"

Adam advanced, glowering at her. "The scar you're so obsessed with can get her out of that wheelchair!"

"Will she thank you when your precious experts leave her scarred *and* crippled?" Louise asked harshly. "No guarantees, remember?"

Adam shook his head sadly. "You won't even give her hope, will you, Louise? I want my daughter to *walk* into her future! That makes it worth the risk."

"Whose risk, Adam? Not yours. You won't have to look into *her* mirror either!" Louise's body was rigid with anger.

"Your values leave a lot to be desired," Adam said and started to turn away. "Go back to your parties, Louise."

Aldora gasped as she saw Louise move, saw the woman catch Adam full in the face with the flat of her hand.

Adam turned back to Louise, stared hard at her for a long moment, the angry red mark from the blow deepening against his tanned jaw. Then he silently stepped over and held one of the doors open.

Grant edged closer to Louise. "I'll show you out," he said, his voice commanding.

Louise tossed her cape carelessly over one shoulder. She let her eyes rest on Aldora once more and then travel pointedly to the cedar cane that leaned against the bench. "I had assumed you forced this surgery because you were tired of nursing cripples, Adam," she said sweetly. "I was wrong; you seem to have a penchant for them." She glided easily through the doors and let them swing behind her.

Adam seemed about to go after her, but then he turned a tortured gaze on Aldora. "I'm sorry, sweetheart," he said softly, his hands and shoulders lifting in defeat.

Aldora rose to put her arms around him. "It's not important," she said, leading him gently to the bench as Grant disappeared through the still-swinging doors. She glanced at Julie. Her friend threw her a knowing look and followed Grant.

Moments later Grant and Julie returned and Grant nodded meaningfully at Adam. Before he could recount his talk with Louise, a green-clad surgeon came smiling into the room. "Good news," he announced, holding out his hand to Adam. "Jessie's doing wonderfully. She'll be out of recovery in about three hours."

Tears stung Aldy's eyes. She saw the joy and relief flood Adam's face as he pumped the doctor's hand. His eyes searched the surgeon's.

"Complete success, Adam." The doctor looked at Grant. "Take him for coffee. Jess will be a while getting set in ICU."

Grant nodded.

"Thanks, Sam," said Adam. Grateful tears welling in his eyes, he grabbed Aldy and followed Grant and Julie to the cafeteria.

INSIDE the quiet of the intensive care unit, Grant and Julie waited to see Jess. Only two visitors, five minutes out of each hour, so Adam and Aldy went in first.

"How's she look?" said Grant, jumping up and rushing to face Adam as he came out of Jessie's room.

"She's not really—" Adam was still fighting the fear he'd felt at Jess lying so still and pale.

"She's fine," Aldy said, taking Grant's hands. "It's a rough surgery. Takes a day or two for the shock-gray to wear off." She smiled at Adam. "Her heart's strong, pressure's normal."

Julie looked at Aldy. "You wouldn't just be—"

Aldora put her arms around Julie. "No, I wouldn't!" She shook Julie gently and grinned. "She's not about to carry on any deep conversations after nearly seven hours of anesthesia!"

Adam smiled, ran his fingers through his hair. "Aldy's right," he said. "I expected the impossible. She's fine."

Grant hugged Julie and grinned. "If you two want to get some rest," he said, "Julie and I can wait on our own."

"No chance!" Adam said. "We stick together."

When Grant and Julie came out of Jessie's room, Julie's cheeks were wet. She sniffed and rummaged for a hanky.

"What's wrong?" Adam said, instantly alarmed.

"Nothing," Julie said, blowing into her handkerchief, "she's so. . .I'm glad she's okay."

Adam smiled and wrapped his arms around Aldy. "Without you, sweetheart," he said, "we wouldn't have got her this far."

Aldora squeezed his waist affectionately. "Go get

some sleep, darling," she said. "Jess will be groggy all through the night."

Grant and Adam walked toward the elevators and Julie lingered with Aldora. "Come on, I'll buy," she said, steering Aldy to the nurses' lounge.

"So, that's it," Julie finished.

Aldora sipped thoughtfully at her coffee and tried to absorb the picture Julie had drawn. Louise: willful, spoiled, selfish, turning every event to her own advantage. But Aldy kept seeing a frightened, lovely woman who feared desperately the loss of all she felt she really had: her beauty. A lonely woman who feared the same for her daughter.

"Will she try to make trouble for Adam and Jess?" Aldy asked.

"That's the last thing Louise wants," said Julie evenly. "Louise wants everything to be 'pretty.'" Julie slid her chair back, walked around the table to Aldora. "Official action against her, charges, she'd be mortified!" Julie grinned and accepted Aldy's grateful hug.

The two women walked arm in arm to Julie's car.

"See you tomorrow," Julie called as she dropped Aldy at her porch stairs and drove off.

Aldora waved until the Mustang was out of sight and then climbed slowly to her front door. Falling exhaustedly onto her bed, she prayed that Julie was right about Louise.

ALDORA shelved her own work and put off the job offers that began to arrive per Ellen's prediction. She spent each day at Jessie's bedside, joking, sketching, playing verbal games, encouraging the child to fight off the easy, semiconscious drifting that most postoperatives succumbed to. The more Jess asked of herself now, the less her therapist would have to demand from her later.

Each evening Aldora worked diligently at her art. The

portrait of Adam at the helm of the *Amara* was nearly complete and Aldy started roughing in the portrait of Grant and Julie. Working from the photo of them embracing by the bowsprit, she knew it would be a treasured wedding gift.

Adam came by late in the evenings after settling Jess. The two of them would sit over mugs of hot tea and discuss Jessie's progress, Aldy's growing store of paintings for the show, and their own hopeful but uncertain future.

"Look, Aldy," Adam reasoned, "Doctor Sam says it's a complete success. I say we tell her about our plans now."

"Give her a chance, Adam. She has to start walking on her own, begin to believe in her own recovery first."

Adam got up, impatient with it all and paced around looking at Aldy's paintings. "Well, at least let me start helping out with the bills. You're not doing illustration now, you're caring for Jessie. It's only fair."

Aldora shook her head. "Adam, we've been over this ground before. I have enough from the murals to carry me for the present."

Adam took her hands in his. "You should be pouring all your effort into the painting," he said firmly. "This show will be the making of you! They'll clamor for more and you'll have nothing left to sell the throngs." He grinned at her.

"Oh, Adam," Aldy said softly, "you know the most uncommon thing in the world is to have a sell-out at one of these gallery presentations." She protested his confidence but a part of her glowed with pride at his active support of her talents.

"I only know that the most 'uncommon thing' around here is for me to win a discussion point with you." Adam grabbed her arm and dragged her against his chest. He kissed her hard and released her all too soon. He pulled on a sweater and carried his tea mug to the kitchen.

Aldy hated to see him leave but the strain of tending to the Foundation's business all day and Jessie's needs all evening was beginning to show as lines around his eyes, a hollowness in his cheeks. Aldora walked him to the door.

As the day of Jessie's "first walk" drew near, Aldy spent a part of each day coaching, preparing Jess. They spoke frankly about the problems as well as the rewards involved in rehabilitation. Aldy told Jess of the pins and needles she would feel in her feet and legs and spent time patting and slapping the soles of Jessie's feet so that their first contact with the floor would be less of a shock. It would hurt a lot at first, Aldy admitted, but she also promised that it would get better rapidly.

When the big moment arrived, Jess had four anxious bystanders and two volunteer therapists in the room. Adam, Grant, Julie, and Bill watched; Aldora and Ellie coached and encouraged as Jessie's physical therapist strapped her into her brace for the first time.

Jessie's first steps were slow and shaky. Being upright for the first time in twelve days left her sick to her stomach and dizzy. But she took five wobbly steps before asking to lie down again and her audience exploded from breathless anticipation into riotous cheers.

"It does make you sorta sick," Jess said meekly and grabbed Aldy's hand as the therapist removed the brace.

Aldora nodded, her voice quavering as she remembered her own first walk. "You did just great!" she said, recognizing Jessie's monumental gallantry.

"You took as many first steps as Aldy," Ellie encouraged.

Jessie grinned at her.

The hospital ordered guest trays for all visitors and Jess beamed proudly as she presided over her "first walk" celebration dinner.

Adam tucked her in for the night and drove Aldy

home. "She's gonna make it," he said happily as he walked Aldy up her stairs.

Aldora switched on the lights and set the kettle on the stove.

"We're nearly home free," Adam said as he slid his arms around her and proceeded to greatly interfere with her efficiency in the kitchen. His arms were tightly about her waist, his chin on her hair as she tried to fix their tea and set out dessert. "Leave that," he whispered huskily and moved his hands to her shoulders. Turning her to face him, he kissed her deeply as his hands explored her body, fired her desire. Aldy could sense the liberated longing in his touch now that the ongoing concern over Jess could be pushed to the back of his thoughts. Her senses rejoiced in the way the troubled, tired mask slipped from his face at her caress.

Mouth still on hers, he lifted her in his arms and carried her toward the bedroom in an unspoken request. He placed her gently on the bed and his eyes were urgent, pleading, as he slowly began to unbutton her blouse, pull it free of her skirt.

Aldy's slim fingers aided his efforts and then nimbly unfastened the buckle of his belt as she drew him onto the bed next to her and shrugged her clothes from her body.

She lay back against the pillows and let her eyes travel the lean length of him as he finished removing his clothes and came to lie beside her.

"God, but you're lovely," he whispered as his tongue teased her neck, the hollow of her throat, and trailed toward her breasts. He drew her over onto him and pressed her firmly against the hard muscles of his chest. Adam's hands flowed over her and followed the curve of her waist, pausing to cup her hips and draw her closer still, before his mouth captured hers in soul-stirring rapture.

Aldy's whole body was aching with need and she

moaned and pressed herself against him, shifting her weight, arching into the shelter of his body.

Adam wrapped his arms around her shoulders and ran his hands down her back to the small curve of her spine. His fingers encountered the thin scar that ran down to the cleft of her buttocks. "Don't let me hurt you," he said, suddenly easing his embrace, restraining himself with obvious effort.

"Adam," Aldy said, wrapping one leg over both of his and running the sole of her foot seductively along his thigh and calf, "I won't break, really I won't." She smiled at his concern and leaned to flick at his mouth with the tip of her tongue.

"You keep that up," he growled as he tumbled her playfully, gently, onto her back beside him, "and all thought of being gentle with you will go by the way." He bent to nip her shoulder and a pleasure-filled laugh bubbled from Aldy's throat as Adam slid his palm along the inside of her thigh in a teasing caress. As he possessed her with his hands and mouth, Aldora surrendered willingly, all the fears and longings that she'd ever fought against or concealed began to fall away at his touch.

Aldora ran her hands along the hard length of him and moaned her pleasure as she pulled his weight onto her slight body.

Adam started to resist her direction. "I'm too heavy," he began and was saying something about her back, but Aldy never let him finish the remark. Made bold by the fire he'd fanned with his teasing, she pressed her mouth over his and wrapped her arms firmly around his shoulders. One leg encircled his hips, commanding him to join in the love Aldora wanted to share. She lifted her body to meet his and Adam groaned his suppressed desire as he answered her great need with his own.

He was tender, passionate, forceful, by turns and he inspired Aldy to unimagined joy as they expressed their hopes and dispelled their fears in the intensity of their love.

Soon Aldy lay in Adam's arms, her head pillowed on his shoulder, her fingers drinking in the textures of his skin. And Adam gazed at her with fascinated wonder as he stroked her and whispered her name over and over against her tousled hair.

Chapter Eighteen

When Jess was allowed to go home, Aldora presented her with a long, narrow, lumpy package.

Jessie tore away the wrappings and squealed her delight at the hand-carved cedar cane. "It's like yours!" Jess said, waving the stick at Aldy.

"Naturally," Aldy said. "Couldn't have our 'accessories' clash when we go to therapy."

Jessie smiled triumphantly as Adam and Aldy escorted her to the hospital exit. The nurse helped Adam settle Jess in the camper of Bill's pickup, and with Aldora hanging backward over the front seat speaking words of encouragement through the boot opening, Adam drove them slowly home.

During the next two weeks Aldora took Jess to therapy every other day. She worked out with her as promised, then took her to the park in the afternoon. They sat in the shade of the giant trees and worked on Jessie's drawing and painting lessons.

"You're learning to paint as fast as you're learning to get around," said Aldy when she came to pick Jess up one morning. She held up one of Jessie's paintings that she had matted and framed the night before as a surprise.

Jessie chatted happily all the way to the hospital.

Aldora was helping Jess dress after her hot pack treatment. They were ready to go to the rehabilitation room when Aldy heard a harsh laugh directly behind her.

"How biblical!" said Louise. "The lame leading the lame."

Aldora turned to find Louise staring down at them.

"Mommie!" Jessie shrilled. "I can walk!" Jess

grabbed her cane and started to maneuver proudly for her mother.

Aldora stood frozen as Louise leaned over and tugged the pullover Jess was wearing firmly down. Her mind raced frantically as she tried to think of some way to get Louise out of here before she made another disparaging remark.

"Both Adam's girls have matching canes, I see," Louise said quietly.

Jessie, ignorant of her mother's sarcasm, was about to remark gleefully as she stepped closer to her mother and held up the cane for inspection.

Aldora saw Louise's shocked look as Jessie's sweater crept up over the back brace and showed the still-red stripe that ran down the child's spine.

"And matching scars too, I suppose," muttered Louise shakily as she yanked the sweater down over her daughter's hips.

Aldora's heart leaped painfully as she saw Jessie's eyes fill with tears. Louise's angry protest had hit home. Aldy wanted to strike Louise, wanted to drive her away from Jess, silence her. She started forward but Louise anticipated her.

"Don't move," she ordered, putting herself between Aldora and her daughter. "Stop, darling," she said, dropping to one knee beside the sobbing child. "Momma'll take care of it." She patted Jess as she tugged at the stubborn sweater again. "Mama will get you the best specialists to cut away that horrid scar, just like they did for Mommy." Louise smiled and bared her neck for Jess to see.

Aldy saw Jessie's eyes go wide with fear. "No, Mommy, no!" she pleaded. "Aldy's scar is tiny! Mine will go away too!"

Hearing the mounting panic in the child's voice, Aldy grabbed at Louise's arm, yanked her away from the hysterical Jess. "Don't mention more surgery to someone who's been through what *we've* been through!" she snapped. Aldy laid special emphasis on the plural as she wrapped a comforting arm protectively around Jessie's shoulders. "Don't worry, honey. She didn't mean it. No more surgery, Jess," Aldy soothed.

Jessie clung to Aldora and muffled her sobs in Aldy's hair. Out of the corner of her eye, Aldora saw Louise go white with anger as she watched her daughter take Aldora's words over her own. Surely Louise would leave now, thought Aldy frantically; she must see that her power over her child had dwindled past having any other effect but frightening the girl half to death.

Aldora was totally unprepared for Louise's next statement.

"Of course, darling. You listen to Aldora. She has all the expertise." Louise smiled at them.

Aldora looked up, astonished by this reversal.

"You want to be so honest with her, tell it all," said Louise, fixing Aldy with a malicious stare. "How does Adam like *your* scar?" she rasped. "He was always such a perfectionist. Does damaged merchandise affect his lovemaking?"

Aldora was struck speechless. Rage and humiliation sent hot blood to her face. How could this woman say this in front of her own daughter? Aldora fought for words and control as Louise hurled insults at her rival. No longer aware of Jess, uncomprehending of the kind of love that transcended physical imperfections, Louise flung her final comment at Aldora and left before Aldy could achieve that control.

Jessie burst into hysterical screams.

Two nurses rushed in past the retreating Louise, then one ran for a doctor. Jess was given a mild sedative so that Aldora could get her home.

Throughout the drive Aldy coaxed but Jess remained wooden. Her eyes stared vacantly out the window, her face averted.

Adam had been notified and was waiting when Aldy pulled up to the front door and climbed from the car.

He was about to run to Aldora when he caught her warning look and went to Jess instead.

Confused, Adam lifted Jessie gently and his eyes begged explanations Aldy couldn't provide as he carried Jess up to her room.

Adam carefully removed Jessie's brace and tucked her under the covers. Staring numbly, the child accepted her father's efforts. Adam gave her two small white pills and sat by her bed until they took effect. Then, almost dragging Aldy out into the hall and down the stairs, "What the hell happened?" he raged desperately. "What did Louise say?"

Aldora felt the tears start. She could barely find the courage to repeat those awful words, but Adam had to know. She took several long breaths and shakily recounted the incident.

Adam's eyes filled with black, helpless rage as Aldy quoted Louise's parting shot. A strangled cry of anguish escaped his tight lips as he slammed his fist down on the coffee table. "That bitch!" he swore softly. "That unfeeling, vicious bitch!"

Aldora clenched her hands into tight fists and shoved them deeper into the sofa cushions.

"She told you I'd do what?" Adam asked in shock.

"That you'd get sick of tending *two* cripples and send Jess to live with her mother," Aldora repeated tightly.

Adam swallowed hard. "Jess knows better!" he cried, his eyes searching Aldora's frantically.

"I'm sure she does, inside," Aldy said softly. "But just now it's touched a nerve. Give her time, maybe—"

Adam buried his face in his hands and cried brokenly.

Aldy moved closer, cradled him. "We'll work it out," she murmured. "It'll be all right, darling." She kept holding him, speaking softly. She prayed her words of hope were not empty promises. "Jessie's tough. She'll pull out." Her heart ached at the thought of all the painstaking work that had built Jessie's trust over the past months. It made Aldy nearly ill to realize that it was this Louise's threat had shattered. That it was she, Aldora, whom Jess now feared.

Slowly, Adam collected himself. "Sorry, sweetheart," he said quietly. "I just—" Emotion threatened to overwhelm him again. He put his hands on her arms. "What if Jess can't accept us now?" he said.

"We'll shelve our plans," Aldy answered. "She'll grow secure in time."

Adam looked hesitant. "But if she continues to see our getting married as a symbol of her own rejection—"

"Adam!" Aldy said firmly. "I won't marry you if it means Jess has to live in fear. She's accepted it the way it was; it can stay that way."

"But you've asked so little, you're entitled to—" Adam floundered and pulled Aldy against him dispiritedly.

"We're not entitled to joy at Jessie's expense," Aldy said. "I have my work. I have you, our love. It's more than I ever expected. God willing, I'll win Jessie's trust again."

Holding her at arm's length, Adam smiled and shook his head. "Pretty hard stuff yourself," he whispered, striving to find strength in the levity of his old endearment. "A hard woman, I could hardly do without." He drew her close again. His mouth, hungry, grateful, found release against hers.

Chapter Nineteen

Aldora fought her way through each succeeding day. The frustration of combatinp Jessie's fears tightened her own back into knots of pain and the strain sapped her strength. She and Adam had to appear before a judge to offer just cause for the enactment of a restraining order against Louise. Jessie had to be constantly coaxed, coddled, reassured, before she would even return to her prescribed therapy. And all this while Aldy maintained rigid vigilance to keep her own relationship with Adam pushed firmly into the background.

Aldora missed Adam fiercely. Their time together was sparse and rushed, definitely contraband. By the end of each day her body ached with more than the rigors of her physical exertion, her emotional tension, she ached with need for Adam's gentle touch, his caresses. Seeing him only from a distance, in Jessie's company, was playing havoc with her senses. The slightest touch of his hand as he helped her with Jess sent desire coursing her veins with an urgency she hadn't known existed.

Ellen came to therapy at first, provided what support Jess would not accept from Aldora. Then, gradually, Aldy was able to make some small inroads into the frightened child's confidence. As Jess recovered, Aldy began to take her back to the studio occasionally after therapy. She worked at her easel while Jess sketched at the drafting table. Aldy strove to include Jessie in all the preparations for the upcoming exhibit. She had Jess help with the final selection of works to be presented, and gratefully heard Jess trumpet her delight when Aldy insisted that a portrait of Jess be included in the catalog.

Down at the boat, Aldora posed Jessie, standing with her father as Adam hauled in the sails. She snapped photos to guide her in her work and her heart ached as she recalled the first time they had all been on the *Amara Alexandra*. The longing she saw in Adam's eyes as they sat across the table in the galley stirred Aldy's blood and she had to fight to force herself to eat normally and chat with Jess.

On the drive home, Jess in the front seat between them, Aldora ached to lean against Adam's side, touch his shoulder, feel his lips on hers. When Adam and Jess dropped her at her door, she smiled and waved and retreated tearfully to the diversion of her darkroom as soon as they were out of sight.

Aldora watched Jessie's face come smiling up through the developer as the child stood proudly by her father and helped him with the rigging. Knowing how Jess felt at being able to stand, to help, eased Aldy's pain as she looked at the tall, laughing man and realized that, in this shot, his expression of joy was exclusively for his daughter.

Aldora collected the prints from the dryer and started up the front stairs with heavy steps. Her brave words to Adam rang deafeningly in her ears as she climbed. "I have my work. I have you, our love," she had told him. It wasn't quite like that, she thought bitterly. As she stepped onto the porch she was almost resenting her own resolve. *It's* not *enough,* she thought desperately. *I want Adam. I want him here, close to me, holding me.* Tears ran down her face as she placed the photos on the table and fixed a cup of tea.

She sat sipping at the steamy liquid, ignoring the way it seemed to turn bitter in her mouth. Sighing heavily, she rose, put the cup in the sink, and carried the photos up to the studio. Tacking her selection on the corkboard, she roughed in the beginnings of the portrait of Jess and Adam, flipping on the Daysor light as evening brought deep shadows to the room.

Wrapped in the buffer of concentration, Aldy didn't hear the front door slide open, didn't hear the soft tread on the stairs until Adam slid close to her and pulled her from her stool. "God, I need you," he whispered as he held her urgently against the hardness of his body and kissed her lips.

"Adam," she murmured when she could speak again. "I need you too, but Jess?"

"She's asleep. I told her I had a meeting at the hospital." He grinned at her. "We have some time." He led her to the sofa at the back of the studio and his hands eagerly stripped her smock from her shoulders as he drew her down on the cushions.

"I've missed you so much," Aldy whispered as she slid her hands over the coolness of his skin and tasted the tangy after-shave clinging to the base of his neck with an eagerness in her mouth she'd not known before.

Their bodies sought each other with a new frenzy born of enforced separation and as Adam entered her, she made small animal sounds of joy and responded to his hunger with eager and eloquent movements.

Their lovemaking had a drugged insistence that did not fade as they lay in each other's arms, spent, but not yet sated. "I can't get enough of you," Adam murmured as he kissed her cheeks, her eyelids, the corners of her mouth.

Aldora didn't want it to end. The unrelenting hands of the studio clock were soldiers marching on the fortress of her love. A single tear escaped the corner of her eye and Adam felt it and brushed her cheek with his fingertips.

"It's not easy, is it, sweetheart?" he said, gently drawing her over onto him, pressing her slight weight against him. "God, I don't want to leave you!" He rocked her tenderly.

Aldora, unable to deny her own desires, clung to him, relishing the closeness, the feel of his body pressing on hers. Gone was the iron will that had placed Jessie's welfare ahead of theirs for so long.

Adam sat up and reached for the phone, dialed.

"Margaret, it's Adam," he said, holding the phone in one hand while stroking fresh desire into Aldora's body with the other.

"I'm at Aldy's, you can reach me here if Jess wakes." He recited her number and dropped the receiver back into its cradle. He looked tenderly at Aldora and she rose and led him down the stairs, turned back the bedcovers, and crawled in to sleep beside him.

When Aldy opened her eyes again, Adam was looking at her through the darkness of the room. She smiled and snuggled happily against him. He began to make love to her, this time more slowly, languorously, ravishing her with more than hard passion. His hands were slow on her body and his lips were insistent as they expertly teased her into full wakefulness. No frenzied coupling this, but an impassioned expression of all any man could feel for his woman.

"It's nearly time," Adam said as they lay together in the darkness. He brushed the back of her neck with kisses. "I can't be caught sneaking in, shoes in hand," he whispered, trying to ease the pain of parting with his teasing words.

Aldy watched as he left the room. She heard him go to the studio. When he came back, he was dressed to leave.

Sitting on the edge of the bed in the gray light of dawn, he embraced her and tucked the sheet around her shoulders. "Go back to sleep, sweetheart." He pressed a last kiss into her palm and was gone.

Aldora rolled over into the lingering warmth his body had left behind and buried her face in the pillows. As she heard his car pull away, she wished a number of thoroughly uncharitable thoughts about Louise.

DURING the next two weeks afternoons were reserved for exclusive attention to the portrait of Jess and Adam. As hard as Aldora and Ellen made Jess work in the therapy room, Jessie pressed Aldy harder back at the studio. She insisted that Ellen could handle her therapy two mornings a week so that Aldy could devote more time to the painting.

"You and your dad will steal the show," said Aldy as Jessie posed one afternoon for a few color corrections. "Another stroke here and there and you can take this home to show your father." Aldy noted Jessie's happy smile. "Don't squirm, Jess. You'll have two noses if you move now," Aldy teased.

Jess laughed. "Daddy'd have to kiss me good-night twice," she offered.

"I bet he wouldn't mind," said Aldy easily. She stared hard at the canvas, didn't look at Jess directly.

"I bet he wouldn't," said Jess thoughtfully. She turned toward Aldy and looked up with more self-confidence than Aldy had seen since the incident at the hospital.

"Hey," Aldy cried. "I said don't move!" Aldora masked her own leaping hope with a mock scowl and Jess resumed her pose.

Adam smiled widely as he saw the covered canvas in Aldy's living room.

"You have to collect us all, Daddy," said Jessie brightly. "We're having an unveiling!"

Adam grinned and started for the painting.

"No peeking!" Jess yelped. "You take me, Aldy can get the canvas."

Adam looked at Aldora. Seeing her nod, he scooped Jess into his arms and carried her down the stairs. "Be back in a minute," he called over his shoulder. "Don't carry it, Aldy."

Adam bounded back into the house and grabbed Aldy in an ardent hug. Feeling her momentary resistance, he glared at her. "She's in the car," he snapped. Then softening: "She'll never know."

Aldy grinned and pulled him down to her, kissed him deeply. "Is that better?" she teased.

Adam moaned and nibbled her neck. "I wonder how long she'd stay in that car?" he mumbled meaningfully.

"Adam!" said Aldy in mock alarm.

He laughed, released her, and picked up the painting. As he tried to lift a corner of the covering sheet, Aldy slapped his wrist playfully. "Jess said no peeking!"

Aldy grabbed her purse and sweater off the kitchen chair and followed Adam out to the car. He was getting so edgy about concealing his affections lately. Aldy hoped he wouldn't force information on Jess that she wasn't ready to handle.

Jess supervised as Adam placed the painting against the wall in the entry hall. "Stand back," she said and took one corner of the sheet in her hand.

Adam stepped back and waited.

His mouth opened and a warm cry of pleasure escaped as Jess took the cloth from the portrait. He moved closer, looked at the laughing child standing by his side on the deck of the *Amara Alexandra*. "It's fantastic!" he said reverently. "Just fantastic."

"It's my first *standing* portrait!" Jess said excitedly. She threw her arms around Aldora and squeezed. "And Aldy did it!"

"She sure did, pumpkin," said Adam quietly. "She did it all." The double meaning leaped across the room as he gazed tenderly at Aldy; his face held love and thanks.

"Oh, Daddy," said Jessie, catching his meaning. "You're right!" She hugged Aldy harder. "You worked so hard."

"*We* did, Jess," Aldy countered. "And it's *not* work when you care about someone."

Jess giggled her joy and begged hot chocolate in the library. It was the first time the three of them had done this sort of thing since Jessie's reversal. "We can hang the painting in there until the show," Jess suggested hopefully.

Later, Jess in bed, Adam drove Aldy back home. "I

think she's finally come around," Adam said as he pulled into Aldy's driveway and stopped the engine.

Aldy nodded. She told Adam of Jess's comment in the studio that afternoon.

"Home free!" Adam said eagerly. He grinned and pulled Aldy to him.

"It's a promising *start,*" Aldy said. "But we mustn't rush her; she'll let us know when she can handle more." She hated to dampen Adam's hopes but Jess was so very fragile right now.

Adam scowled but silenced Aldora's protests in a most effective manner. "I won't allow it to take much longer," he said as he pulled his lips from hers. "I can't take much more of this." He started to lead her toward the bedroom.

"Adam," said Aldy, holding back. "Jess knows you're here. She's probably waiting up for you to come back, look in on her."

"Dammit!" Adam said angrily. "How much power am I supposed to give a ten-year-old over *my* life?" He dropped Aldy's hand as if she'd burned him. He strode a few paces away and turned.

Aldy went to him, put her arms around his neck. "Please, Adam," she pleaded. "I know, but give her just a little longer."

Adam pushed her hands away. "You're getting overprotective, coddling her!" His face was set, grim, as he faced Aldora. She could read the hurt in his eyes.

"Adam." Aldy felt fears threaten. "We're *so* close! Please, don't spoil it."

His face softened at her plea. He took her in his arms. "I'm sorry," he said, kissing her cheeks, "I just want you so badly. I want to be with you. I'm not iron-willed, you know." He pressed his mouth against hers with hard desire. His hands slid up under her sweater and easily unfastened her bra, smoothed the bare skin of her back. Lips still on hers, he moved his hands to cup the fullness of her breasts.

Raw passion roared through Aldy at his touch. Her nipples hardened as his thumbs brushed over them in an urgent command. He drew his mouth from hers. "I'll be back," he whispered and bolted down the stairs to his car.

Aching with longing, Aldy left the porch light on, the door unlocked and walked weak-kneed to the bedroom. She pulled off her clothes and slid between the cool sheets.

It seemed forever until she heard Adam's firm step on the stairs, then he was dropping his coat on her chair and moving to the bed. He removed his clothes slowly, deliberately taking his time, making her wait, watch him. Then he drew back the sheet and let his eyes caress the gentle curves of her hips, her waist, the high firm swell of her breasts.

Aldora held out her arms to him. He moved purposefully to the edge of the bed, took both her hands in his, and drew her over to him. "You'd best not have spent all your energy on Jess and painting," he warned and then he covered her mouth with his and lay beside her. In the soft glow of the bedside lamp Adam taught Aldora an unexpected corollary to the adage about patience and virtue.

JESSIE continued to progress as the date of Aldora's art show drew closer. A few sessions with the staff psychologist were added to Jessie's therapy schedule and she was responding openly in dealing with her disability. She even began to look forward to her group session once a week with the other children in the rehabilitation room at the Foundation. She beamed with pride when she told Aldy that the others had praised the murals and described her own pleasure at telling them the artist was her art teacher *and* a personal friend.

A little at a time the strong stuff Jess was made of carried her farther from her fears and insecurity. She was beginning to accept the fact that her father just might have enough love to include both his ladies in his life.

On the eve of the gallery show Jessie was radiant as she took her father's arm, and with Aldy at his other side, they escorted Adam up to the gallery steps and into the exhibition hall.

Jessie helped Aldy hand out the catalogs, and whenever anyone would inquire about buying the portrait of Adam and Jess on the boat, she'd tell them it was already sold and then wink delightedly at Aldy as the client displayed obvious disappointment.

Adam and Jess took Aldy to a fancy supper club after the show. They were joined by Grant, Julie, Bill, and Ellen. Everyone cheered the sucess of the show and heralded Aldy as a rightful heir to the fine-arts throne.

Aldora blushed furiously, held up her hand in protest. "Stop," she cried. "My head will be too big to fit through my studio door!" She tapped her glass. "An announcement," she said. "Julie, Grant, that portrait of you on the boat is your early wedding present. Take it home with you."

Julie shrieked her surprise and Grant's grin lit his face with emotion. They both embraced Aldy until she thought she'd suffocate.

"I'm running out of storage anyway," she murmured modestly when they praised her generosity.

"With tonight's sales?" Adam said quickly. "You'll have more room than you know what to do with." He winked at Jess. "Especially since that one of Jess and me goes back to the library wall tonight."

"I'm glad we got a painting while she was still a starving unknown," Bill said jokingly. "After tonight you'll be the only one who can afford her work, Adam."

Aldora blushed happily.

"I know what she can paint to fill the space," Jess said mysteriously.

Six faces stared into hers. "What, honey?" Aldy asked.

Jess shook her head. "I'll show you tomorrow," she teased and pressed her lips together tightly.

No amount of wheedling could pry Jessie's secret from her that night. She went off to bed clutching her hand over her mouth and shaking her blond curls adamantly. "Good night, Daddy," she called from the top of the stairs. "Night, Aldy." Eyes sparkling mischievously, she gripped her cane and walked to her room.

The next afternoon Jessie leafed slowly through Aldora's photo file. Her smooth brow puckered in concentration, she searched the shots Aldy had taken on both trips to the *Amara,* while Aldy watched with ill-concealed curiosity.

With Julie called out of town on a job, and all the arrangements awaiting Aldora's attention, she hoped Jess wouldn't want a full-size painting of her father's beloved ship lying at anchor. That would definitely fill the space in her studio, Aldy thought with justifiable alarm. It would also fill the wall in Adam's office that now displayed only the serigraph of that anonymous schooner. Watching Jess sort through the pictures, Aldy became more and more sure that that was what Jess had in mind. Jessie had said she didn't want to tell last night because it could be a surprise for her father's birthday. Aldora gulped at the thought of trying to complete such a mammoth work by the middle of July and still helping Julie with the wedding arrangements as promised. Completion by the fifteenth or twentieth would allow time for it to dry for the final varnish by the twenty-sixth, but Adam still might have to accept a slightly damp present. Aldy was running through these mental calculations when she heard Jess's eager cry.

"Here it is!" Jess held a photo out to Aldora and grinned impishly. "Do this one next!"

Aldora took the photo and stared at it. Her heart beat triple-time and her throat constricted with emotion. "Are you sure, Jess?" she asked feebly. "This one?" She held the photo up for Jessie's confirmation.

Jessie's curls bounced wildly as she nodded her head in exaggerated insistence. "It should have been in your show."

Aldora looked at the picture Grant had taken of her at the wheel of the *Amara* with Adam's strong arms wrapped tightly around her and his handsome face looking happily down into her own as the white sails billowed behind them.

"Will you?" Jess prodded.

"I'd love to, Jess. But why should it have been in the show?" Aldy all but held her breath as she hoped and waited for a reply. Was Jess trying to tell her she was no longer so frightened of sharing Adam with her?

"Well," Jess said slowly, "everyone else was in the show. Me and Daddy. Uncle Grant and Julie. This is the only picture that you're in." Jess looked again at the photograph.

Aldy's heart thudded a bit more heavily. Maybe it was a reaching out, she prayed, and maybe it was what Jess said: the only shot of her Jess could find. She leaned over and hugged Jess hard. "I'd love to do that one, honey," she said as she clasped Jess with slightly trembling hands. It had to be significant that Jess wanted it for her father's birthday. It had to.

"All the great artists in your books do self-portraits," Jess babbled happily. "Even the one without his ear."

Aldora chuckled. "Van Gogh," she said. "Do I have to cut off my ear first?" she teased.

Jessie giggled and shook her head.

Aldora ached to ask Adam what he thought about Jess's choice, but she couldn't spoil Jessie's surprise, couldn't betray the child's confidence.

Chapter Twenty

By the time Julie's wedding plans were in full swing, Jess was one of the most enthusiastic participants. In spite of all the makeup work she owed her home teacher, Jess insisted on helping Aldy with the endless errands that went with arranging a large wedding and reception. She raced through her studies and then worked diligently on the guest lists: sorted the reply cards, checked the names against the master list, helped select type for the placecards on the reception tables. Her growing affection for Aldora and her desire to see the portrait finished by her father's birthday led Jessie to push herself to new independence.

Jessie suffered through her tutor in the mornings and then, twice a week, she took a cab to her therapy appointments and her sessions with the psychologist, begging Aldy to wait with the wedding chores until she returned.

Even with all Jessie's help, Aldora was totally exhausted at the end of every day. The painting was off to a flying start, most of the wedding chores were complete, and Aldora dragged painfully off to the spa after dropping Jess at home. She stripped down and plunged into the cooling water of the pool and did ten laps before her muscles began to uncramp. As she sank gratefully into the hot tub Aldy thought about how happy Karen had looked when she'd told Aldy she was taking a leave of absence to elope with Chuck. She'd miss Karen when she went to manage her husband's new spa for women in September, but she was delighted to see that Karen's dream had come true. Thinking of Karen's joy made Aldy wish that she and Adam could have more

time together too. The last week had been a rough one.
Adam had been able to get by only once, and Aldora,
exhausted from taking Jess around all day on errands
and several hours in front of her easel, had fallen asleep
on his shoulder almost in midsentence. Adam had been
very understanding, tucked her into bed, and smoothed
the dark circles under her eyes with his fingers as he insisted that she get some sleep. . . alone. He'd kissed her
tenderly but she sensed his disappointment from the
slight slump of his broad shoulders as he straightened
and walked out of her bedroom. In spite of the guilt she
felt at his sacrifice, she was asleep before his car pulled
from the drive. "Oh, Adam," she muttered, climbing
from the swirling water. "I warned you I had definite
flaws." She toweled herself dry and dressed hurriedly.

When Aldy drove up to her house, Adam's car was
parked out front. She jumped from the car and ran up
the stairs.

Adam greeted her with a hug and pulled a bunch of
fresh-cut flowers from behind his back. "Put these in
water before the heat of my passion wilts them," he
teased and nibbled at her earlobe.

Aldy laughed and hugged his neck, leaned against
him as they went into the house.

"How are you, love?" he said, searching her face for
signs of well-being.

"Fine," Aldy answered. "Won't fall asleep on you,"
she added, grinning wickedly.

"I want to tell Jess," he said, slipping an arm around
her shoulders and leading her to the sofa. "She's doing
so well; she's excited about the wedding, about you. It's
time." He smiled down at Aldora.

Aldy looked at him. "Adam," she said. "It's *Grant's*
wedding she's excited about; we can't spoil it for her."

Adam pushed her down onto the sofa. "Aldy," he said
firmly, "she's had plenty of time. We have *our* lives to
consider." He looked pleadingly at her, took her hands
in his. "I can't wait any longer. I won't go on like this."

"What do you mean?" Aldy asked. She slid her arm around his waist. "We have so much already, let's not ruin our chances over a few weeks." She burrowed her head lovingly against his shoulder.

"No," Adam said, pulling her firmly around to face him. "Look at you," he said sternly. "This schedule, the work with Jess, our sneaking around like this was some back-street affair. It's killing you! When I do get over here to see you, you fall asleep before I get my coat off."

Aldora went rigid. Tears stung her eyes as anger surged through her. "Oh, so that's it!" she cried. "I warned you you didn't know what it would be like to get involved with me. I told you I couldn't do it *all*! You said it was enough!" She jumped up and ran for the bedroom. Adam's complaints about her lack of stamina weren't something she wanted to stay and listen to.

Adam was too quick for her. "Aldy." He grabbed her. "Wait. I'm not criticizing you, dammit!" He held her arm in a forceful grip.

"Let go of me!" she yelled. "I knew you wouldn't stand for it when my obvious inadequacies began to interfere with your creature comforts," she blurted angrily.

Adam's hand fell to his side. His face twisted with anguish and his eyes were hard jade chips as he stared at her. "Funny," he said stiffly. "I had the absurd idea that *your* 'creature comforts' were being interfered with as well!"

Aldora stared at him; her mouth opened but she couldn't seem to force any words out of her tight throat. "I didn't mean it that way," she stammered. "Adam—"

He stared at her. "When you can make a choice between your overprotective concern for my daughter and your love for me, let me know." He turned and strode angrily toward the door.

Aldora saw him slide it back forcefully and she watched mutely as he stepped onto the porch and was gone.

WHEN Jessie's cab honked the next afternoon, Aldy limped to the porch and asked the cabby to help Jess up the stairs.

"What's the matter?" Jessie asked, her frightened eyes taking in Aldy's painful stance.

"Don't worry, Jess. It's just a setback, too tense I guess. I'll be fine." She smiled tiredly.

Jessie sat at the kitchen table, but fear still showed as she watched Aldy ease herself into the chair.

"Don't look like that, Jess," Aldy said firmly. "My surgery wasn't as successful as yours. You won't have this problem, not ever!"

Jessie looked unconvinced. "We had the same operation. . . ."

"Jess!" Aldy took her hand. "I explained. *My* bones didn't fuse. *Your* last X rays were beautiful! A perfect fusion!"

Jessie's eyes were bright with unshed tears.

"Jess, if my little setbacks are going to upset you so, make you doubt your recovery, then maybe it would be best—"

"No!" yelled Jess, anticipating Aldy's statement. "I won't stay away! I want to help." She got up, came around the table, and hugged Aldy awkwardly. "I just got scared for a moment. I believe you," she said, sniffing back her tears hastily.

"Okay," Aldy said. "We can do the lists for the wedding. I can sit down for that."

"I guess you won't be able to work on the painting," Jess said softly.

"Maybe tomorrow, Jess." Aldy patted her shoulder. "It'll be done in time."

Jess smiled. "I'll call a cab to get home," she offered. "You rest so we can paint tomorrow."

Aldora nodded and watched Jess dial the number. Her throat constricted as she heard Jess's newly independent voice give the information to the cab company. *She's come such a long way,* Aldy thought happily. *I can't jeopardize her progress, not for anything, not even for Adam.*

They chatted while Jess waited for her cab and Aldy's resolve grew stronger as she watched the small figure being helped down the stairs and into the waiting car by the uniformed driver.

A week before Adam's birthday the painting was complete and drying on the easel. Aldora had dragged through her days, putting on a false smile of good cheer when Jess was around and suffering Adam's cool manner with well-concealed anguish whenever he ran into them at the house. Just the sight of him sent torrents of longing flooding through her, but his formality tore at her heart and quenched her desire. Now she didn't know how she would get through the birthday party that Jess was chattering about as she helped Jess up to her room. She heard the heavy front door swing shut at the bottom of the stairs.

"Daddy!" Jess cried excitedly. "We were just talking about you."

Adam smiled and took the stairs two at a time, leaned to hug his daughter as he reached the landing. "You were?" he said, looking at her. "What'd you say?"

Jess grinned. "I can't tell," she said. "It's about your birthday."

"Oh, secrets!" said Adam, playing to her hand. "I may have some plans of my own, you know." He grinned at Jess.

"What, Daddy?" Jess stared anxiously at him.

"Well, maybe *I* should have a secret or two," he teased.

"Daddy!" Jess cried, tugging at his hand in frustration. "Tell me!"

Adam chuckled. "I'm taking you two lovelies to

dinner at the beach," he said, glancing up at Aldora.

Aldy heard Jessie's delighted squeal but her eyes were locked on Adam's. The beach! How could he take her back to the beach now? Now with that icy reserve, when the last time they dined at the beach.... Aldy felt her stomach tighten as Adam looked at her levelly, half hearing Jessie's question.

"Well, pumpkin," he said, still looking at Aldy, "the last time Aldy and I had dinner at the beach, you didn't get to go along." He looked down at Jess. "So I thought I'd make it up to you."

"I'd better get going," Aldy said over Jessie's excited babbling. She felt that she'd collapse if she had to stand around listening to any more chatter about surf-side restaurants and walks along the shore afterward. Part of her was happy for Jess, rejoicing that the girl would be able to walk along the sand with them, but another part wanted to slap Adam for this travesty. She turned toward the stairs.

"Aldy." Adam put a hand on her arm.

His touch was gentle, soothing. It sent sparks flying as he ran his fingers along the inside of her elbow. She turned back. "Yes?"

Adam was looking at her with an unfathomable expression. His mouth smiled at her but Aldy wasn't sure if the smile reached his eyes. "Wear that lavender dress for me, will you?" he said smoothly. "I'll pick you up at seven."

"I'll be ready," Aldy said with as much composure as she could manage. She went quickly down the stairs before she could say any more.

If her aged Volkswagen had had the power, Aldy was sure she would have laid rubber all the way out that elegant circular drive. Her hands clutched the wheel frantically and her palms were slippery with perspiration as she turned onto Sunset Boulevard and headed home. What was he doing this for? Tears ran down her cheeks and she swiped angrily at them as she drove. The lavender dress, she thought miserably, what other symbols of better times would he spring on her in this apparent bid for revenge? He had told her to call when she could choose. Well, she hadn't been able to choose. Not between a father and his daughter. He was crazy to have asked it of her. Did he think taking Jess with them to their private, romantic spot could make her jealous of the child? Could maybe force her to choose? The inside of her arm where Adam had held her and let his fingers trail expertly against the sensitive flesh still tingled and Aldy rubbed the spot, trying to erase the sensation. She'd give the devil his due, she thought hostilely, lavender dress and all, but she'd do it for *Jess*!

As Aldy slipped into the lavender jersey, she shuddered and nearly snagged the zipper with her trembling fingers. "Damn you, Adam Holcomb," she muttered as she struggled with the fastenings. If Jess hadn't been so wildly happy as she'd helped Aldy wrap the portrait this afternoon, Aldy would have canceled out on the whole phony evening. "You want games?" she mumbled, looking in her mirror. "You get games!" She unbuttoned the front of the dress so that it plunged a bit more daringly and ran a brush through the silky length of her freshly washed hair until it shone. Then she placed delicate silver hoops at her ears and applied lip gloss to her mouth with painstaking care. She examined the effect. Her eyes looked enormous and the strain of the last few days had put hollows in her cheeks that emphasized her high cheekbones dramatically. She brushed a touch of blusher over them and switched out the bathroom light. She grabbed her white crocheted shawl off the bed and wrapped its laciness around her bare shoulders, lifting her chin fractionally as she started out to the living room.

"Good, you're ready," Adam said, letting himself in the front door. "Jessie's in the car." He put out his arm and tucked Aldy's hand possessively into the crook of his elbow. Without trying to conceal the pleasure in his eyes, he bent to give her a light kiss on the cheek.

"Happy birthday, Adam," she said pleasantly. "That goes in the trunk." She motioned to the wrapped painting.

Adam's smooth manner faltered a little as he looked at her beribboned package. He let go of her arm and picked up the present. "Bet it's a teakettle," he said, shaking the package gently.

Aldy laughed, but her mind whirled. How on earth could she present him with a portrait of the two of them now? "It's all Jessie's idea," she said quickly. "This is the picture she requested the night of the show." She fought a wild desire to go and throw her arms around Adam, rush to him and straighten things out at any cost.

Adam grinned and motioned to the door. "After you," he said, holding the present carefully and trailing Aldy down the stairs.

Adam put the package in the trunk and slid behind the wheel. "We'll have to hurry if we're to get this home and still make our reservations," he said, looking down at Jess.

"You can't see it till after dinner," Jess insisted.

Adam looked at Aldy. "It'll be okay in the trunk?"

She nodded and Adam turned onto the freeway ramp leading to the beach.

Jessie teased unmercifully, "You'll never guess," she said as Adam made wild attempts to discover the contents of the mystery package.

All three of them were laughing by the time they got to the restaurant. Adam gave his name at the door and they were shown to a sheltered little table that overlooked the shore. The sunset over the water promised to be spectacular and Adam settled back in his chair and ordered for them.

Jess looked a bit sad as the waiter brought her her Shirley Temple.

"What's the matter, Jess?" Aldy said quietly.

Jessie looked up from her drink. "Nothing really, just that the last time we all did this I...Daddy had to carry me." She smiled uncertainly at Aldora.

Aldy patted her hand. She knew how Jess must feel: liberated at last from the wheelchair, but also from the extra attention it had caused her father to lavish on her. "Lucky thing, lady," she said, looking around the room. "It'd be a tight fit for your old chair; we probably couldn't have got next to the window."

Jessie grinned at this. "You're right," she said, looking around the cramped quarters. Then Jess went rattling on about the water and the waves as Aldy, only half listening, thought again how very fragile Jess still was, still so indecisive about the giant step she'd taken and how it would affect the rest of her life. Aldy glanced at Adam. He was smiling at Jess, sipping at his drink and watching where she pointed out the window. Aldy's heart lurched a little as she looked at his strong profile, his warm smile. It was just like the smile he wore in the portrait out in the trunk of the car. She loved him beyond reason, but he couldn't make her choose between him and Jessie. No matter how lovely the dinner, the atmosphere, the walk along the beach later.

"Aldy?" Adam was speaking to her and she looked up hastily.

"Sorry," she mumbled. "What was that?"

Adam smiled indulgently at her. "The lobster or the combination plate?"

"Oh, lobster's fine," she said quickly. At least if her appetite hadn't improved by the time the lobster arrived, no one would be able to tell if she couldn't really do it justice, she thought prudently.

When the waiter returned to their table, Adam gave the orders and called for another drink for himself. He smiled at Aldora. "I sure do like that dress," he said as he leaned back in his chair and cast an exaggerated glance over Aldy from head to toe. He raised his glass to her and drank.

Aldora blushed and mumbled something in the way of a thank-you and sipped nervously at her own ginger ale. What was he up to now? Aldy's feelings were really muddled. Adam had been so formal ever since that awful blowup and now he was behaving as if nothing had ever been said. Was he that good of an actor for Jessie's sake? Aldora didn't believe it was possible. Adam's smile seemed genuine; his touch was affectionate. Maybe he had resolved something inside himself, she thought with a sudden, sinking feeling. Maybe he'd decided that he could get along very well without hearing her choice. He had done just that for those four years before she'd met him.

The waiter brought the salad and Aldy did no more than push it all around her plate as she watched Adam, in his newfound friendliness, keep up the conversation much as he had on that first evening when Grant had been occupied with Jess and Adam had entertained Julie and Aldy single-handedly.

When the main course arrived, Aldy grew nearly ill looking at such a huge lobster and knew she'd never even make a dent in the food on her plate. She picked diligently at her dinner and tried to keep up with the ongoing chatter in spite of the hard lump that visited itself on her throat every few minutes. By the time the plates were taken away, Aldora knew that she would never be able to survive the transition from lover to friend where Adam was concerned. Not even for Jess. If that was how it was to be, she'd wait until Jessie was completely recovered and then she'd leave. Maybe move back to New York for a few years. Anywhere was better than here. Better than hanging on as a "friend" until Adam started bringing new prospects home to meet his daughter! "Excuse me, please," Aldy said and Adam stood as she left the table and walked quickly to the restroom.

When Aldora returned to the table after collecting herself and dabbing at her eyes, Adam and Jess had the walk along the beach all planned.

"Just a little walk," Jess explained. "Daddy wants to open his present." She winked at Aldora and urged her to finish her coffee.

Adam and Aldy helped Jess down the incline to the beach and Aldy told Jess to set her own pace until they reached the hard packed sand. "It's tricky in the soft stuff," Aldy coached. "Lift your cane higher, less drag."

Jessie wobbled a bit at first but soon got the hang of hacking through the soft sand and eagerly headed for the shoreline.

Adam took Aldy's arm and held out his hand. "Shoes?" he said, smiling down at her.

Aldy braced against his arm and took off her sandals, handed them to Adam who tucked them in his pocket. Then he slipped an arm around her and they followed Jess toward the water.

Jess turned around, came to them. "Can I wade a little, please, Daddy?" Her eyes sparkled and she hung on Adam's arm until he consented. Adam knelt to help Jess with her shoes and socks.

"Okay, pumpkin," he said, grinning. "Have fun."

As Jess scrabbled down to the water's edge, Aldora noticed with some alarm that Adam was steering her gradually toward the abandoned lifeguard station. "We'd better stay closer to Jess," Aldy said and started to turn back toward the shore.

"She's fine," Adam said, exerting slight pressure to redirect Aldora's retreat. "We can watch her from here," he said, brushing sand from the wooden ramp, settling himself, and pulling Aldora down next to him. "That's more like it." He leaned back against the planking.

Aldora could hardly breathe. The blood roared in her ears and she felt light-headed. It seemed like a lifetime since Adam had brought her here that first time. She longed to let herself go, lean into him, wrap her arms around him, but Jessie's shrill voice, her laughter, wafted up the beach and insinuated itself between her and Adam. She looked at Jess, waved. She knew Jess couldn't possibly see her, wasn't even looking her way, but it helped to strengthen her resolve. She'd not be lured into choosing in Adam's favor by moonlight and a set of apparently overactive glands!

"Thank you, Aldy," Adam said softly, taking her hand in his.

At the touch of his hard, cool palm Aldy felt more confused than ever. "For what?" she said, trying not to notice how Adam held her small hand in both of his and caressed her fingers, the back of her wrist, as he spoke.

"Just about the best birthday present a parent could want." He nodded to the shore. "I've dreamed about being able to send my daughter off to play along the water like she did when she was small." He had a wistful look in his eyes. "I just never really believed it could be more than a dream until you came along." He gave her hand a squeeze.

Aldy didn't know what to say. "Jessie's tough, she'd have come around. She's a fighter."

"Speaking of fights," Adam said, grinning at her, "is ours over?"

Aldora looked away from him. She couldn't find the right words.

"Hey, you were probably right. I have no patience. It's worth the wait to see her like she is tonight." Adam drew Aldy's hand closer to his face and kissed the palm.

The movement of his lips on her skin sent shivers of excitement through her. She looked over at him. "I won't choose," she cautioned.

"Aldy," Adam said, raising his voice to a new firmness, "I just agreed with you and apologized."

"You won't push her?"

Adam shook his head and put his arms around Aldy.

He drew her close to his body. "You're beautiful, except for that thick head of yours." He chuckled and snugged her tightly against his chest, tilted her face up to his. His mouth was only moments from her own.

Aldy's protest hung stillborn on her lips as Adam covered her mouth with a compelling kiss. Every fiber of her trembling body cried out the rightness of that moment.

"We'll do it your way," he murmured as he held her more tightly and ran his hands tenderly, teasingly, then demandingly over her throbbing body. Gradually, his kisses gentled, grew sweet, sensuous, searching. His teeth nibbled at the fullness of her bottom lip and Aldora ran right out of resistance. Her arms went up around his neck and her fingers laced themselves into the thick hair at the base of his head. She parted her lips and loosened all her pent-up longings.

As Adam's mouth lingered on her hair, her ear, the sensitive spot he knew so well at the nape of her neck, Aldora knew she would have done anything he asked of her, and done it willingly. Adam seemed about to speak, but Jessie came squealing up the beach waving something in her free hand.

Adam released Aldy from his embrace but his arm stayed around her shoulders and his hand continued to caress her bare arm as he turned his attention to his daughter.

"What is it, Jessie?" he asked as she came to the foot of the ramp.

"Look, Daddy," she said, still panting from her labored hike up the softer sands, "a whole clam shell. It's still attached!" Jess held it up to him.

"A real beauty, pumpkin," he said and offered the shell for Aldy's inspection.

Aldora noticed the way Jessie's glance took in Adam's arm around her as she turned the shell over in her hands and praised Jess for finding it. The look Jess wore made Aldy think of the look Julie had had that day she'd come upon Grant with his arm over Aldora's shoulder in the office. "It's great, Jess," she said, covering her unease. "It'll be perfect for some watercolor studies at your next lesson," she spoke lightly, hoping a mention of her place as Jessie's teacher would distract Jess, make her put the event of coming upon that embrace in second place.

"Can we go now?" she asked anxiously. "Daddy hasn't seen his present yet." Jess looked from Aldy to her father, her eyes bright with excitement.

"Sure, Jess," Adam said.

"I can't wait either," Aldy added as she slid from Adam's side and started to pull herself up with one hand on the ramp's rail.

Adam sprang to his feet and helped her. He had a reluctant look in his eye as he released her hand and bent to help Jess with her shoes. "Better get these on before we get to the steeper path." He rolled one of Jessie's socks onto his thumbs and held it out for her foot.

"I'll get sand in them, Daddy," Jess complained, obviously not anxious to relinquish the freedom of going barefoot in the moonlight.

"We'll dump 'em out at the car." Adam put on her shoes while Jess balanced on one foot and then the other by leaning against Aldy's shoulder.

Aldy retrieved her sandals from Adam's pocket and slid into them as they walked to the car.

By the time they had reached the house, Jess had extracted promises from Adam related to daytime trips to the beach, swimming, sand castle building, picnics. More promises than there was time to keep. She rushed ahead to the front door, urging Adam to bring the package to the library.

"Uh-oh!" said Adam, grinning. "It must be a painting!" Then to Aldy: "Jess puts all our paintings in the library." He laughed and carried the package up the stairs.

"You'll never guess what it's of," Jess taunted as Adam set the painting carefully on the floor by the couch.

"Say when." He looked at Jess, hands poised to tear at the wrappings.

Aldora watched them and knew she was right to protect this fragile independence in Jess.

"Open it, Daddy," she squealed excitedly.

Adam's strong fingers pulled the paper from the painting with infinite care. He began to smile as he saw his own figure and recognized the setting, but his smile faded to stunned wonder as he pulled the wrappings from the rest and saw Aldy's likeness in the circle of his arms. He stared at Jess. "Jessie," he whispered. "This is *your* choice?" His eyes were searching, hopeful.

Aldora caught her breath. No, she thought, not now! She could see he was desperate to place the same wishful meaning on Jessie's selection as she had wanted to do at first. He'd promised! He'd said he could be patient. Aldy's heart seemed to stop as Jess nodded at her father and she saw Adam gather Jess in his arms, tears standing in his eyes as he hugged her.

The expression on his face as he looked at Aldora over Jessie's shoulder sent a chill to Aldy's heart. She didn't know how to prevent Adam's saying what he was most certainly going to say to Jess in the next moment. Her mouth opened, but like a nightmare scream, no sounds came out. She wanted to run, to clap her hands over her ears and make sure that the words Adam was about to say about their wedding were never heard. She was frantic. Sure that Adam hadn't seen Jessie's faintly reproachful look when she'd come up from the beach, hadn't heard Jessie's momentary sadness as she'd mentioned her father carrying her into restaurants. She began to claw desperately at the corners of her mind for some conciliatory remark to throw Adam's declaration into reverse.

"How about three weeks after you get your back

brace off?'' Adam said, looking at Jess, his eyes sparkling with love and anticipation.

Aldy gasped audibly. He was going to ruin everything! This was Jessie's day, her surprise for her father, she'd never forgive them!

Jess looked bewildered.

"For the wedding day, for Aldy and me," said Adam softly. "You can be a bridesmaid and the dress won't even have to be fitted around your back brace," Adam offered. He looked at Jess anxiously, small doubts crept in at the corners of his eyes as she pulled away from him and turned a wondering expression on Aldora.

Aldy blurted out the first thing she could think of to gainsay Adam's foolish haste. "We can put it off, Jess. There's no rush. Weddings are such a lot of hard work. You've found that out helping with Julie's wedding." She rattled on searching for some sign of acceptance, some softening in Jessie's eyes.

"No," said Jess firmly.

Aldy's heart all but stopped. She'd warned Adam not to rush the child. "No what, honey?" she said gently, forcing an easy tone and a smile.

"It's *not* work when you love someone," Jess said and smiled at Aldy.

Aldora leaned down to hug Jess, tears running openly down her face.

Adam grinned and took both his ladies in his arms for a long moment. "I guess that date's all right?" he said softly against Aldora's ear.

"Oh, yes, Adam! Yes!" Aldy smiled through her tears and put one arm tightly around Adam's waist. She still hugged Jess with the other. The portrait caught her eye for an instant and she realized that the joy she'd captured with her brush, she'd also captured with her heart.

Enter a uniquely exciting world of romance with the new

Harlequin American Romances. T.M.

Harlequin American Romances are the first romances to explore today's new love relationships. These compelling romance novels reach into the hearts and minds of women across North America...probing the most intimate moments of romance, love and desire.

You'll follow romantic heroines and irresistible men as they boldly face confusing choices. Career first, love later? Love without marriage? Long-distance relationships? All the experiences that make love real are captured in the tender, loving pages of the new **Harlequin American Romances.**

What makes North American women so different when it comes to love? Find out in the new **Harlequin American Romances!**

Send for your introductory FREE book now!

Get this book FREE!

Mail to:
Harlequin Reader Service

In the U.S.
1440 South Priest Drive
Tempe, AZ 85281

In Canada
649 Ontario Street
Stratford, Ontario N5A 6W2

YES! I want to be one of the first to discover the new **Harlequin American Romances.** Send me FREE and without obligation *Twice in a Lifetime.* If you do not hear from me after I have examined my FREE book, please send me the 4 new **Harlequin American Romances** each month as soon as they come off the presses. I understand that I will be billed only $2.25 for each book (total $9.00). There are no shipping or handling charges. There is no minimum number of books that I have to purchase. In fact, I may cancel this arrangement at any time. *Twice in a Lifetime* is mine to keep as a FREE gift, even if I do not buy any additional books.

_____
Name   (please print)

_____
Address   Apt. no.

_____
City   State/Prov.   Zip/Postal Code

_____
Signature (If under 18, parent or guardian must sign.)

What romance fans say about Harlequin...

"Harlequins are the best."
—D.L.,* Tampa, Florida

"Excellent...very good reading."
—K.R.P., Burlington, Vermont

"...fresh and original...tremendously romantic."
—F.V., Abbotsford, British Columbia

"...Harlequin makes me relax and dream a little."
—S.L., Aurora, North Carolina

*Names available on request.

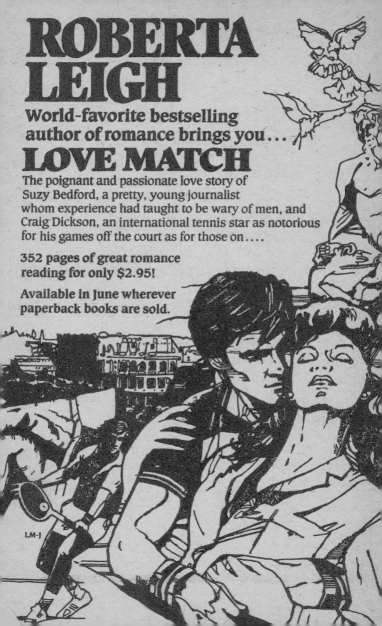

ROBERTA LEIGH

World-favorite bestselling author of romance brings you...

LOVE MATCH

The poignant and passionate love story of Suzy Bedford, a pretty, young journalist whom experience had taught to be wary of men, and Craig Dickson, an international tennis star as notorious for his games off the court as for those on....

352 pages of great romance reading for only $2.95!

Available in June wherever paperback books are sold.

LM-J